TAPOUT

What Reviewers Say About Nicole Disney's Work

The Clinch

"Wow. What a great sports romance. Eden Bauer, reigning UFC featherweight MMA champion faces brawler Brooklyn Shaw in a knock down battle which leads to so much more. Not only is this a fascinating romance with heat and heart, but new to me author Nicole Disney writes with passion and skill. The fight scenes are easy to visualize, the passion these women share is explored, and their emotions are raw. Fabulous read. You don't have to be a mixed martial arts fan to appreciate the dedication and desire needed to be the best of the best, even if it means facing off against the woman you love."—*Late Night Lesbian Reads*

"Wow. Where did this come from? I love sports. And I love sports books if they aren't surgical, exact, or expansive on the actual sport aspect. But there is something so intriguing about this mixed martial arts world, that I was completely engaged. Sizzling chemistry, though. That car scene? You can't see me fanning myself, but oo la la."—*Bookvark*

"I'm not an MMA fan, but I loved this book. It's the perfect mix of action and romance with some family drama thrown in for good measure. I love so many things about both characters. The chemistry between the two of them is really steamy and I loved how there is balance between tension, desire and love throughout the storyline. The descriptions of the MMA action really make you feel like you're in the heat of the moment with them, somehow without feeling too violent, which really impressed me. Disney has created something special here, and even if you don't love sport, or martial arts, I highly recommend you try this, it's a definite re-read for me."—*LGBTQ+ Reader*

"I had no idea what to expect from an MMA romance novel. But what I didn't expect is that I would be so involved in it. This book made me sit up on the edge of my seat and hold my breath a couple of times. The way Disney writes about fighting is both beautiful and realistic. Coming out of an MMA fight battered and bruised doesn't quite cover it and that's what Disney lets you read about. Eden and Brooklyn are both great characters. What you see is not always what you get and it was fun slowly peeling off all of Brooklyn's layers. I would definitely recommend this book."—*Karin's Lesfic Book Blog*

"*The Clinch* is an incredibly vivid rivals-to-lovers sports romance, charged with immediacy. All the sports scenes were written with such intensity that Eden's exhaustion was clear with all the muddled thoughts and I felt myself holding my breath in expectation of the next jab, hook, or kick. *The Clinch* is a tension-filled romance with heavy themes, and I definitely shed a tear or two while reading."
—*Hsinju's Lit Log*

"I adored this story. It had heart, emotion, and an undeniable passion where both characters were concerned to succeed, whatever the dream may be. …I highly recommend this story to anyone who likes an angsty, passion filled romance, with a little good rivalry and healthy sportsmanship thrown in for good measure. Very excited to see what Nicole will bring us in future stories."—*LESBIreviewed*

By the Author

Hers to Protect

Secrets on the Clock

Shadows of a Dream

The Clinch

Exposure (Co-written with Kimberly Cooper Griffin)

Tapout

TAPOUT

by

Nicole Disney

2025

TAPOUT

ISBN 13: 978-1-63679-924-7

This Trade Paperback Original Is Published By
Bold Strokes Books, Inc.
P.O. Box 249
Valley Falls, NY 12185

First Edition: September 2025

Credits

Editors: Ashley Tillman and Cindy Cresap
Production Design: Susan Ramundo
Cover Design By Tammy Seidick

Acknowledgments

Thank you always Radclyffe, Sandy, and the entire Bold Strokes team for building this beautiful community and giving our stories a home. I am so honored and happy to be part of this group of incredibly talented and kind people.

Thank you to Ashley Tillman for stepping in as editor on this novel. Your insights made the story shine, and if it weren't for you, I still wouldn't know my millennial language is aging, which is just tragic.

Thank you to Cindy Cresap for being my long-time editor and the copy editor on this project. You've been making me a sharper writer for years.

My warmest gratitude to Z, for coming into my life and seeing the best in me in a time of chaos and loss. You always see my vision and help me bring it into focus, even if you do argue with me about my totally awesome character name choices.

I am so lucky to have grown up surrounded by a beautiful and supportive family. Thank you to my mom, Terri, and my aunt, Patty, for being two of the coolest women I've ever met, and for loving and supporting me my entire life. Thank you to my dad, David, who was so proud of my martial arts he once entered me into an impromptu talent show and then traversed much of the state of Tennessee looking for a blue belt to make sure I got to wear my correct rank. I hope you're watching, and I hope I still make you proud. Thank you to my amazing grandmother, Mimi, who read all my work despite having severe eye issues that made the task no small labor. I miss you terribly every day.

Last, thank you to every single person who read and loved *The Clinch*. This book would not exist without you.

Dedication

For the warriors.
To the instructors, coaches, and training partners
who've stood beside me throughout my martial arts
journey—you are my mentors, my teammates, and my
friends. Being in your company has made me better in every
way. I hope this story honors your strength and character.
Oss.

CHAPTER ONE

Some fighters are born with thunder in their hands. Some are phantoms, always disappearing at your fingertips. Others are zombies sent to break your will with unyielding indifference. Some are psychics who know your thoughts and read your soul, and still others are time travelers from an era of unbound violence, primal and ruthless. Sometimes breaking people is the family business. A legacy inherited in blood and anointed like a crown.

We come to it as a calling. As a salvation. A habit.

I wish I could say I am any one of those warrior essences. The fact is, I didn't come from the womb swinging. I grew up small, wiry, and silly. Even now the closest thing I have to killer instinct is a smart mouth, and that's not doing much for me from the cold tile of the bathroom floor where deep breaths and not puking have become an either-or situation.

I hear time and space in voices, my moment stalking closer, marked with the eruption of cheers that mean a fight is ending. Space closes, focuses, out from the voices by the octagon to the gentle tap on the bathroom door and Eden's voice.

"Laila? You're up next."

"Okay" is not sufficient at this point. I should be out there moving, staying warm, and listening to Eden's last pieces of advice, not lying here like a croissant having a panic attack and calculating my chances of army crawling out of here undetected through the air vents.

"Let me in, Laila. I can help you."

"I can't do this."

I've fought before. Many times, in fact. Just never in front of the most influential people in the sport. People who can change my life on a whim. Never in front of millions of television viewers.

"Open the door."

I'd tell her to kick it down, but she might do it, so I muscle through the symphony of inner whining and stand. A wave of hot nausea fumes into my throat and nose. I could just about convince myself I really am too sick to fight if I didn't know better. A more promising way out than the air vent, but still wishful thinking.

I open the door and digest Eden's expression. People usually tell me I look like a ghost when I feel this lightheaded and horrified, but she doesn't.

"You're okay," she says instead. I try to slide down the wall, but she seizes my arm and pulls up. "Nope. Stand with it. Look at me."

I'm already looking at her, but I will my eyes to focus. Long dark hair, pretty mouth, a sharp intelligence in her eyes but a kind expression. Eden's been my coach for ten years, my best friend for at least four. She's the greatest UFC champion of all time turned full-time coach and has been ascending to one of the best of those too for the last few years.

The first pro fighter she took on, Brooklyn Shaw, became the featherweight champion and hasn't relinquished the title since, and she's not the only star in Eden's stable these days. Brooklyn managed to steal Eden's heart while she was at it, no easy feat, and now the two are a force I'm unbelievably lucky to train under and call friends. However, in this moment, all I can think is I doubt Eden ever had to talk Brooklyn off the floor before a fight. They're both card-carrying warriors, and for all the kindness Eden is capable of, I have a hard time believing this is anything less than pathetic to her.

"I'm sorry," I say.

"Everything you want is on the other side of this moment," she says.

I breathe. The oxygen quakes through my chest and arms. I'm shaking. I've never wanted anything like I want the glory of a victory in the UFC cage. I want the vision I've cultivated for so long. To dominate. To land a right hand so clean I get a walk-off knockout. I want to scream from the top of the octagon cage with a bloody fist in the air. I want to bring home a UFC contract and change my life in an instant of precision and power. I want to feel the ache of combat in my bones tomorrow and laugh with friends over every turn of the fight.

But I don't, and I mean I really don't, want to step out of this fucking bathroom.

"This is sick," I say. "How is this a real thing?"

I'm not built for this, never have been. I'm not vicious; I'm ridiculous. The first time someone pushed my little brother around, I called that bitch a twatsack cumstain and became a hero for all of five seconds before she smashed my head into a pole.

I'd like to think a decade of martial arts training has changed my susceptibility to having my head rammed into permanent playground fixtures, but I can't be certain. The person across the octagon won't be any ten-year-old named Muffin Top Molly.

"Laila, you will never forgive yourself if you don't go out there," Eden says. "Once they close the cage, you'll know what to do. You're trained for this. You earned this."

"Blue corner, two minutes!"

I look down at my gloves and verify they are blue. The crowd isn't big. This venue isn't made for the giant audiences of the pay-per-view events, just a handful of people for each fighter and the staff, yet their voices rising in anticipation in the next room give me a shot of adrenaline anyway.

"What if I lose?"

"You won't."

"What if I do?" In front of everyone. Every friend and family member I have. Every training partner. Every deadbeat in my neighborhood. Every family with a TV on while they eat dinner. Every school kid who's walked by one of my posters. Even Muffin Top Molly, I'd bet. Eden grabs my shoulders.

"Just go hard. Give it everything you've got, and you'll be proud."

"Blue corner!"

The barking voice belongs to a staff member in black who's craning around the corner looking ready to fight me himself. I look to Eden again.

"Who do you want to be?" she asks.

"Okay."

"Okay?"

"Let's go."

"Let's fucking go." She slaps my shoulder and pushes me through the doorframe.

I try to absorb her energy and multiply it. I will it to bring feeling back to my fingers, but they're cold and slow. I push through the double doors that separate backstage with Eden and the rest of the entourage of coaches and staff at my sides. Blue and red lights tint the short walkout tunnel. Eyes are on me. Cameras. A few whoops sound even though I didn't bring anyone except my team. Dana White, the president of the UFC, sits at his table cage-side ready to watch and decide my fate. There's no turning back.

They signal me into the octagon. My legs are shaking. The canvas is spotted with blood from victors and vanquished both. My opponent makes her walk to the cage next. For how conditioned I supposedly am, standing takes a heroic effort, so how can I hope to complete three five-minute rounds of the most physically demanding sport I've ever been rash enough to pursue?

"Stay loose," Eden says through the cage from my corner. Hah. A drop of advice against the hurricane of chaos in my mind. I try to shake out my arms, and they fall like bowling balls to my hips.

Then she steps into the ring. Tabitha. The Alley Cat, she calls herself. A play on Tabby, I think, but she does also look like the kind of person to lose a piece of her ear in a parking lot. She's built. Wide shoulders, thick thighs, cut arms, belligerent face. She's stoic and hard, looking at me with sharp eyes between sharp brows and cheekbones.

"This is yours, Laila. Put her down and take it."

Eden's last piece of advice rattles through me. I'm not here to be afraid. To survive. To escape injury. Not lose. Not be humiliated. It's all wrong. You don't get the dream just by showing up. You have to put them down and take it. Pry it from their frantic fingertips. Strangle it from their gargling throat. I have to be more than this.

The ref makes eye contact. "Are you ready, fighter?"

I nod.

"Fight!"

I step forward on trembling legs.

CHAPTER TWO

One week earlier

Emerald Tiger sits half a block down the road silhouetted by an ugly industrial orange dusk. Vic lets her feet clap hard on the downhill sidewalk and pulls a strip of cherry-red hair behind her ear so I can see the minutiae of her sassy expression.

"It's bad luck to celebrate before your fight. You should wait until you win," she says.

"Maybe we'll have another party after," I say.

"Then why have one now?"

"I thought you wanted to come."

She more or less invited herself when I mentioned it, and she'll brag about being at this event later but doesn't see why that should stop her from mocking it now.

"I'm just saying you haven't done the thing yet. Celebrating now is like admitting you might not get to later. You should be hungry before a fight, not satisfied."

"Just play nice, okay?"

"Of course I'm going to play nice," she says.

The bell that sounds when I open the door feels too quaint for the pterodactyl this little martial arts caterpillar has become. The front room has the same plain pine desk and modest Taekwondo space where I went from a clueless teenager who had to be reminded not to dance in class to an Emerald Tiger black belt. Chatter comes from the MMA room in back. I kick off my shoes before walking across the blue and red mats.

"Come on, you'll like the MMA room," I say.

Vic responds to strength more than harmony. The MMA add-on is much newer and tougher with its sleek black mats and vibrant emerald tiger head painted on the back wall, not to mention the championship belts on display, including the most coveted UFC championship belts.

Eden might've underestimated herself with this add-on as it's still not big enough to accommodate as many fighters as she could attract, but she says she likes having a smaller, elite group of select fighters. I'm lucky to be one of them but acutely aware it would not be so if I weren't one of her original students. Most of my teammates are already in the UFC while most of the ones who aren't are signed with Bellator, a smaller but still major promotion. Being the team's little sister isn't the worst thing, but I want to be more.

"There she is!"

The boys all throw their hands up and whoop as I come inside, a dozen muscled, perfect bodies horsing around and laughing as they point at the congratulations banner. Eden rounds the corner out of the supply closet, and a bright, warm smile glows from her.

"We almost thought you weren't going to make it to your own party." She sets down a tray of comically healthy snacks and comes to hug me.

"Of course I'm here."

Eden offers her hand to Vic, who shakes it like she's never completed the gesture before. Their energies couldn't be more different, Eden bright and professional while Vic's reservation almost reads as suspicion.

"Eden Bauer."

"Yeah," Vic says.

I elbow her. "And this is my friend Vic."

"Oh yeah, sorry. Vic. Nice place."

"Thank you."

"I've seen you fight. You're pretty good," Vic says.

I scoff at the dramatic understatement that is "pretty good," but Eden doesn't miss a beat.

"I enjoyed my time in the octagon, but I'm happy to be coaching talents like Laila now. Do you fight at all?"

"Just my share in the street, and I'm good friends with Harlow."

I've never heard Vic mention anyone named Harlow before, but the information seems to mean something to Eden, and I'm not sure she loves it.

"I see. How has that been for you?" she asks.

"It's great, but don't worry. She isn't coming."

"I'm not worried."

Vic smiles and thumps her hand down on my shoulder like it will break the tension. I'd really just love to know what the fuck is going on.

"Well, Laila loves it here," Vic says. "I've wanted to at least see the place for a while."

"I'm glad you made it. We're all excited for Laila."

"You're expecting a win then?"

Eden's body language tenses. I can tell she's had enough of Vic, but her friendly, "Of course we are," is controlled and restrained.

"Vic thinks it's bad luck to celebrate before I win," I say. "That's why she's asking."

Eden scans her before speaking. "Becoming a professional fighter is a long, bloody road, and just as mental as physical. It's important to feel your successes. Getting a spot to fight on *The Contender Series* is one of the biggest opportunities the sport has to offer. She gets to fight in front of the world and the UFC president. A great performance is a ticket straight into a UFC contract."

"Sure, but an opportunity doesn't mean anything until you bend it over and make it yours."

"It means something," Eden says. "It's not like signing up for karaoke. It's earned. She'll be spending all next week in Vegas shooting interviews and getting her head right. She deserves a deep breath now."

Vic's smile creeps across her face like her lack of response is a favor rather than a surrender. I shouldn't have brought her. She'll never understand what Eden is saying. Respect in her life is bought in blood and cash, not effort.

"Well, I'm sure you know best, Champ," she finally says.

"Enjoy the party." Eden points to the cooler at the end of the table against the wall. "There's alcohol in there for anyone who isn't competing soon."

She leaves before either of us reply. When I look over my shoulder, I see she's joining Mateo, who just entered, no doubt to tell the fifteen-year-old who is her cherished protégé and basically adoptive son that he is not allowed access to said alcohol.

Vic follows my gaze and takes a long moment before looking back to me. "Are you sure she's thought through this matchup?"

"She doesn't get to pick my opponent."

"Yeah, but does she think it's a good one?"

I try to mask my frustration though I'm not sure I do the job. "Of course she does. Some people actually believe in me."

"Come on, you know I'm just watching out for you. You've talked about it? You're sure she wouldn't feed you to the wolves?"

"Vic, it's been a long time since the playground. I have skills now. And yes, Eden cares. If anyone would know if this were a good idea, it's her."

She rolls her eyes. "Whatever, I could take her."

A laugh bursts like a balloon in my chest. "You could not."

"Oh please, she's flesh and blood. I could too."

"Vic." I put my hands on her shoulders. "That is the greatest female fighter of all time. She would barely notice you were trying."

"That's your problem, putting people on pedestals."

"You have no idea what you're talking about." And I breathe easier, because even though I act like I barely notice Vic's doubts and criticisms, I do notice. It's nice to hear her say something stupid. To remember she really doesn't have a clue.

She's a tough girl and a loyal friend. There was a time when I needed her to pull girls off me by their ponytails. A time when her signature strategy of slinging them to the ground by shirt or hood or hair and soccer kicking them in the face was the pinnacle of martial arts to me, but her chances of doing that to Eden are zero. Her chances of doing it to anyone I've ever shared the cage with are zero. Her chances of doing it to me are zero. I don't need her to approve of my party or my coach or me. I'm one victory away from doing more than she ever dared to dream of. When I do, I won't be a silly little thing to chastise.

Chapter Three

The air hisses like white noise. Muffled in stereo. Tabby's bully face glares across the space between us, her confidence bordering on smug. Scattered cheers dot the room.

It's common though not required for fighters to touch gloves before engaging, but Tabby runs through that tradition. I barely get a step off the fence before her shoulder hits my sternum and her weight slams me into the cage, which has less give than you'd imagine. It's my ribs that sag and creak.

She uses her full weight and strength to pin me to the cage, pushing like she wants us both to explode out the other side. Her arms scrape down to pick up my right leg for a takedown, and only then do I finally move. I try to slide my hands under her arms for double underhooks. I've barely threatened to accomplish the maneuver before she abandons her cause in favor of straightening up and socking me in the face.

Her glove lands with a blunt thunder impact on my ear and silences it. An uppercut follows, muted. My head snaps up like I don't possess a single neck muscle. A cross glances off my glove and blasts my face. And then she's plowing me into the fence again, only this time I'm bleeding onto her back. Did she break my nose? Already?

Her arms constrict around my waist, and she tears hard to her left. I step to catch the weight too slow and too narrow, and she drags me over the top of my planted foot with ease. She's strong and moving with malicious abandon.

My knees smack together as I land. A sharp clang of bone pain rings through me. The impact rattles through my whole body. Just as I realize I need to fight for position Tabby is lunging to secure dominance. The top of her head bashes my nose, and my eyes fill with tears as her legs slap down on either side of me.

This can't be happening.

She's taken mount even though I'm on my side rather than my back, and the fists start coming.

"Get out of there, Laila. You've got to move!"

Eden is screaming at me from my corner. I watch the drops of red dotting the canvas.

Tabby's fists land like a meaty baseball bat. Not sharp like arrows but disorienting like a wave you didn't see.

Move. For fuck's sake, I have to move.

I haven't so much as thrown a punch, and from here, pinned on my side, there is no punch worth throwing. I have to get up.

I shift my hips backward to destabilize her base, a first step, but her knee wedges against my spine and her arm slithers between the canvas and my neck. Her fingers dig into my shoulder, and she pulls me toward her as she falls to her side. She moves me as a solid, resisting block and slides so she's strapped onto my back.

Her left calf clamps across my waist, and she levers the back of her right knee over her left ankle to secure the body lock. She squeezes so hard I have to warn my body not to puke, but thank God I finally have the presence of mind to put my hands where they belong before it's too late. I protect my neck as she tries to slide her arm around it for a choke.

My hands slam onto her forearm just in time to pull and lock it to my chest where she can't crush my throat.

Her right hand punches me in the side of the face, but I stay fastened to the left. I turn my head away so she'll quit catching my damaged nose, but if I let myself get distracted for even a second she'll get what she's really after. A rear naked choke.

"Break the body lock!" Eden shouts.

Eden's call confirms I'm still a step behind. It's what I'll need to do to get Tabby off my back, but it's taking one hundred percent of my effort just to not get submitted. I can't even block the punches, let alone pry her legs off me. This can't be happening.

I'm outside of myself. Watching on TV. Watching my bloody desperate body as Tabby slings it at will. I'm screaming at the TV. For fuck's sake, shift to your right side. Put pressure on the body lock. Tuck your chin and use your left hand to stop the choke. Use your right hand to pry this body lock apart. Don't just lie there getting humiliated. Bridge. Turn into her. Explode. I would explain it all to the TV so well, so just *do* it.

But back in my body I know I can't. If I let go of this fucking wrist with either hand it will slide into place. She'll choke me out. I know it. So, I hold fast.

I feel her frustration with the way I've stagnated her wrist, the crowd's frustration with the way I've stagnated the fight. I know something is coming, yet it does nothing to help me resist her rag-dolling me back onto my side, and it does nothing to stop her elbow from slamming into the side of my head.

I fight to curl into a turtle position on my knees and elbows, not a good position, but better. It will give me at least some amount of protection and structural stability, but she lunges onto my back before I can get my hips far enough back to resist her. She slams me forward flat onto my stomach, using her legs to stretch me out.

Her hips drive down while her fists fly. I try to show enough signs of life to keep the ref from ending the fight, but there's nothing I can do. Not really. I can't hit her. Can't lift her. Can't even fucking see her. I try one more time to come up with an explosion of energy to free me and am shocked when my hips turn.

She's off.

But then the cage door opens. Eden and the cutman are on the way in. I didn't break free. I was saved by the bell.

"Sit," Eden commands me.

I stumble onto the stool. A shock of cold hits my back as she presses an icepack between my shoulders. The cutman rakes down my face with a cloth and shoves cotton swabs up my nose. I wince and pull back from the painful intrusion, but he holds my face and tries again.

"Hey, look at me," Eden snaps.

I'm ashamed to look at her, but I don't dare disobey her.

"Listen to me, fuck that round," she says. "It's dead. It's gone. She came out hot and overwhelmed you, but you're coming back out on your feet with your hands up. You've felt it all. Now make her feel you. I need you to initiate. If you get in a bad spot, I need you to get out like you're on fire. Don't let her settle in. Don't accept anything from her. Break free and ram it back in her face right away. This is your fucking fight. You decide what happens."

I nod, willing my eyes to stop watering.

"Laila, I need you to want it. Do you want it?"

Chapter Four

One minute can save you. It can pull you from the throat of a predator. It's long enough for your coach to whisper the perfect secret in your ear or scream the obvious in your face. It's enough for the cutman to control your bleeding. Enough to cool your temperature and lower your heart rate. It's even enough to convince yourself the next round will be different.

I stand across from Tabby. The weight of my shoulders depresses my spent lungs. She looks fresh bouncing in place. Her eagerness puts a metallic taste in the air, a bullet in the chamber. I have to make her stop knowing what she thinks she knows. That it's over.

"Are you ready?"

I nod at the ref, and the round starts.

I move through my exhaustion. I don't know how. I just do. I meet her in the center because I have to. There is no other script. I keep my hands up even though they're made of lead. I move my feet even though they're magnetized to the canvas. Tabby swings for the rafters. I pull back just in time to feel the wind of her fist passing.

She swings again. A left hook from the parking lot this time. I duck under it and throw my right hook into her body as hard as I can. The solid slap of impact is so satisfying I throw it again, but it's too greedy. She drops her elbow to block and cracks me with her other hand. My nose gushes again, the patchwork from my corner a quick bust.

Tabby powers forward, crowding me into the fence. I tell my feet to move and circle out, but they're too slow. I end up on my heels as Tabby shoves me. I see her knee hurtling toward my face just in time to throw my forearms up. It shocks my bones and shoulders. She socks me in the stomach, then the side of the head.

Her arms wrap around my leg for a takedown. Her shoulder drives into my hip as she fastens my thigh to her chest. I hop on one foot searching for a point of balance, but the strength difference is more pronounced than ever. I'm too exhausted to sustain a challenging resistance.

I drive my elbow down onto her back, not because I think it will stop her or even do serious damage, but because it's the only thing I can do. Try to glean the smallest satisfaction. She takes the elbow without reaction and finishes ripping my leg toward her and to her right to drag me down. She drives her shoulder into my chest when I land so hard it feels like it'll collapse.

"Get up right now, Laila! No rest! Don't let her settle!"

Eden is crystal clear. She wants a scramble, for me to escape in the messiness that occurs when you hit the ground before Tabby can put her knees and elbows and hips in all the right places to render me immobile.

The thing is, I'm already immobile.

Just this bulldozer shoulder in my chest has my shoulders flat under a thousand pounds.

"Move, Laila!" Eden screams.

Of course I want to fucking move, Eden. You don't know what this is like. Except she does, and she would find a way, and I hate her for it.

"Hip out!" she screams.

Tabby is driving her upper body into me so hard it's true, my hips aren't locked down, but as soon as I try to move them Tabby slams her hip onto mine and starts pounding me in the face. I search for the open spaces, alternating my movements to wherever I can find them, but all these little efforts are not culminating into anything.

I take five punches looking for an inch, and in an instant, she takes back three. I heave for air but get blood down the back of my throat instead. I choke and turn, heave again and feel a glove clap over my ear. I fling an elbow over my shoulder and miss. She climbs on top of me in mount. Just like the first round. Me, awkward on my left side. Her, thick thighs latched onto my ribs holding me under her.

I stay alert and cover. She grabs my wrist and goes to pry it away from my face. I lock my arm in a strong acute angle she shouldn't be able to overcome, but slowly, painfully, she does. The drag of her dismantling my defense is a building wave, the strike to my face a lightning bolt. My head slams the canvas and my vision swirls.

She moves to do it again. I'm so focused on covering my face I don't see it coming or register it when her weight lifts and shifts. The pressure on my ribs intensifies, then releases. The relief is short. The back of her leg slams across my face, and she wrenches on my wrist so hard there's no hope of holding it to my chest. I try to catch my right arm with my left to pull it back, but it's too late. She pulls back with all her weight, my wrist locked to her chest. She lays my elbow across her hip in an arm bar.

She bridges up against my elbow, pulls my wrist down. I try to sit up to chase the joint and relieve the pressure. I try to twist to do what's called a hitchhiker's escape, but her leg holds my face down hard. I'm in too deep. I'm extended as far as I can go, and she's hipping up in a steady motion that has more than enough left to snap my arm.

I feel it stretch. Lock. A stab of pain.

It's lose or break my arm and lose. There's no wiggling, no burst of power, no bell that can stop it.

I tap.

Going unconscious or letting someone severely injure you rather than tapping out has never been something I thought made losing any easier or cooler. Yet when I do tap out now, when the ref's hand lands on my elbow to save it from further damage and end of the fight, shame comes like a wall of water.

Tabby's leg drives into my face one more time as she launches off me. She raises her fist and shouts to the crowd. I've seen a thousand fighters celebrate victories. I've celebrated my own. You don't realize how personal it feels to the one lying on the canvas bleeding. She's excited for her win and to get a UFC contract. It has nothing to do with me. She doesn't say fuck you, you fraud ass flower, you quitter, but that's what I hear. "Good fight" never sounded so ridiculous.

Eden shows up at my side and kneels next to me. She puts her hand on my shoulder. "Are you hurt?"

I shake my head. Between the blood and exhaustion and tears trying to form, there's fire in my throat.

"Let's get you up."

I cover my face, try to pass it off as holding my nose while I press the tears away.

"Come on, Laila. It's almost over. Stand for the announcement. Grace in victory and defeat."

To say I'm not in the mood for her fucking wisdom doesn't say it, but Eden pulls my arm to help me up. The ref tows me to the center of the octagon by my wrist. I want to yank it away as if that'll change anything. The announcer recounts what everyone just saw.

"After two minutes and twenty-four seconds of the second round, your winner by submission, Tabby, the Alley Cat, Santos!"

The ref raises her hand. Drops my wrist. I head for the cage door and hear Tabby telling her coach the fight was "no problem."

"Oh, fuck you," I say as I go down the steps. I see Tabby's family hugging as I pass the seating area, and I think they should fuck themselves too even though I know that's not reasonable.

I don't even realize Eden is right on my heels until I get backstage and try to rip my glove off so hard I turn into her, but she doesn't seem surprised by the outburst.

"Okay," she says. "I'll get them."

"I got it," I snap, but she goes to her bag and fishes out scissors anyway. I rip the gloves off but am trapped in the tape. Eden watches me struggle, and it feels good to yank on the tape with all my strength even though it's only less likely to tear now that I've bunched it up. My body is screaming at me for asking any more of it, and I finally stop and hold my hands out for her. She doesn't move until I look up.

"It's going to be okay," she says. "I know it feels like—"

"You have no idea what this feels like," I snap. "You were undefeated. You never lost and you really never got fucking humiliated and thrown around like a fucking crash test dummy."

"You think I've never lost a fight?"

"Not like that. Not that badly. Not in the UFC. Not on TV. Not when it was deciding whether or not you have a future."

"This is not the end, Laila. It's one fight. I know it's a big one, and I know this sucks, but you will get another opportunity if you take this and learn from it and come back strong."

"Why didn't you just tell me I don't have it? How could you send me out there just to get smashed like that?"

She pulls back like I smacked her.

"I wouldn't do that," she says. "You do have it. Laila, you cannot let one loss make you doubt everything. You have to be stronger than that."

"You think I don't see the difference between me and everyone else in your gym? You think I don't know I'm the weak link? Your little nobody stray you have to humor because I stumbled in the gym before it was what it is now?"

"That is not true," Eden says.

"Oh please, you can barely get it out."

She reaches for my shoulder, but I swat her hand away. I can't look at her. I can't stand her. She let me believe I could do this. She's a former champ. She knows exactly what it takes. There's no way she didn't know I'm not at this level.

All the doubts I've tried so hard to silence over the years wash me away in a flood of shame. Ten years of training under the best in the world made me a better fighter than all the shitbags on my block. Good enough to not sweat a scuffle at a concert or pry Vic off me when her play fights turn too real. It made me good enough to win five amateur fights with people who just wanted to say they'd done it once and even two regional pro fights. She made me good enough to think I could overcome not being a natural, but that's not true.

Ten years of the best training in the world just to be good enough to be spat out by the first person I come across with real talent. Everything I've tried to kill in myself, my smallness, my weakness, my unseriousness, my fear. It's all alive and well and writing on the wall that I will never be elite. Eden should have just told me before I poured a decade of my life and all my hopes into it.

I storm over to grab my bag and sling it over my shoulder, abandoning my need to get the tape and gauze off my hands. I go to pass her to leave, and she tries to stop me.

"Laila, you can—"

I push her. Hard. She steps back, stunned, but isn't even close to falling over which just makes me madder. I push her again. Her eyes finally darken, and she tosses the scissors to the side. Something shadowy inside me shoots to attention with mischievous joy, and I raise my hands to push her a third time even though I know she could annihilate me. I think I want her to annihilate me.

But she just grabs my wrists with maddening restraint and speaks in a low voice.

"Oh, now you want to fight?" Her eyes burn into me, and she slings my arms away. I push past her and kick the back door open.

There. It's all destroyed now.

CHAPTER FIVE

The screaming crowd is so loud in my head that coming back to the silence of my living room is a hollow piece of death. The muffle of my roommate's TV and an occasional passing car confirm life continues around me, but I'm a set boulder in a river.

Nothing like a silent room to show you how loud your mind is, and how many useless objects you've accumulated. Somehow on my lifepath I became the type of person to have a Samurai sword in the corner. It's not even a corner that would make for a quick retrieval in an intruder situation, and it is neither sharp nor strong enough to cut a man down anyway. I haven't touched it since I put it there three years ago to announce that this is the home of someone with ancient warrior wisdom both poetic and fearsome.

My fraud couldn't have spread far as people are more likely to interpret it as the memorabilia of a twenty-year-old dude who smokes too much weed than they are to mistake me for a Samurai.

A pain shoots through my cheekbone and bores in between my eyes like it's telling me to quit focusing. Just crawl back into the fuzzy numb crackle. I point my phone camera at myself. I look the same as I did yesterday. Dark blues under both eyes. Swollen. All the bruising and pain of a broken nose only it isn't. Sanity might say that's a good thing, but the way I see it, the least she could have done is broken it. Nothing more humiliating than being less injured than you thought.

A burst of percussion erupts on the front door. Only Vic knocks like that. Only Vic comes by unannounced. She tries to come in, but it's locked. There's the thunk of the door stopping on the deadbolt and then the thunk of her body against it.

"The fuck, let me in!"

I strain against my stiff, angry muscles to stand and open the door. She grimaces when she sees my face.

"Yikes."

"Fuck off."

"You fuck off, what am I supposed to say?" She squeezes around me to get inside. "Why are you trying to lock me out?"

This is not a neighborhood where you keep your doors unlocked, but she's also right I wasn't hoping for company.

"I'm recovering. Baths. Ice. Rest. It's what you do."

"Fuck that, you need air. And life. Let's go out. You want to dance?"

"Vic, I can barely walk."

"Bullshit, I don't see any crutches. You're just sore. Let's do something."

"Vic."

"Listen, you little shit, we're not going to just stare at your wall and mope. It's bad for you. We're going out."

My cell vibrates, the loud rattle obscene across the cheap IKEA coffee table. I reach out to silence it when I see Eden's name. Vic leans forward with interest and points at the screen.

"What's up with that? You're not talking to coach lady? I thought she had you on a leash."

"Well, she doesn't."

There's an edge in my voice, but the way she leans back like I just threw a grenade is an overreaction.

"Damn, you two got beef, huh?" she asks.

"Is it a crime not to answer your phone?"

"No, just not like you."

She slumps onto my couch, sinking into the deep cushions. She's in baggy pants and a hoodie. Her hair is long and straight, mostly black with a few stripes of red. She has the cutest dimples that make her look sweet though she's more often salty. She raises an eyebrow as a thought comes to her. "I thought you'd already be back in the gym honestly."

"It's been three days."

"Exactly."

"What do you want me to say, Vic?"

"The truth. There's some word around town."

She grabs the bag of pistachios from the coffee table and dumps a handful of the most expensive snack I own into her palm.

"What kind of word?"

"That there's beef in the air." There's pistachio in the air the way she's talking with her mouth full.

"What are you getting at?"

"I want to take you to the Yard tonight."

I fall onto the couch beside her. My muscles are on fire. Tender and warm. My quads feel like they've been through a cheese grater, and my arms feel like they'll rip off my body under their own weight.

"There is no way in hell I'm dancing tonight, Vic. You don't understand."

"Please, like I've never woken up after a fight. And the Yard isn't for dancing. You'll like it."

"What is it?"

"Fights."

"What do you mean fights?"

"Underground. Remember a while back I told you I was going to take a neighborhood fight?"

I glance over. My traps are so tight I almost think my neck won't even do it, but it does.

"Yeah, but nothing ever came of it. That kind of thing always falls apart."

"Not Harlow's things."

"Who is this Harlow person you're suddenly such good friends with?"

"It's not sudden. It's just a different circles thing."

I don't think of myself as a possessive friend. I assume Vic is at the center of many a circle given her pervasive restlessness. It's for the best she pursues her more mischievous urges with other people. Yet I do find I have some distaste for this Harlow. Why the mystery? Why have I never been invited, never even heard of her? Is that even a real name? If there's any circle I should be part of, it's the fighting circle. Why have I been excluded?

"Not tonight," I say. "Another time."

"Tonight."

"I'm dead."

"You're not. You're pouting. Take your ass back to the gym and make up with Eden or come to the Yard with me, but this hiding in your cave shit has to go."

"You're not my fucking boss, you know?"

"Maybe I should be. I told you not to have that stupid party. Now look at you."

"This is not because of the party."

"Tell yourself what you need to, just put your shoes on. We're going to watch some fights. Maybe it'll remind you you're not the first person to get cracked and you can stop whining."

"Fuck you," I say it slow to drive the point home.

"Come on, tough guy, stand up and say that to me." She jumps up and boxes the air. She looks playful, but I know from experience she's got about five seconds of that in her before she gets competitive, and I don't even want to play fight right now.

"Come on, don't be a wet mop," she says. "Your nose isn't even crooked. You're still pretty. What else do you want? Let's go have some drinks and watch other people scrap for once. You can cry later. It's even more pathetic in the dark."

"You are such an ass. And what do you even mean underground fights anyway?"

She smiles as she grabs my shoes from the corner and throws them at me. Moving my arm fast enough to catch them shoots a loud pang of tenderness through me.

"See? You're curious. Shoes on. I'll show you. I'll even get an Uber so you don't have to walk, Princess."

"Will there be blood?"

"Oh yes."

I slip my shoes on, and she flashes rock horns at me. Getting in the low-ride Uber car involves more or less collapsing, but she actually holds my arm and tries to help me. The drive is less than ten minutes before the car slows and Vic says to jump out. Whatever this is, it was right under my nose.

The block is residential. Nothing resembling a venue, and I would argue nothing resembling a real home though there's plenty of life around. People walk down the street like it's not meant for cars, drinking and smoking and laughing. It's like a world apart with a sense that help couldn't get to you if you needed it. I hook Vic's arm.

"Is this legal?"

She laughs and repeats the word, "Underground."

It's not the answer she's pretending it is, so I simplify. "What are the chances we get arrested tonight?"

"Laila, when has going to jail ever been my way of cheering you up?"

She's never called it fun, but it wouldn't be the first time she went to jail. "This looks sketchy."

"Look, it's invite-only, and these are not sloppy people. You'd never heard of it, had you?"

I shake my head.

"See? It's cool. It's a real professional operation, just underground. So you know the first rule."

I roll my eyes at the *Fight Club* reference and don't bother reminding her the rules of Fight Club were created to be broken by anarchistic maniacs.

I follow her down an alley that is the exact kind of place you grow up being told to never go. She sweeps her arm through overgrown bushes next to a garage door that's missing a panel.

I climb over the thorny brush vowing to never place this kind of trust in her again. "This is so busted."

"Really don't know what you thought underground meant."

When we emerge from the brush, she turns onto a back porch that is made of a couple sheets of stained plywood. A guy in all black greets her with a clipboard. I'd say he looks like a bouncer except he's too small for the stereotype. Five foot five, a hundred twenty-five pounds after a few cheeseburgers. His lumpy cauliflower ear suggests he can likely handle himself just the same.

"Vic and a guest," she says.

He scans his clipboard.

"I have you. No guest."

"I know, but she's cool."

He tilts his head as if to say she knows better.

"Hey, I fight here," she says. "I'm allowed to bring a guest."

"You get one guest on nights you fight, with notice. Not anyone any time." He glances at me as if to say it's nothing personal, but also that he couldn't care less if he ruins my night. I'm not sure I care either at the moment. This place looks like a crime scene, and it hasn't even started yet.

"Harlow will clear it," Vic says.

"Will I?"

The voice comes from the other side of a screen window inside a structure you could probably have called a house once. I'd kind of assumed the trek around back was due to a structural instability in the building itself, but this daring soul is inside, and it's too dark in there to see her.

"Hey!" Vic says. "Got a fresh one for you. Laila Moretti."

I feel like I hear footsteps for a year even though the walk from the window to the door can't be more than five feet. The sliding door scrapes across the track. and for someone with no expectations I am locked with surprise.

Harlow steps outside with the ease and presence of someone in charge. Long blond hair frames her face and intense, bright eyes scrutinize me with penetrating efficiency. Her body is strong and athletic, and she moves it with the same casual authority that took over this situation.

"Laila Moretti," she says. "A little far from home, aren't you?"

It's been a long time since I was asked what I was doing on the wrong block, which would be unsettling except I actually am very much in my neighborhood. Yet, somehow, I know that's not what she means.

"Things aren't great in Wonderland right now," Vic says. "Just showing her what's out there."

Harlow appraises me again, a smile playing at her barely parted lips. My skin tingles as I remember the bruises and swelling under my eyes. I wouldn't mind not resembling Quasimodo if she's going to insist on looking at me like that.

"Rough fight," she finally says. My ears burn. Of course she watched. Who didn't.

"Not my best night."

"I hope not."

"Look, I'll just go," I say.

Vic grabs my arm and holds me in place. "Come on, we just want to watch the fights, Harlow. She's cool, I promise."

"It's fine," I say. "They don't want me here. I'll go."

"You can watch," Harlow says. "Just as long as we're crystal clear. No videos, no pictures, no running your mouth to anyone, and I am not recruiting you."

Why the fuck was that last comment necessary?

"Please, you would be so lucky," I snap.

"Would I?" Harlow's smile takes over her face, and even though it's beautiful it makes her look more intimidating rather than less. I bolster my resolve and nod with more than a little attitude.

"I'm a pro. I just fought for the UFC. I don't need your little sideways comments just because I had a rough night. If I did want to fight for you, you'd be stupid to say no, and you know it."

"It's not a crime to be outmatched, Moretti, but my people go down swinging."

"Your people are a bunch of gutter scrappers passing the time while they're out on bail."

"Hey!"

"Not you," I shoot at Vic, but really that's not a terrible description of her.

Harlow smirks. Something about it is maddeningly authentic. Like she actually is untouchable. "You're pretty trigger happy on the talk, aren't you?"

"Come on, guys," Vic says. "She's obviously not trying to fight tonight. We just came to have a good time and watch."

"Go on and watch." Harlow tilts her head toward the yard. I hate that she pulls off that attitude so well, like her face is built for it. Probably one of those faces that looks good no matter what. Some people can do that. No makeup, silly face pictures, snort laughter, cussing someone out, always hot no matter what. Meanwhile I can manage to look like a dork in high-end lingerie.

Vic pulls me from where I'm planted resenting Harlow her ability to pull off lingerie, which is neither proven nor my business.

"Oh, and, Moretti," Harlow says. "If you're going to call them gutter scrappers to their faces, you'll want to watch your ears. There's a bite bonus tonight."

She disappears back into the shack of a house before I can decipher what she means.

"Come on, we already missed the first round while you two were measuring your dicks."

"Did she say bite bonus?"

"It's over here."

Vic yanks me toward the gathered crowd in the middle of the expanse of untended earth. They're pressed up to a chain link fence that has been shaped into a loose interpretation of a circle, their bodies swaying to the beat of scattered jeers. I have to watch the ground we're crossing or risk peril, the least of which would be twisting an ankle in a hole, but more likely cutting myself on some rusting piece of debris.

When we reach the fence, I realize two things. One, there are two behemoth men inside that fence throwing meaty fists at each other's thick skulls, knuckles wrapped in just one layer of gauze splotched with red. Two, the people around the fence are not only gathered against it—they're holding it in place manually.

Vic squeezes into a space, pulling me with her. The man on her left knows her, nods at her arrival and angles his body so we can fit, but neither of them bother with pleasantries before shouting into the ring. Circle? Fence? Whatever they call it, it offers no protection. The ground is dirt pocked with clumps of growth. The chain link, aside from not being secured, has no padding on the beams. The size of the circle is whatever the audience morphs it into as they sway and yell. Curiosity shoots through me as I process the rawness of what's happening.

The bloodier fighter must be six four. A bald, translucent white, tattooed Goliath without expression. He lunges at the other man, still an easy six two but fatter with a hairy chest and a twisted, ripped scowl. Their chests slam together as the bald one locks his enormous hands onto the other's neck and slings him into the fence. The impact knocks me stumbling backward. My body protests the forced effort to keep my feet, but my soul comes alive. I'm both amazed the others held it in place and certain they wouldn't be able to if these monsters crashed into it hard enough. Vic waves at me to come back.

"You'll get used to it. You have to brace for it."

"Can they really bite?" I scream over the chanting voices.

"What?"

Before I can ask again, the bald Viking starts pounding his grounded opponent, who raises a pathetic arm to guard himself. He scrapes on his back toward the middle of the ring, but the behemoth drops his knee on the man's face, driving down to hold him still by his face and beating his stomach. The man's legs flail, but he's fastened to the earth under two hundred sixty pounds of mean. The hairy man on bottom tries to wrench his assailant's foot the wrong way, but big boy lifts up, then slams his knee down again on the man's face. A river of blood flows from under his knee.

I press against the fence, my heart pounding as I take in the scene. This is the truest version of fighting I've ever witnessed. MMA sacrifices pieces of reality to the sanity of basic safeguards and the street loses integrity to the chaos of panicked intervening friends and surprise weapons. But this. This is a fight, in all its bloody chaos, with all its animal urges accounted for.

The Viking postures up and lifts his foot to stomp, and the man on bottom yells "tap," pounding the ground for good measure before the shoe can land. The victor lifts both arms over his head and screams a guttural roar.

Chapter Six

The heat of beaten bodies fumes from the earth like fog in a graveyard. The cage is empty, a rusted combat shell. Spots of blood dry into dark dots of battle rain. The people have dispersed. The loud ones and the drunk ones and the jokers drained into the street and now it's all money changing hands in shadows. I scan for Vic, who was in just such a conversation five minutes ago with some guy, but now she's nowhere.

I've never struggled to find my place in a room. For better or worse, approachable has always been one of my leading qualities, but no one looks open or friendly or even like they're having fun. Instead, it only feels darker and more illicit with every passing minute.

My stomach sinks. My heart beats faster as my new role of lost puppy embraces me. An odd feeling. As if I don't know my way home. I can behave after dark as well as any woman who grew up hearing about the things that happen after midnight, but this yard of glass and thorns is a menacing mouth ready to taste me. I don't know whether to worry or fume that Vic has vanished.

I survey the corners again, listen for her voice. *God damn it, Vic.* I spin straight into a hard body. Harlow's hard body. I bounce off her, stunned and embarrassed. She looks stunned too, and something tells me that expression doesn't grace her face often.

"Shit. Sorry."

"You look like you're about to make a run for it, Moretti. You okay?"

"Have you seen Vic?"

Understanding fills her face, and I know Vic is gone before she answers.

"She was walking off with Sam like fifteen minutes ago. Was she your ride?"

"Who the fuck is Sam?"

Her eyes are so expressive I can see how belligerent she finds the question.

"Are you serious?" I try instead.

"I could be wrong."

We both know she isn't wrong, but I want an explanation I know she can't give. For what was so pressing to my friend who dragged me here that she would ditch me now without a word.

"Vic can be a bit of a wild card," Harlow says. Her face is full of calm sincerity that pulls me back into my body. She's tall and solid and somehow comforting even though she makes me self-conscious in a way I don't understand. There's a bright, almost reflective quality to her blue-gray eyes. Looking into them, I get the feeling she knows Vic much better than I realized.

"Sure, if by wild card you mean stinking rotten egg asshole."

Harlow beams. "You have a way with words."

"I have a way with ridiculous situations. I guess I can stop waiting around like a dipshit. Thanks for letting me crash the fights. Vic obviously sprung it on you like the rotten ass she is."

Harlow smirks. "Stick around another few minutes. I'll give you a ride."

She offers all smooth and casual, yet my response still comes out like a choked sputtering engine. "She wasn't my ride, really. We took an Uber. I can walk home. I'm close."

She tilts her head and clicks her tongue. "You know better than that. It's late and sketchy out there, and I'd be willing to bet your legs are still too shot to run if you needed to."

I scoff in exaggerated offense. "My legs are fine."

"Your legs were shaking like a Chihuahua at a fireworks show when you came in here."

"Fuck you." I punch her arm. When my fist connects it jolts me awake to the fact that I don't know her like that, but she's smiling with a grounded comfort.

"Fine. Thank you. Sorry," I say.

"Don't be. You can help me fold this if it's really eating you up."

She grabs one end of the chain-link fence and nods at the other. I grab the next panel, walking it flat against hers, then pull in the next.

"So," she says. "How'd you like it?"

"Uh, what?"

"The event."

"Oh. It was interesting."

"Interesting?" She raises an eyebrow, good humored but so sure of herself. Of course interesting isn't a strong enough word for what I just witnessed. It was brutal and lawless and infiltrating anything so clandestine is exhilarating. It was real and raw in a way that transcends savagery.

"Did the gutter scrappers entertain?" she asks.

I sigh and press the next fence panel to her chest, look straight into her beautiful eyes. "It's possible I shouldn't have called them that."

She smiles. "It's possible?"

"Anyone who steps into the cage deserves respect. I know that. Even if it is in a backyard."

"Is that you trying to be nice?"

I can't help but smile because she's right, that was a sad attempt at manners if that's what it was.

"They entertained," I try again. "They fight hard, like you said. The gore of a street fight, but some of them have some real skills."

She grabs the stacked fence by the sides and picks up four panels in an easy motion before carrying it off to a shed in the back, not even having the decency to struggle. Apparently, she doesn't just look strong. She returns and takes another stack of the remaining panels before it occurs to me to help her. I'm just standing like an idiot watching her muscles flex when I realize I was probably supposed to do that.

"So, you're a fighter or what?" I call to her back.

"You think so?" she returns over her shoulder.

"Well, are you?"

She disappears into the shed for a moment, reemerging dusting her hands off on her jeans.

"Car is this way."

I roll my eyes as I follow her. I'd be willing to bet that's a habit of hers. A tingle of mischief flares at the prospect of trying to pry something real out of her.

She rounds the house to the opposite side where an old Mercedes sits in overgrown weeds looking like it might've sprung from the earth itself.

"Does it run?"

"If it likes you." Harlow winks and opens the driver's door as I realize I've managed to insult her again. I kick myself and slide into the passenger seat thinking maybe it's best if I stop talking. The interior is really nice. Black leather and more gadgets than I expected. Maybe it was just the surroundings that made it look like it might have a hornet's nest in the back.

"Where to?" she asks.

"To the right, then left at the light."

The car comes to life with a spirit that confirms it probably doesn't in fact have to approve of your personality to do so.

"It's a nice car," I say. "I didn't mean anything by that. I don't even have a car."

Harlow puts it in drive before she looks over. "I don't blame you. It can be a pain parking the thing."

"I can't afford it," I say. The fact that my lack of a vehicle isn't a trendy New York decision but a direct reflection of my financial prowess feels like a truth that has to be expelled like a demon.

"Why not?"

The question disarms me. I used to have a car, but it was a beater, and when the transmission gave out a year ago neither fixing nor replacing it was an option. "Because they're expensive. Apartments are expensive. Training more than you work is expensive. Supplements and high-quality food are expensive. Phone, internet, and electricity—"

"Got it, sorry. I just figured you were bankrolled out of those kinds of worries with your gym doing so well."

"Well, it's not my gym. It's my coach's gym."

"But you work there. I just figured Eden took care of you being as close as you are and having so much time in."

"I work the desk. It's not a glamorous position. She pays me three times more than she has to and gives me a lot of free private training, but I'm still not rolling in it."

"Understood."

"She's a good person."

The brake lights ahead of us illuminate her face in red as her eyebrow raises. "I'm sure she is."

"So, what's the deal with you two?"

"What deal?"

"You obviously have some sort of deal. Why aren't you allowed in the gym?"

"I'm not allowed in the gym?" she asks.

"Vic made it sound that way."

"Did she?"

The brake lights flare again and accentuate the contours of her strong arm. I find myself wanting to test the power of it. I grab my wandering mind. There is palpable weirdness around Harlow and Eden. I'm not imagining it.

"Are you playing dumb with me?"

"What's *your* deal with Eden?" she asks.

"She's my trainer and my boss and my very good friend."

"Yet things aren't good between you."

"Says who?"

"Well, Vic made it sound that way." Harlow seems tickled to echo me.

"Is never answering a question some kind of sport for you?" It snipes out harsher than I intended, and the way her face turns serious makes me regret that she didn't miss it.

"My fighters aren't broke," Harlow says.

I sigh at the non sequitur and want to tell her she's only gotten away with being this frustrating her whole life because she's gorgeous.

Something tells me the response isn't meant to be as evasive or as pointy as it strikes me. I called myself broke and she basically said I shouldn't be, yet all I heard was that I'm a loser and my friend is cheap. I search for some kind of peace offering.

"Yeah, well, maybe I'll come fight for you then."

She scoffs. "Why would you do that, Miss UFC?"

I scoff back like it's a contest. "You saw my fight. My chances with the UFC are shot."

"For a mortal, maybe. But you're on the Eden Bauer train."

"What does that even mean?"

"She's their darling. She'll get you another chance," she says.

"That's not how it works."

She smiles again, like it's just for her, which makes me realize I might be watching her face more than you could strictly call normal. I look back to the road and realize she passed my turn, which makes a lot of sense since I've neglected my one job of directing her.

"The next left."

"Being the darling is everything," Harlow says. "It's more than winning, even."

She says it like a known fact, and I don't know what to make of that. Eden was a darling, if by darling you mean well-liked, but she was also undefeated, so you can hardly separate the two. In any case, I am not a darling. I'm nobody.

"What are you insinuating?"

"I'm not insinuating anything. I'm saying it's a business, and your trainer happens to have made the UFC a truckload of money. If she asks them to give you another shot, they will. Maybe not tomorrow, but it'll happen. If you want the UFC so bad, just stick with her."

Horrified sounds dramatic, but a huge piece of me is exactly that. Every aspect of my training has imbued martial arts, particularly competition, with a near sacred eminence. It cannot be faked or counterfeit. There is a single and direct route to the top, and that route is to win. No one can do it for you, but do it enough, and you will rise to the peak. Fail to do it enough and you will disappear. It's pure and fair and objective and one of the few mammoth ambitions that is not subject to simply knowing the right person. Yet here she is saying it is, and with an unnamed authority I don't understand.

"Left," I say, and she smirks because of course she knows I just doubled back, but she doesn't comment.

"I'd hate to see how you take bad news," Harlow says.

"Sorry, but getting a free pass in a year or two because my coach is famous isn't exactly good news to me, even if I believed you, which

I don't. And don't worry, I got your message loud and clear that you don't want me fighting for you both times you said it. You think I suck. You don't have to pretend to be doing me a favor. My place is right here, you can stop."

She comes to a stop. I can see she feels bad, but the idea of her trying to comfort me just sounds even more embarrassing than this whole night has already been. In just a few hours I've managed to show up at her event an uninvited, shaky, bruised, televised loser, get ditched by my own friend, admitted to being too broke to own a car, forgotten where I live, and been snubbed by a backyard organization that was beneath me three days ago. I open the door and spring out as fast as my shaky Chihuahua legs will let me.

"Moretti," she says. I close the door, cringing at myself for doing it as it clunks shut, but she doesn't miss a beat in rolling down the window. "Laila, wait. Come on."

I close my eyes and turn back because as much as I want to storm off, it's too petulant even for me. That and I like the way my first name comes out of her mouth. I lean down and look in the car window.

"It's fine, Harlow, really. Thank you for the ride."

"The deal with Eden is that she and I have an agreement. It's complicated, and it's ancient history, but it works. It's the most important part of my end of that deal that I do not recruit her students. That's why I'm not offering you a fight. I don't think you suck."

"Agreement? What agreement? How do you even know each other?"

"Did you hear the I don't think you suck part?"

I breathe through the need to squeeze more information from her throat. "Yes. Thank you. I think."

"Good night, Moretti."

She pulls off before I can answer, which is infuriating in ways I can't even put my finger on, the least of which being that we're back to Moretti already.

CHAPTER SEVEN

My roommate is a recluse. She works from home and spends her free time gaming from that same computer, which means she seldom leaves her room. It's rare to so much as catch her in the kitchen for a snack. I suspect she snuck a mini fridge and hot plate into her room to avoid me, which is too bad since I'm delightful.

This means when she does finally tap on my bedroom door, it can only signal one thing.

"Do you have rent?"

"Simone," I say. "Faithful roomie, gamer goddess, when have I ever not had the rent?"

"Is it about to be right now?"

"Let's talk about what we mean by have."

She rolls her eyes. "As in have a check to put in my hand in the next six hours."

I bite my lip. "Is that the King James translation?"

"So, no?" Her face and voice are in perfect sync in their boredom with this conversation, as if this is chronic and predictable even though I've never been late. I do act like it's a minor miracle every time I pay for something, so I guess I don't inspire confidence.

I flop my head against my bed pillow. "Ugh, hold your panties. I just have to go get my check from work, which I really didn't want to do today." I should have switched over to direct deposit ages ago, but between how much time I've always spent at the gym and mobile deposits, it's never hassled me enough to do so.

She shrugs, unmoved. "It's Bentley you'll have to ask for an extension, not me."

Bentley is the landlord. Young guy as far as crotchety landlords go and nice in between fussing about women's hair in shower drains and unapproved painting. I once told him I was going to make my room hot pink. He failed to identify it as a joke and nearly had to be restrained. Bentley and Simone have that in common—a lack of appreciation for my humor.

Obviously I'm not going to ask for an extension when the rest of the money I need is a five-block walk away, but the fact that she seems to think I might makes me want to mess with her.

"Would you go get it for me? I don't want to see my boss today." I manage to keep a straight face through her looking at me like I'm a pain in the ass little sister who doesn't understand the world yet. She's really pretty, actually, though I hardly ever notice anymore. Long black hair, deep brown skin, thin and gangly but in a graceful, majestic way.

"I really doubt they're going to release your check to me, Laila."

"I'll write you a note."

"I still don't think—"

"Kidding, Simone. You'll have it within the next six hours."

She goes back to her room as I shake my head at the weirdo. She's low on the challenge scale so far as roommates go, agreeable, reliable, predictable. She never steals my food or leaves her shit everywhere or brings creepy people over. She doesn't play her music too loud, and I've never walked in on anything kinky, but not being able to summon a reaction from her even when I want to can be boring. I'm often reminded by friends in worse situations that boring and sane are not bad qualities in a roommate, but I suppose I'm prone to loneliness, especially lately.

One might say that makes today the perfect day to go to the gym, but I'm terrified to face them. Any of them really, but especially Eden, who is there all day on Fridays. It has to be done, though. This is what happens when you put too much of your life in one basket. My dream job, my day job, and my social life are all one and the same, and that's a lot to fuck up at once.

I push into my shoes, muscle through the lingering ache in my body. I make a big show of leaving, trying to catch Simone's eyes, but she can't be bothered.

The later it gets the busier it gets at the gym, but trying to dodge Eden isn't an option. With the level of my chaos being what it was the last time I saw her I don't imagine it matters what time I go. She'll find a way to step out and ask what the fuck is wrong with me regardless. I know I would.

The five blocks go fast, and when I step inside, I lock eyes with her right away. God, she couldn't even have the decency to be in the back. My heart skitters. She looks taller than her actual five ten, or maybe I just feel smaller than my actual five five.

"Hi," I finally say in what only manages to manifest as a whisper.

She holds my gaze for a long breath, then nudges her head toward the mat. My heart cracks as I realize she's letting me come train. Without so much as an apology, she's ready to let me back on the mat, and I'm going to let her down again. Harder.

"Can we go to your office?" I ask.

She steps off the mat and crosses the short distance to her office barefoot. I close the door, delaying in any way I can until I have to face her. Somehow in all the hours dreading this I haven't come up with a plan. I'd love for her to start, but I know she won't. I'm the one who owes her an explanation.

"Eden, I'm not proud of how I've handled things." My voice shakes, and I pause to try again. "After all you've done for me, pushing you was fucked."

She looks at me with intensity I can't withstand. I can't even call it anger. Just power, and I wilt, my eyes dropping.

"Are you okay?" she asks.

The question is so far from anything I expected it makes tears spring to my eyes. My throat practically seizes trying to regain control, but the tears spill over anyway, and I shake my head.

"I can't do this. I know that now."

I've already mentally separated from this place. From my dream. From her. Some small piece of me still wants to hear something that fixes it from my instructor who's always had all the answers. Yet I know no matter what she says it won't pierce the cold, hard ice of reality.

"You're hurt, Laila. Injuries are part of our world. Sometimes we forget the worst ones aren't always physical, but you will heal."

"I don't belong here."

"You do."

"I don't, Eden. I got demolished. It wasn't close. And who is she even? She's unranked. If she can do that to me, how can I keep lying to myself?"

"She's new, but just like you, she wouldn't be there if she wasn't skilled. It was one fight, Laila. One hard fight. She had a good night. You had a bad one. It happens."

"I'm the weak link here too. Everyone is nice about it, but I'm a mascot."

"What are you talking about? You smash people all the time."

"I'm talking about the pro team."

"You mean the one with mostly rock-solid men?"

I shake my head because I know she means well, but it lands flat. Just a flash of memory of Tabby crushing me to the canvas so hard I thought my stacked shoulders and hips would crush to dust is more powerful than anything she can say. I was helpless, not even competitive. I know the truth now, and there is no unknowing it.

"Just get back on the mat," Eden says. "Once you get past that you'll feel better, I promise. Don't go hard, don't think about what's next or your last fight. Just be with your people and do what you love. We'll figure the rest out when it's time."

"I just came for my check, Eden. I'm not coming back."

Her eyes harden, and I see a flash of anger. I brace for her to tear me to pieces, but just when I think she might, she goes to the safe and retrieves my check. She extends it toward me.

"I'm sorry," I say. "I came to say that too."

She nods but doesn't answer.

"And I'm sorry I didn't give notice. I never meant to let you down like this. I just have to figure my life out now."

"And you're going to do that unemployed and alone?" she asks. "You think Vic is going to pull you out of this?"

"Believe it or not Vic knows a thing or two about being down and out."

"And that's something you want to learn? How to be down and out?" She looks so disappointed. "You're better than this, Laila. Vic doesn't want you to succeed. She was knocking you every chance she got before your fight. You going to let her tell you what you're capable of?"

"You barely even know her," I say with way more feeling than I have any right to given I still owe Vic a good sock in the jaw, but it's not about Vic. "Have you stopped to consider that I'm not capable? I'm not you. I know you can't comprehend this, but not all of us can just make it. Sometimes it's not in the cards. And when I spend fifteen years of my youth and life and health on this and don't make it, then what do I have? Besides a fucked-up body and a busted bank account?"

"You're right, Laila, there are a lot of really valid reasons to choose another road. Giving up on yourself over one fight just isn't one of them. Do you still want this or not?"

"It doesn't matter if I want it. You can talk shit about Vic and Harlow if you want, but you don't know what it's like to fail. Everything you touch turns to gold and I'm happy for you, but I'm not you, and you can't fix that."

"Harlow?" Eden's brow creases with suspicion and surprise. "Is that what—"

"God no, that's not what this is about. She's worse than you with the silent monk bullshit. I don't even know what your problem is with each other. I just know you can't understand what I'm going through."

"And she can?"

"I don't know." I don't notice my hand has found my hair until I feel the tug of my fingers. The truth is I have no reason at all to think Harlow might understand, or that she would want to spend any time trying. Why even bring her up? Am I trying to piss Eden off even more? "I don't know," I repeat. "Probably not."

Eden sighs and pushes off the desk she's been leaning against.

"I think this is a mistake, but you know that. If it's really what you want, I wish you well."

"I'm not a fighter." My voice cracks again.

"No one can decide that but you."

Thank God she knows I've decided and doesn't force me to say it again, but when she pulls me into a hug the tears spill onto her shoulder.

"Thank you."

She nods and issues one last instruction. "Just be careful of your friends."

Chapter Eight

People act like wanting to get hit for a living is so unimaginable yet will turn around and work in a restaurant as if that isn't torture. If you're not sweating over open flames and burning yourself on searing pans, you're probably slicing yourself open or shish-kabobbing yourself on hidden pointy things under disgusting dishwater. You can escape that if the rancid smell of emptying grease into dripping, eroding bins is your thing, or there's hauling heavy dishes to the back where you get to scrape children's booger cocktails from plates.

If you're remotely attractive or socially competent they'll put you in the front of house, where you'll be verbally assaulted and psychologically abused by people fresh out of church who hate their spouse and tip in change. In those sweet moments where the sadistic sociopaths known as customers finally leave, you'll enjoy a full five seconds of peace before some over-eager twat in a collared shirt comes along trying to prove they're earning their one dollar an hour more by saying something like "if you have time to lean you have time to clean."

If you don't decide prison is a better fate and murder this individual, you'll now be acting like a fucking meth addict for the next four hours pulling down vents and disassembling equipment so you can scrape mystery black shit out of crevices that were never meant to see daylight.

I'd say there must be something to being the owner that makes it all rewarding in some way, but my uncle has owned this nightmare for ten years and looks just as miserable in his Charlie's Chicken memorabilia as the rest of us. His bitch list includes unreliable employees, anyone else having the audacity to sell chicken within a one-mile radius, and the fragility of managing food costs when the dipshit cooks can't hit a correct portion despite having a scale beside them.

My uncle has told me since the day he opened the place that I have a job with him if I ever want one. Don't get me wrong, I'm grateful he made good on that without qualm or question. I'd be lying if I said I knew the going rate for a chicken girl, but I'd be willing to bet it's even less than he's paying me. Again, I'm grateful.

I'd also be lying if I said I didn't fantasize at least eight times a day about the one-sided violence I'm capable of imposing on these unsuspecting brats. Every time a customer gets a smart mouth about their overly precious order, or a cook expects me to grovel for a fucking side of ranch, flashes of me Sparta kicking them in the chest hard enough to send them across the room fill my mind.

"Excuse me? We've been waiting for like, ever. Does anyone even work here?"

She's in her late twenties and wearing a tube top in a chicken joint at two in the afternoon—a story I don't need to hear.

I see my abandoned profession everywhere. It amazes me how antagonistic people are willing to be without a single combat skill to their name. It would be child's play to throw a rear naked choke on this woman. Drag her to the ground. Buckle her knees with a blow to the liver.

"Yes, I'll be right with you!" I motion for her to calm her britches into one of the cheap plastic seats.

I'm really not as violent as all this. I'm a lover. A joker. Is it possible I simply miss fighting already? It's only been a month. All the bruises have just finally faded. Is that all it takes to forget the hyperventilating mass I was on that bathroom floor? Or is it just that this woman poses no threat to me? Am I just a bully? Eager to use my skills only on people who have no hope of reciprocating? That won't do.

You can't be a tough guy part-time, and you're not a tough guy at all for being able to sucker punch an unsuspecting chick who survives on fried chicken and sarcasm. I can't keep seeing myself as something I'm not. I have to let Laila the fighter go. I'm Laila the chicken girl. Not a title I would have picked, but if you're going to be a quitter, the least you can do is own it.

"Okay, what can I start you with?"

She rolls her eyes to signal I owed her an apology, but I just poise my pen over the pad until she relents and orders a spicy fried chicken sandwich and fried Oreos. The truth is most people are Sparta-kicking themselves in the chest anyway with these food choices.

"Coming up."

I turn just in time to catch a flash of Harlow and Vic coming through the front door with two other people. Cold dread sucks the life from me. My legs feel weak as I scramble around the kitchen wall before they can see me. I hope before they could see me anyway, unless of course they saw me flee, which is even worse.

I look for someone, anyone, to bribe with my entire day's wages in exchange for getting me out of this, but there's no one. It's a skeleton crew as it often is. I'm fucked.

I look down at my uniform as if I don't already know how ugly it is. The world's least flattering, shapeless, rough fabric. Deep blue with red hems and a yellow cartoon chicken in what can only be described as a roadrunner pose. I'm responsible for my own pants as long as they're black, and though I own many pair that make my ass look great, alas, it's laundry day. I'm wearing the ones that are around a decade old and have patches of faded color that make them look dirty even when they're not. This is the last place I ever thought I would care, but life never misses a chance to add insult to injury. I look like this is actually my natural habitat for God's sake.

I dip into the bathroom and rip the hat off. The chances my uncle will be around to chastise me in the next hour are nil. I wet my hands and try to make my hair stand in its usual way. Of course it doesn't want to, but it's better than the hat. I pull open the two buttons available to me on my shirt even though I don't have enough chest to fill it that high. Some skin is better than no skin.

I breathe and try to channel the confidence to go out there and take their order without literally dying from embarrassment. From the brink of the UFC, to disgraced loser, to chicken girl. I set my jaw and armor up. When I pull the door open, Harlow is there, standing in the hallway. I freeze as we lock eyes. The urge to sock her for looking so good competes with the urge to paint a picture or write a song about it.

"What are you doing here?" I can't hide that I'm furious at her for being that hot in my presence at this particular moment.

"Uh, eating, hopefully," she says. "I thought I saw you, but I wasn't sure."

I throw my hat at the register like she won't see it even though all it does is draw her attention to it. She cracks a smile.

"So, it is you."

I sigh. "Yes, it's me. I'll come take your order, just give me a second."

"Hey, I'm sorry if we're invading your space. We come here all the time. It's kind of a hot spot for the Yard followers. I didn't know you worked here."

"It's new." And temporary, I want to say, but I'm not sure if that's true.

"Vic is out there," she says.

"I'm not supposed to hit the customers."

Harlow laughs, and that sound is so nice I forget to be embarrassed for a second. "Want me to hit her for you?"

"Nah, I'll have the guys spit on her chicken."

"Yikes, remind me not to mess with you."

"If you need reminding, I can't help you."

She smiles again before she drops her voice to a more serious tone. "Are you okay?"

There's a feeling in the back of my throat I would describe as approaching tears if I wasn't willing to claw out my own jugular to make sure I don't do that. It's never been hard for me to cry, but lately it's been flat out excessive.

"Sure. Of course. Why?"

"This just doesn't seem very *you*. Last time we talked, you had some kind of situation going on with your boss, and now you work here. I'm just doing some basic math."

Her brow is soft under a backward hat. She's wearing the hell out of that thing with her long blond hair left down. Maybe I should've worn my hat that way, though I doubt I'd have the same results. She leans on the wall, indicating she'll wait for an answer. I can't help but notice how long she is, how athletic. And now I find she can do basic math too.

"I'm not fighting out of Emerald Tiger anymore. Or at all, actually."

She nods, looks me over. "You couldn't keep your job at least?"

"I quit."

I catch a brief but transparent expression that says loud and clear how stupid she thinks that was. It makes me irrationally mad considering she didn't even voice it.

"I had to, okay? I can't be around that and not be in it. Just over and over again not being allowed to forget about it."

"Okay," she says. "Sorry, I just thought it would be better than this, but you know what's right for you. I'm just glad you weren't fired."

"Of course, it was better than this." I'm not sure why I'm so mad.

"Well, can you get the job back?"

"Probably," I snap even as guilt washes over me looking at her poor confused face. I sigh. "I'm sorry. I'm being irrational."

"I'm getting used to it."

"Fuck you." I laugh and she cracks a beautiful genuine smile. "I just can't go back. It's hard to explain."

"I get it," she says. "More than you might think. I just didn't know you had this hidden talent for fried chicken."

"More like a hidden uncle and an empty bank account."

"A hidden uncle? Like on house arrest?"

Now it's my turn to smile and hers to look embarrassed that her mind went straight there. "Have some wild relatives, do we?" I ask.

"One or two."

"He owns the place. My uncle. So, easy job. That's all."

"Your uncle is Charlie?" she asks.

"Tony."

"Okay," she says. "And Charlie is?"

"A name that goes well with Chicken."

She cracks another smile that makes me realize that smile, that mouth, might be the feature that makes her so damn sexy. Her eyes are such a beautiful bright color between gray and blue you assume it's that, but that smile, the way the corner of her mouth is always pulling into a smirk like she's thinking something dirty, it's making me dizzy.

"You're kidding," she says. "There's no Charlie?"

"There's a Charlie," I say. "His name is just Tony. No one wants Tony's Chicken."

"Got it." She laughs. "Well, as fun as your uncle sounds, if this isn't what you want and you need to make some money another way, all you have to do is call."

My brain glitches at the ease with which she offers it. Like it's nothing. Like she's swimming in so much money she could be rid of some without noticing. My mind catches up with how Harlow makes her money and how I'd have to make it from her.

"I know I gave you shit for not offering me a fight, but the truth is I can't take it anyway. I'm not fighting anymore."

"I didn't mean a fight, Moretti. I heard what you said. I mean working with me. Helping to set up and tear down events, getting fighters where they need to be, that kind of thing. I mean it doesn't pay as much as a fight, but it's not half bad compared to this. I've got one coming up Saturday. I could give you five hundred for the night. Cash, no strings."

"Five hundred?" It would take the better part of a week to make that here, and I know I don't do much in the way of keeping that fact off my face. "Seriously?"

She shrugs. "Sure, if you want."

A sweet little voice tells me it pays that much and pays it in cash because it's fucking illegal, but that soft little girl voice gets trampled by the money goblin holding out its greedy fingers for phone and grocery money. Then comes Eden's voice, telling me to be careful of my friends. I'm sure this is exactly the kind of thing she means, but Harlow's eyes are so kind and the pressure nonexistent. She's offering to help me, and I want help.

"Okay, that would be good."

"Yeah?"

"If you're sure. If you really need the help. I'm not an orphan, don't put yourself out."

"I'll pick you up at eight."

She's backing away before I figure out how to thank her, her eyes sparkling like she can read my mind and doesn't need it.

"These idiots will be happy with four number fives to go," she says. "I'll come back here and get them from you in ten and get them out of here so you can have your place back."

Oh Christ, she's an actual angel. I don't even have to see Vic or deal with the ridicule that would definitely follow.

"Now I officially owe you."

"Oh, and the hat was cute," she says. She winks before she disappears around the corner. A mixture of awkwardness and satisfaction makes me feel like I might implode. I pick my hat up off the register and put in their order, realizing by the time I'm finished that I still haven't stopped smiling. Maybe *that's* what Eden meant by be careful of my friends, because the way Harlow makes me feel— aside from exciting and safe and frustrating and intriguing—it feels dangerous.

Chapter Nine

Harlow's Mercedes is even prettier the second time around. I don't know if it was the darkness or my preconceived notions that made me see it so differently on the side of that abandoned house in the weeds. It's so nice it doesn't even look out of place when she pulls into the garage of a luxury high-rise, though I feel out of place enough for all of us.

"What are we doing here?"

"The event is on the roof," she says.

She always calls it the event. Never the fights, which is how I've always referred to such events, even of the fully professional and sanctioned variety. I wonder if it's part of the secrecy canon to never call this what it is.

"Really?" I ask. "They're not always in the yard?"

She beams at me, clearly amused I ever thought that was the case.

"You haven't seen anything yet." She pulls two bags from the trunk and hands one to me before heading for the leasing office, which is closed. She punches in a code and the pad lights up green.

"Do I want to know how you got that?"

She smirks and takes me to the elevator, where she punches in another code to activate it, then selects "R," the button above fifty.

"One of my investors has a connection to the building and volunteered it as a location."

"Investors?"

She shrugs, a small admission that might not be the most straightforward title.

"There was a time when all the fights were in the yard. It might not be much to look at, but it's mine, and for a long time it was all I had. It's part of the lore now. It's a badge of honor to see a yard event, to fight in one. It's tradition that new recruits have their first fight there. Those nights are my gift to the neighborhood, but events like this one…" She finally looks over and meets my eyes. "This is where the money happens."

"Your gift to the neighborhood?" I manage to stifle my natural scoff because there's nothing in her tone that suggests she's anything less than sincere. Even so, I see a defensive bristling in her eyes.

"That's right."

The elevator climbs past forty, and I wonder if that warm fall scent is coming from her or if it just permeates out of the walls somehow. It occurs to me too late that elevators are intimate and maybe this ride would have been more so if I didn't have this relentless tendency to antagonize her.

"What do you mean, exactly?" I ask.

She analyzes my face before she answers. "Yard events are free to attend. People bet if they want to, but they don't have to spend a dime. That's one thing, keeping it in the neighborhood for normal people. Then there's the fighters. I pay every fighter for every fight, and I pay them well. Way more than they'd get as an unknown at another organization if they could get in at all."

I nod. I have a dozen easy challenges to what she said, but I don't know if I actually believe them or if it's just become sport to me.

"Look, I know how it must look to you," she says. "I know it's grimy and unpredictable and dangerous, but I give people real money, and I give them a chance. You know how much both are worth in our world."

The elevator door opens before I can answer. A view is a given on the fifty-first floor, but I didn't expect anything so spectacular. It knocks all the words out of me. The city lights are a galaxy of fireflies, and the cars so far below are the breathing lifeblood of this colossal organism we live inside. I feel so cozy in my smallness and so connected in the complexity.

"You like it?" Harlow asks, like it's a gift.

"It's amazing. I'll take two."

She shakes her head and walks into the closest thing to a clearing. There's a grill, tables, chairs, but I see where this is going.

"We moving all this?"

"Yep."

"You sure you don't want them to just have at it in the pool?" I nudge my head toward the sparkling water that's illuminated from the bottom and surrounded by tropical flowers that have no business surviving in New York.

"That would be pretty slow moving," she says. "Maybe we could get something going over the firepit, though."

"A burn bonus?" I'm still trying to figure out if that bite bonus she mentioned back in the yard was a real thing, but she reveals nothing with that playful expression.

"We'd better stick to this area."

"Is there a rule not to throw anyone off the roof at least?"

She rolls her eyes. "Yes, there's a no blatant murder rule."

"Going soft?"

"What do you take me for?" She hands me a chair to put me to work, and I take it with a smirk that I hope has the same effect hers so often do.

"So…" I clear the last chair and move to help her with the grill.

"Yes?"

"On a scale from one to Pablo Escobar…"

She shakes her head again, but I catch her smiling, and it sends a little zing down my spine.

"Are you asking about the organization or me?"

"Both."

"I don't know." She lifts the grill, and I have to scramble to pick up my end and follow her before she just does it herself. In fact, I imagine she could do all of this herself quite easily. Whatever she claims, she's doing me a favor with this job. "One, I guess."

"One?" I ask.

"On the Pablo scale."

"That's it?"

"Well, considering there's no drugs or murder or international empire, yeah."

"Sure, but one? I mean there has to be at least some bribery, money laundering, tax evasion?"

She raises an eyebrow, and I almost miss that it's playful until she says, "Do you *want* me to be Pablo Escobar?"

I open my mouth to respond, but a voice that isn't mine fills the air. Probably for the best.

"Heya, Harlow."

Harlow beams as she sets down the grill to greet the woman who's approaching, and I find myself wishing she'd beam at me like that. I produce more head shakes and eyebrow rubs. They hug, and it finally occurs to me this could be a girlfriend. There could be a girlfriend. Why wouldn't there be? God, she's beautiful. The girlfriend. The woman.

"Laila, this is Davina. She's our doctor for the night."

"Doctor?"

Beautiful and a doctor. Great. But, sure, the Pablo Escobars of the world do tend to have their choice in women even if they're ugly, and Harlow is anything but ugly.

"In case someone gets hurt," Harlow says.

My mind clatters trying to catch up. Things fight for the top of the list. The fact that this is someone working the event, not necessarily a girlfriend wins even though that should be less important than the fact that Harlow has actual medical staff present. That's a given at a professional fight, but I hadn't even entertained it would be possible here. Maybe she really is a one on the Pablo scale, and maybe I need to throw out everything I think I know already.

"That's great. I didn't know you had a doctor."

"We have refs, too." Harlow winks. I know there's a ref, but as usual Harlow is letting me know she misses nothing and saw my surprise at the civility glowing from beneath this underground world.

"Sam is on his way up," Davina whispers to Harlow loud enough I can hear. Harlow nods and makes eye contact again before pointing at the clubhouse.

"We'll have the fighters staged in there. You can take these bags and get organized. There's a fight list in there, but they should all know who they're fighting and when. Five minutes between fights from the time everyone is off the floor. You're just helping things flow. Jake should be up any minute. He'll want the guest list, which is in the bag too. He'll take care of the door and security. I'll be around if you need anything. You know how to wrap hands, obviously?"

It takes me off guard, but I manage to nod.

"Great, you can wrap them then or watch their coaches do it. Sometimes they get fussy about the particulars, just do what they want. They can go bare knuckle too if they prefer. We're just making sure they're not putting shit in there they shouldn't be. Nothing sharp, nothing heavy, nothing that isn't gauze or tape."

"Got it."

"Great, have fun."

She disappears to the elevator in a manner that makes me think I'll see very little of her for the rest of the night, leaving Davina and me staring at one another.

"First time?" Davina asks.

"Working, yes. I think it's really cool you do this. Making it safer."

She picks up the side of the grill Harlow abandoned and helps me move it to the clubhouse. "It's not the worst way to make some extra cash, and Harlow has always been good to me."

"You've known each other a while, then?"

"Forever. Here they come." She nods at the elevator as the light indicates it's on its way up. "Better get that stuff into the back."

I scramble to gather the bags by their straps, more distressed than I might've guessed at the threat of being insufficient at this job in any way.

I make three trips that should've been five and am waddling under the weight when a voice drags through the air.

"Well, who's this?" A male voice full of money and cigar smoke. I hope he's talking about Davina and keep my head down, but shoes fill my frame of vision. I can tell they're designer shoes hand made in Italy or some shit even though I don't know jack about shoes. His legs are cloaked in suit pants that have the same look, understated yet loudly well crafted.

I resist the urge to pretend I'm slow enough to still be clueless. I'm socialized enough to know that while Harlow would likely prefer me to be out of sight, she'd prefer even more for me not to insult the money, and this man is obviously money.

"My name is Laila. I'll be helping out this evening."

He looks me over and shares a private laugh with himself. His suit is immaculate, all black, his hair deep black too and airy in a way that makes him look younger than his face says. Designer sunglasses, shiny watch, smug expression. I never like this type of guy, which is a shame since my life would probably be a lot easier if I did.

"You can call me Sam," he says. "Where do I know you from?"

"I don't believe you do."

"No, no, I'm never mistaken when it comes to people."

I remember with anguish that I've been televised, a state of affairs I still haven't adjusted to.

"I guess you might have seen me on TV. I was on *The Contender Series*."

He squints like he's trying to see it. "No, no, I know what it is. You were in the Yard not too long ago. With Victoria."

My mind glitches, grinds, then finally connects this Sam with the Sam Vic disappeared with that night.

"Yeah, I guess I was. We didn't meet. I didn't realize—"

"I noticed you," he says. "You were noticeable. Out of place, covered in bruises, limping. Lost."

"I wasn't lost."

"You were," he says. "But you aren't anymore."

"Well, nice to meet you."

"I hope to see you in the ring soon. It's not every day we find a lost UFC fighter. Imagine the possibilities."

He turns his palms up to display whatever vision he sees, then backs away to bring a gorgeous woman with cascading hair to his side. He knows exactly who I am, and he saw my fight, all right. I don't like the pretense. Or the condescension.

I huck the bags over my shoulder again and retreat to the clubhouse. The space swells with people, the elevator making the fifty-story journey in just a minute and unleashing ten new guests every time it does, all dressed to the nines.

I find the fight and guest lists, along with wraps, tapes, gauzes, braces, Vaseline, cotton swabs, shirts, signs, cards, and all manner of first aid including adrenaline and even Narcan, which I can only hope is on hand because of audience activities more than fighter ones. To put it mildly, Harlow does not want anyone dying on her watch.

The other bag is more of a fighter's playground with hitting pads, extra gloves, towels, and all manner of warmup toys. Even when the fighters and their coaches, if you can call them that, start to fill the clubhouse, no one seems to notice or need me. They let me wrap their hands, then go back to their routines.

"Laila?"

I spin toward the familiar voice, both relieved and irritated to hear her.

"What're you doing here?" I ask.

Vic puts her hand on her hip and looks me up and down. "I think that's my line. How'd you get in?" She drops the attitude, which was apparently meant to be playful and pulls me into a hug.

"You think I can't swing an invite without you?" I've been so annoyed with her over ditching me for Sam, and for not trying harder to reach me to apologize, but now that I've met Sam, what I feel is closer to concern.

Vic looks around and seems to process the room, then snaps back to me. "Wait, are you fighting?" She grabs my forearm with urgency. I can't tell if that would be exciting or horrifying for her.

"No, I'm working."

"Oh, sure, that makes way more sense," she says with thick sarcasm. "What the fuck do you mean?"

"Harlow offered me a job for the night, and I'm broke, so here I am. What are *you* doing here?"

She wasn't on the fight list, though apparently, she does fight here sometimes, a secret I'm not sure I'm over. Vic gets in street scuffles often enough when she turned up banged up, that story never went questioned, but now I'm wondering if it's been this all along. I've seen her get into many a fast-food dining room brawl, but this is another thing.

It's no surprise Vic is snitch proof, and I know Harlow's enterprise is not a half-hearted secret, but a true one. Yet, I feel like a smaller part of Vic's life than I ever guessed. Ever since we met in first grade on the playground, we've been each other's backup every time either of us was summoned to answer for ourselves with our fists. As a small but mouthy kid, I did spend my childhood getting Vic into more fights than I got her out of, but I never failed to show up, and I didn't think she'd ever do a thing like this without wanting me there.

Even knowing Harlow's explanation, that as an Emerald Tiger student I was specifically excluded, I can't deny my ego is wounded and my friendship up for inspection.

"I'm cornering a friend." Vic waves a young woman over. Woman being generous because this girl can't be over eighteen.

"Hi," the girl says. She looks athletic. I'll give her that. Tough too, which is a quality you shouldn't be able to describe in physical terms, yet we all recognize it.

"Hey. You must be the third fight."

She nods. There's only one female fight on the list, so she can only be Sophie or Katarina.

"I'm Sophie."

"I'm wrapping hands when you're ready," I say.

"Wrap her now," Vic says. "You should hold pads for her for a minute, Laila. She has a nasty hook. You'll like it."

"Oh," I say, not sure if that's something I'm supposed to do or not. I imagine I'm supposed to represent a neutral presence, but I think I'm also a whatever-gaps-need-to-be-filled kind of hire. Vic's expression shows no indication it's a controversial request, so I wrap the girl's hands and hold the pads. "The first fight is soon, so I only have a minute, but go on."

I hold the mitts, and when her gloves make that crisp, solid slap into them, a little surge of electrical excitement shoots through my body. I let her fire off another four shots before throwing my arm at her head to duck, which she does seamlessly before bobbing back up and throwing the hook again. It is a nice punch. Crisp. Strong. Everything where it should be.

"Nice, right?" Vic asks.

"Very nice," I confirm, surprised I really mean it. This girl has training. Real training. Which I admit is more than I expected from the fighters here.

"You should come out with me to corner when she's up."

"Oh, I doubt I'm supposed to do that. I'm working, Vic. I'm here for all the fighters."

"Do it."

I hear the voice before I spot where it came from. Then I see a woman stalking toward me. I can only assume this is Katarina.

Sophie's opponent. She's bigger. Taller and stronger and wider. I don't know how the weight classes work in this organization or if they even exist, but she's got pounds on this girl and years too. Her hair is dyed bright green and braided with loose puffs at the ends. Her skin is tatted to just about a full body suit including a few on her face.

"I don't give a shit if you corner her," Katarina says. She closes the distance until she's too close. "There's nothing some UFC reject can say to save her from what's about to happen."

I stiffen as my heart rate skyrockets. Confrontation always does this to me. I've never gotten used to it. I've watched so many of the people I grew up around in these kinds of exchanges, and they seemed like they didn't have a single nerve in their body. Vic is gifted that way. Fearless.

"I'm not cornering anyone," I say. "I'm just here to facilitate the fights." I try to keep my voice sincere. I don't like the attitude, but I'm not throwing gasoline on it like I so often do. I can see how she wouldn't like the chumminess she thinks she walked in on. I am the picture of reason and empathy.

"No, I hope you do," she says. "Tell her to just fall down and curl into a ball like you."

"Okay, fuck you and your stupid green hair. You think you look scary? You look like Krusty the Clown, you jackass."

Katarina seizes my shirt, but whatever she plans to do next is interrupted by Vic lunging between us.

"Hey!" she yells. "You already have a fight tonight. If you get all bloody and fucked up now and it gets cancelled, no one gets paid. Let it go."

God, since when is Vic the voice of reason around here? Katarina stares at me while she thinks it over before she shrugs Vic off.

"Fine, but you're next UFC dropout."

The urge to insult her lack of imagination conflicts with the more responsible need to communicate that I'm not a fighter anymore. There is no next for me, and there's nothing to be gained by calling me out.

"I'm just a facilitator."

"I'm going to facilitate your trip to the hospital the next time I see you," she says.

"What the fuck is going on back here?" Harlow's voice is deep and sexy and sharp and slices me in half. She trusted me with such a simple job, and here I am pissing off the fighters enough they feel the need to threaten me.

"I'm sorry," I blurt before I realize it's Katarina she's glaring at, and Katarina is wilting. Maybe I'm imagining it, but I don't only see Katarina submitting to the boss who signs her metaphorical check. I see fear. Harlow commands fear. She holds eye contact with Katarina for another three seconds before she finally snaps to me.

"It's time for the first fight. Are we ready?"

My heart leaps into my throat again as I try to claw the names of the first two fighters from my memory where they were clear as day until Katarina adrenaline rocketed them into space.

A man with gloves, no shirt, a scar over his eye, and somewhere around twelve abs shows up next to me.

"I get to walk out second, right?" he asks. Thank God his last name, Ruiz, is tattooed across his chest, which is enough to bring my brain back.

"Yes, you're second. Stay ready, please. James, we're ready to walk," I say it like I know who the fuck James is when really I need him to identify himself without exposing me as the unprepared mess that I am.

He springs forward, another Adonis crafted from tattoos and muscle. I nod at him, then at Harlow like this success was expected, not miraculously fished from my ass. She vanishes from the clubhouse like smoke without another word.

I turn back to confirm I have James and his coach. "Ready?"

They nod, and I come back to my body enough to notice there's a DJ outside the door cuing our walk, which answers the question of how I'm supposed to know when to go quite obviously. It will be an absolute miracle if Harlow ever hires me again, but at this point I think I'd settle for convincing her I do have a couple brain cells to rub together.

CHAPTER TEN

Just because everyone in the audience is dressed like they'll be swinging by the Met Gala doesn't mean they don't scream and yell at the fighters what they should be doing to win just like any other audience. They lean in during the tense moments, flinch at the big shots, and drink between rounds.

I want to watch these people from the other side of a false wall. It's never occurred to me before. I've always been busy watching the ring like everyone else, or I've been in the ring myself. I never realized what an odd collection of iridescent beetles gathers to watch with their gaping gluttonous eyes. I wonder how much they're all worth. This era's wealth, watching from the podium of the Colosseum.

Katarina and Sophie are up, and they have my full attention now. I walk Sophie and Vic down the pathway first, which is outlined only by an informal parting of bodies that opens as we pass through and closes again behind us like the breath of an alien. It opens again when I go back to retrieve Katarina.

"Ready?"

"More ready than you'll ever be, Ragdoll."

I turn away before my mouth can do what it does. I guess it's a little cleverer than "UFC Dropout" but still elementary.

The DJ plays her song, which is a throwback and a power anthem for women who like to brag about how many men want to have sex with them as if we aren't all fighting our way through a cock gauntlet.

There is no ring. No cage, no fence, no pit, no barrier of any kind. Just a circle taped on the ground and a crowd punctuating that suggestion. Katarina hovers at my side before she steps into the circle. All I can think to do is nod toward the space.

"I'm going to send this one to the hospital tonight," she says in a low voice that is weirdly intimate. "You might be too fresh off your golden carriage to get the picture, but I've fucked up more girls than you and anyone you've ever trained with combined. When I'm done with this little wannabe, I'm going to show you what a real fight feels like."

She steps into the open space with Sophie, who is across the way looking grounded and ready. I lock eyes with Vic and try to judge if her confidence is real or just supportive, but it's impossible to tell. When Vic is in your corner and talking you up, she's on her own supply.

I feel the need to intervene, but even if there was something I could do, the thought doesn't make sense. Sophie wants to be here, and she throws a decent punch. Who am I to say she shouldn't have the chance to slap the drama off Katarina's face?

And yet, there's that awful, nauseating feeling in the air when you know something bad is about to happen.

"Fight!"

The ref steps out of the way, and Katarina goes straight at Sophie, grabbing at her arms. I expected flying fists, and Sophie tries, but Katarina crowds her space too much for Sophie to get a strike with any pop off. She grabs Sophie's forearms and drags them down, then elbows Sophie in the face.

Sophie tries to shake her off, but Katarina is the larger woman by a lot and makes easy work of clutching onto her. She's latched on like an eagle and does the same move again, forcibly dragging Sophie's guard away from her face, then slashing through with an elbow. This time a splash of blood marks the impact.

Katarina wraps her hands around Sophie's throat, a jarring image that makes a flame flare in my chest. You can't simply reach out and choke people Homer Simpson style in the UFC, but here you can. It shouldn't be that difficult to outmaneuver, just insulting. Katarina uses the leverage to drag Sophie's head down while she drives her knee toward Sophie's face. My body tightens like I'll feel the impact myself. Sophie manages to turn her head enough to escape taking it right in the face, but blows to the side of the head can be just as dangerous.

Sophie leaps backward out of Katarina's clutches, but she looks rattled and unsure how to handle this line of attack. She must come from a formal setting. It explains her technique, and it would explain her bewilderment with this style. In a real gym, grapplers use takedowns. This straightforward grabbing and dragging is sloppy and brutish and only possible because of Katarina's size advantage.

Katarina barrels toward Sophie again, who backs away but runs into the ring of people surrounding her. They push her back into Katarina's clutches.

"Head position!" I yell.

A little shot of adrenaline reminds me I shouldn't have done that. I need to stay in my fucking lane, but I can't control myself.

"Head under her chin and frame!"

I grimace. What the hell am I doing? The crowd is so loud I'm sure no one even notices, but Sophie does. She jams her head against Katarina's chest and uses her forearms to brace against her body, creating a strong structure with her arms. She jams her head upward into Katarina's chin, causing her to look up and forfeit her posture and leverage, which neutralizes her strength.

Sophie's execution confirms she's had real training, but it only holds up for a second before Katarina figures out how to turn, drop her hips, and drag Sophie over her thigh, slamming her to the ground. The crowd roars in a satisfaction that can only mean Katarina is the favorite. All that talk about destroying countless women might be true, but I'm about ready to give up my pay for the night for a shot at her. This isn't genius fighting; she's just bigger and meaner, and I don't want that to work, but it is.

Katarina's fists land with sickening impact, and though I can't see Sophie's face from my angle, I see blood on the ground.

"Come on, that's enough!" I yell. The ref doesn't move.

An elbow jabs into my ribs, and it doesn't feel accidental. From someone who wants to see a knockout I imagine or maybe even bet on one. Something about this young woman getting mauled by this brute is twisting a knife I didn't know was inside me.

"She's done," I yell again, but no one cares. The ref finally lunges to stop the fight. As he's closing the distance, Katarina stops punching, yanks Sophie's arm up, and falls back into an armbar, slamming it over her hip without pause and bending it the wrong way.

The ref pulls Katarina off and Sophie yanks her arm back to her chest, her body curling to cradle it while Katarina does a lap around the ring. I know she's looking for me, and I'm ready to be found. I push forward past the block of a man who's in my way and lock eyes with her. She launches over and pushes her middle finger into my face. I slap it away.

"Fuck you. You didn't have to do that, you bitch," I yell.

"I wanted to. What're you going to do about it? Get in here, I'll snap you in half right now."

She pushes me hard enough to throw me off balance, but the wall of people behind me stops it from being effective. I swing for her teeth. It's clearly still all the way in my bones because I don't have to think a thing to do it. It just happens. But I don't hit her teeth. I don't hit her at all, and my mind can't wrap around why at first. And then I'm moving backward. I finally understand I'm being pulled. There's an arm looping over my shoulder to my ribs across my chest.

It's strong and secure and benign, and I can't argue with it even as Katarina and I shout the worst words we can come up with at each other. I smell that same warm scent from the elevator. Feel soft hair brush my neck. It's Harlow. Harlow is pulling me away from Katarina, and God, she is strong.

Katarina pushes into the crowd intent on chasing me down. The moment she steps in reach I send a front kick at her, but it falls just short as Harlow gives me another tug. And then her hands fall off me all at once, and she launches in front of me. She's nose to nose with Katarina, who sputters like a dying engine.

Katarina's eyes bounce from mine to Harlow's half a dozen times before she finds the words.

"She's a fighter, Harlow. She's fair game."

"Did I say she's fair game?"

"She's got a fucking attitude. Anyone who talks to me like that gets set straight. You'd do the same." Katarina glares at me about ready to foam at the mouth.

"She's off limits, Pierce," Harlow says. It stings a little realizing she calls everyone by their last name, and I'm surprised something like that can actually penetrate my thoughts right this second.

"You're really going to talk shit and then hide behind the boss?" Katarina yells at me. "You really are a little coward bitch, aren't you?"

"You wouldn't last one minute in the ring with me, you delusional walrus. Are you fucking stupid?"

Harlow turns toward me now, but I look past her.

"I would annihilate you. I would embarrass you. Do you have any idea who I've fought? I'd spank you like the little brat you are."

Harlow steps closer than I expected, her chest touching mine and her lips against my ear, sending shivers through my body.

"Is this really what you want?"

I can't imagine she's about to throw us in the ring here and now, but I could be wrong, and either way, the question does sober me. I meet her eyes and see an ocean of calm that runs so much deeper than this fury that has me acting like a maniac.

Part of me very much does want to sock the shit-eating grin off Katarina's cocky face. Part of me wants to prove I'm not a coward, and I'm not all talk. Part of me wonders if that urge to hit people I kept rubbing up against at Charlie's Chicken wasn't as simple as job dissatisfaction. Part of me, I admit a big part, really wants Vic and Harlow and Katarina and every-fucking-body else in this God damn neighborhood to know that just because I lost on TV does not mean that any halfwit with a bad attitude could do that to me.

Harlow turns back to Katarina but speaks loud enough for us all. "We have two more premium fights to get to tonight, if you don't mind."

She says something else in Katarina's ear that's just for her, and whatever it was, she absorbs it and heads directly to the elevator. When she's gone, the giggles come back one at a time at first, and then the full buzz returns like nothing happened.

"Go back to the clubhouse," Harlow says in my ear. "Don't worry about walking the fighters out. Jake will take over. I'll meet you back there after."

She disappears into the crowd. I lose track of her almost instantly. God only knows what she's always so busy with, but it's hardly the time to question her. I head for the clubhouse, confused because her breath in my ear sent a current of sensation through my body, yet I still feel like a slapped puppy. Pretty sure I just got fired, which is fair.

The next hour in the clubhouse takes a week, but the place eventually starts to clear out. When the fighters are gone and the chatter is faint, I labor to my feet and return supplies to the bags they came from. I place each item carefully, like an apology.

"You okay?" Harlow's voice surprises but doesn't startle me. It's too soothing to startle me. I take a deep breath and push the emotion away, not sure exactly what it is or where it's coming from.

"Is everyone gone?"

"The last elevator just went down. Why?"

"I was just thinking it's so beautiful out on the roof that maybe it would be nicer if you yelled at me there."

Harlow smiles. "Come on then, trouble."

I follow her out to where she leans against the rail overlooking the city. I've always been a sucker for the lights. Even seeing them a million times, it never stops dazzling me. They're the best up here where they can stay sacred and quiet. Get too close and an argument in the street will pierce the magic, but I'd be lying if I said such things didn't have their own charm.

"You ever look out at all those people and wonder if you're the biggest loser of them all?" I ask. I regret it right away. I don't want to self-deprecate my way around a well-earned reaming, and that came out way more serious than I meant it to.

"No." She takes a second to look over but is smiling when she does. "I'm not even the biggest loser I know, how could I be the biggest loser in all of that?"

"Right. Solid."

"I mean have you met people? Every other one has some secret addiction they spent their kid's college fund on before their wife divorced them, and now they're selling iPhone chargers out of the back seat of their Ford Focus. People are a fucking mess."

"Well, that was really specific."

She laughs. "You're doing fine, Laila. And you don't have to fight Katarina to prove that."

"I'm sorry about all that."

She shakes her head. "Nah, I owe you an apology. She's like that. Always talking a big game, always looking for a good fight and trying to hype it up. I should have known she'd take one look at you and see dollar signs."

I can hardly process what she's saying. "You're not mad?"

"No, but you did get everyone excited about the idea taking the bait like that, and I wouldn't mind knowing what's going on in your head. I thought you were done fighting."

"I am."

"You didn't seem done tonight."

"She busted Sophie's arm on purpose just to be an asshole. The ref was about to call it. She didn't have to do that."

Harlow sighs as she considers it. "Katarina knows how to work this game. She knows how to put on a show, what people want to see. How to stay a premium fighter and make the most money. But yes, you're right. She's also an asshole."

"People want to see an eighteen-year-old with way more potential than Katarina take permanent damage and maybe lose her career because she took a fight just a little too early?"

"People get just as hurt in the UFC every day, Laila. Sometimes it's malicious, sometimes it's just business, but everyone knows what they signed up for. And Sophie's arm isn't as bad as all that. Davina looked at it and thinks it's probably just a partial tear. She'll take some time to heal and come back when she's ready."

"Well, good." I roll my eyes. "That doesn't make Katarina any less of an asshole."

"True." Harlow looks back out at the lights.

"I wasn't trying to fight her. I just can't help my mouth sometimes."

"Or your fists?" Her smirk makes my cheeks warm as I remember I did indeed throw a punch, even if Harlow thwarted its landing. The glow of embarrassment draws my attention to the cool air, and I want to step closer to her, but I don't.

"Yeah, I guess sometimes those too. I can be impulsive."

"Impulsive?"

"Well, yeah, clearly. Reckless. Thoughtless. Stupid."

"Or maybe you're just a fighter who had a really good opportunity to fight. She was asking for it, she's trained, you don't like her, and you wanted it. It can be that simple, you know?"

I narrow my eyes at her. "Wait a minute, are you recruiting me? After all that talk?"

"Why'd you leave Eden?"

"I didn't leave Eden. I left the gym. I left fighting."

"I don't think so."

"Okay, Freud, what do you think?"

She shrugs, turning her palms up, an adorable playful light in her eyes. "Hey, it's not for me to say. I've just held a lot of people back from fights before, and they only come in two types. People who are actually trying to get past you and people who aren't."

I didn't expect her to have evidence behind her theory, and it knocks me off balance. I did truly try to both hit and kick Katarina. I did try to free myself from Harlow's iron grasp, though it was so solid I wouldn't have thought my effort made much of an impression. I'm pleased it did in an odd way.

"Yeah, well a lot of good it did me." I look at Harlow's arms involuntarily as I remember their power and want to feel it again. When I look back to her eyes, they're locked in so intensely a little shot of fear I said that out loud runs through me, but she's just reading my mind. She does that smile again. The one that says if only I knew what she was thinking.

"Don't worry, you gave me a hard time," she says. "You always do."

I laugh. "Me? What are you trying to say?"

"That you're a damn handful."

"Yeah, well you are too. You think just because I haven't had to pull you out of an impulse fight or save you from Charlie's Chicken that you're easy?"

"I'm the picture of easy." She says it with mock offense, but I can see a glimmer of wheels turning. The idea of her feeling insecure seems impossible and endearing.

"You're easy to be around. You're just not easy to know," I say.

"You trying to know me?"

"You haven't noticed?"

She looks back out at the lights in time to further hide an already subtle pleasure in her expression. I laugh as I realize she isn't going to respond and likely won't catch the irony of that, either. I elbow her and look over the rail again too.

"What do you want to know so bad?" she asks.

"So many things. You're very mysterious."

"Pick one."

Questions clash and compete. How and why she started the Yard. If she's a fighter. Where she grew up. Who her family is. What kind of music she likes. If she's single. What her lips feel like.

"How do you know Eden?"

She rolls her eyes. "Really?"

"Yes."

"I thought you two were on the outs. What does it matter?"

"Eden has never done anything but watch out for me, and I've seen her do it over and over again with half the neighborhood."

"Yeah, yeah, I know. She's a saint," Harlow says.

"No, she's just protective."

"And you're wondering why you'd need protection from me?"

"Well. Yeah."

I feel so exposed by the way her eyes are peeling away at me. It isn't fair that I'm an easy read and she's a vault. It isn't equal. I need to expel her from my inner workings, walk her back to the front door of my mind. Humor usually does it. "Listen, I would look for the red flags myself, but I keep getting distracted by your ass."

"You've been looking at my ass?" She grins. I guess that wasn't exactly *un*-vulnerable, was it?

She pretends to look over her shoulder. "Well, how is it back there?"

"It's really nice, you stubborn mother—"

"I'm not dangerous," she cuts me off. "Eden and I used to get along just fine. We even trained together for a short while, but she has a problem with what I'm building here. She's a purist. She wants everyone to walk the path she thinks is right. The one she put you on. You train hard, you come up, you take some amateur fights, you take some regional pro fights, you get a shot with the big boys, make the most of it, and then you waltz off into the sunset."

She pauses for me to respond, but I'm struck silent.

"I think that's great, but that's for the one percent," Harlow says. "The ultra talented and ultra lucky. It's even less accessible now that her gym is what it is, all high profile with elite contenders flying in from around the world. People in this neighborhood can't afford to do things that way."

My instinct is to defend Eden by blurting out all the numbers I know to be true from working there. The massive amount of money she's foregone to teach people who can't afford to pay her what she could charge, but something inside me knows Harlow doesn't just mean money. Money is a central struggle in most people's lives, but people can't afford this in time either, what it takes to train the right way. Or mentally. Emotionally. It takes everything, and most of us don't have enough to give.

"I started the Yard for the rest of us," Harlow says. "The ones the UFC and Bellator are never going to bother with. People who need money in their pocket now, not to quit their job so they can train eight hours a day and pay three gym memberships while their life falls apart on a hope that is never going to happen."

Heat crawls up my neck because I'm not sure if she understands how well she just described me or not.

"That makes a lot of sense."

"I respect everything Eden has done. It's the dream. It's what we all want to do. I just wanted to offer another path. You're dedicating your life to it now. You're risking and breaking your body now. You have bills now. Not everyone can train for years just hoping they'll get a shot and not everyone gets one. And the ones who do don't always make it. I didn't want people to be emptyhanded at the end of that."

"Like me," I say, scolding her just a little for tailoring this speech to me so directly like I wouldn't notice. Only, she looks surprised.

"Yeah, I guess so," she says. "I was actually thinking of myself though."

"Yourself?"

She smirks and elbows me. "Yeah, myself. I wanted to fight for the UFC like everyone else. I got a three-fight contract and a nicer check than I'd ever seen before. Nothing that was going to last forever, but enough to live the life, be a pro."

"Damn, you actually got a contract?" Go figure she was more successful than I was. While I've been walking around acting above all this. "Well, fuck me."

"All that should tell you, Laila, is that there is no magic landmark. I'm sure you thought *The Contender Series* was it, but even if you'd won you weren't guaranteed a contract unless they liked your performance, and even if they did that doesn't mean you'll win any of your fights once you're contracted, and even if you do it doesn't mean they'll retain you, and even if they do it doesn't mean the people will like you enough to turn you into a star, and even if they do it doesn't mean you'll become champion, and even if you do it doesn't mean you won't be a villain or washed up tomorrow. There is no finish line. There is no safe."

Her eyes are hypnotic in their intensity. The idea of "safe" is something I didn't realize I was hunting, but now some emotion between sadness and fear is welling up because I do want to be safe. I want to be saved. Harlow can't do that for me any more than Eden could, and I can't save Harlow from whatever lives in her silence.

"Anyway, I'm sure you can imagine all the reasons Eden disagrees with me."

I laugh because she couldn't be more right about that. Eden believes in perseverance and integrity no matter the cost. She's the kind of person who believes you do, in fact, march into the unknown with no promise of success or reward. She would see this as a cheap shortcut. She would find it small. Not in scope or dollars but in character. She would find it weak to settle. To go underground.

"So, it's nothing personal? She just doesn't like your business?"

Harlow tilts her head in consideration. "They're intertwined, aren't they? When your belief systems clash that way? She basically sees me as a blood merchant."

"Well, that's not fair," I say, surprised how much I mean it.

"She doesn't know me, Laila. Not really." She shrugs in that effortless way of hers, so authentically unbothered, then leans closer. "One of her students asked me for a fight a long time ago. I set it up for him, and he got hurt. That was all she needed to know. She thought he was too young, that I was taking advantage of his desperation and put him in over his head. She thought I ruined his chances of making it for real because he didn't have the stomach for it after that. The truth is he asked for a fight. I matched him with another first-timer in his weight class, and he fought well. He wasn't outclassed, and he wasn't tricked. He went home with more money in his pocket than I'd promised him up front. He just got caught. Fighting is an unpredictable sport. Everybody knows that, but the second it's underground nothing can be that simple and everything is up for judgment."

"That's why you can't recruit her students." I put it together.

She nods. "That is why I can't recruit her students. She told me exactly what she thought of me. I told her what happened and what I was really trying to do with this. We eventually landed on a sort of stay out of my way and I'll stay out of yours thing. I don't touch her students, even if they ask me, and she doesn't report me and ruin my life."

"Nice." I scoff. That's so much to process. That Eden could ruin Harlow's life. That she must believe Harlow to some extent, or she would have. Harlow has an agreement but no leverage. Not that she needs it. Eden won't break her end. Not if the rules aren't violated. But then, my being here could be interpreted as just that. Yet Harlow risked it.

"Fuck." The silence fills as I let all the information settle. I look up and squint at her. "Did you really just say you don't touch her students, even if they ask?"

Harlow rolls her eyes. "You know what I mean."

"Just checking if that was another rule."

"It wasn't spelled out, but I'm sure she wouldn't be thrilled."

"What do you think would be more dangerous? Giving me a fight or touching me?"

"I'm not sure." The city lights play in her bright eyes. "Which did you have in mind?"

I'm so far from ready for what that look does to me. A rush floods my arms and plummets down my body. I want to step closer. Feel her against me. Her soft skin and hard muscles. I want to touch her hair. I want the heat of her mouth to make me forget how cold this roof is getting.

Just as the coiling tension builds to the point it has to spill over, as I'm about to reach for her, an ungodly loud slam makes me jump so high I might've gone off the roof if Harlow didn't grab me. My heart pounds as I look over my shoulder and see the shit bitch security guard who just fucked up my magic.

"What the fuck?" I say. Totally involuntary. The security guard's face twists with attitude.

"You what the fuck. You can't be up here. It's the middle of the night."

Harlow laughs and squeezes my forearm. "Sam knows we're here. It's all good."

"It's the middle of the night," he repeats.

"Sam knows."

"Okay, well…"

"We're about to go," she says.

She meets my eyes and smiles with a mixture of amusement and apology because this guy clearly has no intention of leaving us alone.

"Have a last look at the view while I get the bags, and I'll give you a ride home." She squeezes my arm and heads for the clubhouse. I should take in the view, but I can't help but glare at the security guard instead.

"Really, dude?" I gesture at Harlow, assuming he can add the atmosphere to her jaw-dropping hotness and come up with how much he sucks for this. He cracks a smile and holds up his hands in surrender.

"My bad, okay? Rules."

Chapter Eleven

Simone hates it when Vic puts her feet on the table. I have no idea why. It never leaves a mark, and she's not uptight in any other way, but that one time Simone muttered her annoyance about it under her breath was the closest she's ever come to complaining or to having a quirk. The ruffle in her cool was so out of character it cemented into my mind, and now I can't stand it when Vic puts her feet on the table. I smack her shoe to get her to move.

She rolls her eyes and puts them on the floor. "Yes, Your Majesty."

Vic has no clue this originated with Simone. It might matter to her more if she did. Vic hit on Simone around four times before she realized she'd have more luck seducing the table.

"How's Sophie's arm?" I ask.

Vic shrugs. "It's swollen. It hurts. She'll be out for a while."

"But it's not broken?"

She shakes her head, but my bullshit detector goes off. "She did go to the doctor?"

"And spend all her money on them telling her to put some ice on it and elevate? No."

"But if it's—"

"It's not broken. She'd know."

"Not al—"

"She's a big girl, Laila. She says she's fine. Now tell me what the fuck is going on with you and Harlow? You think I came here to talk about Sophie?"

"Excuse the shit out of me for thinking you gave a damn about your fighter," I say.

"She's not my fighter. She's my friend, and she's good, so stop dodging."

"You still owe me an explanation for ditching me at the Yard. I met Sam on the roof and he's a weirdo. What do you have going with him?"

"That weirdo is filthy rich," Vic says, separating a stripe of red hair from the black and swooping it behind her ear.

"Key word filthy. What, did he pay you a million dollars to go on a walk in the middle of the night? What happened, Vic? I was worried about you. I didn't know anybody, and you just vanished."

She looks at her nails. She doesn't do well with being scolded. Not finding a way to turn the tables and yell at me instead is the closest thing she ever does to admitting she feels bad. Vic grew up watching her father and brother go in and out of jail, both hard men from a hard place who didn't know what to pass down to a young woman other than a credo to not make an easy victim. It's turned out she's not an easy anything.

"Look, when Sam asks you to go have a chat, you do it. That's all I can say."

"Um, no. Cryptic as fuck. Do better."

"It's not your business, Laila."

"Well, then me and Harlow isn't yours."

"There's a you and Harlow?" She raises her eyebrow and beams.

"Don't twist my words. You know what I'm saying."

"Oh, come on. I'm your best friend. If you're not going to tell me, who are you going to tell?" She starts to put her foot on the table again before she remembers not to and puts it back on the floor with a little stomp. Is this person really my best friend? I've never thought of her that way. My oldest friend, maybe, but best? Is this really the best I can do? The guilt I feel over that thought is obligatory at best.

"You first," I say.

"God, you are so annoying. Fine, Sam was approaching me about a fight. He wants to see me in a bigger show."

"I thought Harlow arranged the fights."

Vic nods. "Well, she does. But she's putting together a show people want to see, obviously. Especially the big players. Sam was making it known what he wants to see."

"Which is?"

"Me in a championship fight with Katarina."

My brain stumbles. Vic fighting for a championship is absurd in and of itself, but against Katarina makes even less sense.

"But Katarina isn't even champion, is she?" Katarina did brag about her experience and how many people she's beaten, but I doubt she would have left out the fact that she was champ.

"No. The champ was a chick named Mila. Katarina was champ before her, and she only lost the belt to Mila because she was disqualified in their fight. Mila got pretty hurt, but people dogged her so hard for not being the 'real' champ winning by DQ. She's retiring."

"Oh, that's nice." I roll my eyes.

"We're fighters. It's not supposed to be nice," Vic says. It can be respectful, but I don't even bother trying to tell Vic that.

"What did she get disqualified for?"

"I wasn't there, but I heard Katarina bashed her head into the floor, which is technically a weapon. You can't use objects, just your body. The point is, Sam had the early heads-up Mila is retiring, and he was seeing if I'd be interested in fighting for the vacant title."

"You already said yes, didn't you?"

"Of course, I said yes. I'll make a ton of cash. He already has lots of ideas about how he's going to promote it. Me avenging Sophie kind of thing."

"*He's* going to promote it?"

She rolls her eyes again. "And Harlow, obviously. It's a word-of-mouth enterprise, Laila. Everyone promotes it, and no one promotes it. Sam knows the right people. This is not as nefarious as you're trying to make it."

She might be right. I just don't like how much influence he seems to have—or picturing him pulling Vic down a dark street to talk her into fighting for his entertainment. Against Katarina. Does he imagine her winning or losing this fight that's so exciting?

"And you like your chances?" I ask. She pulls back as if to clutch her pearls.

"Of course I like my fucking chances."

Vic always likes her chances. She'd like her chances against Godzilla.

"Your turn," she says.

I have more questions, but I'm not going to get anything real out of Vic. I think she has to think no one can touch her to get in there, and I can't blame her.

"Harlow." Vic's about to come unglued.

"She found out I was working at Charlie's Chicken and offered me a job helping out with the events."

Vic snorts. "Were you wearing the hat?"

"Shut up, I had to do something."

She raises her hands. "Hey, I get it. You got to pay your bills. Chicken is totally your calling."

"It wasn't for long, and I was lucky to have it, okay? Don't shit on my uncle."

"Hey, I love Tony," Vic says. "The man makes great chicken. That uniform is just public humiliation."

I can't even argue with that. "Well, now I work for Harlow, so it's a non-issue."

"And?"

"And what?"

"And how did you two get all cozy?"

"We're not cozy."

"You're something," she says.

"I'm thinking about asking her for a fight is what I am."

She sits up, her whole demeanor shifting. "Really?"

"Yeah. I mean, with my skills and history and her having a mega underground fighting ring that pays out the ass, don't you think it would be kind of dumb if I didn't?"

She shrugs and leans back again.

"Yeah, I'm going to need more," I say.

"I don't know, Laila. Do I get the urge to get paid, of course. Do I think it's dumb if you just stay a facilitator? Not really."

"What are you saying?"

"Nothing."

"You're saying something."

She sighs. "Look, don't make this a big deal. You just left fighting. All I'm saying is you can make decent, safe money doing what you're doing now. That's what you said you wanted."

"And now I'm saying maybe I want to take a fight and you're looking at me like you know something I don't. What is it? You don't think I can do it?"

"Could you call Harlow and ask for a fight? Of course you could."

"Quit playing with me, Vic. You're saying I can't win?"

"Maybe you'd win, maybe you wouldn't. I'm saying maybe you were right when you decided this isn't for you. It's not for everyone. You have to be a little out of your mind, especially in the Yard, and you're not. If you didn't want to do it in the gym with all the pads and rules and refs and coaches holding your hand, why the fuck would you want to do it in the dirt and broken glass?"

A chill spreads through me the more words come out of her mouth. Having my hand held. That's her take on my career? She's too ignorant to even understand the superior technique or comprehend the level of competition in my world. Everything I've done, and she doesn't respect me at all. Years of professional training, and she still sees me as playing at a simulation of fighting, incapable of the real thing.

"Fuck you, Victoria."

"Fuck me what? You asked me a question. God forbid someone tell you the truth."

"You think you're better than me? Because you fight in fucking jeans you think you're tougher?"

Her eyes flash. She scrunches her nose and holds up her fingers in a pinching gesture to indicate yes, maybe a little. An inferno flares in my chest.

"Are you really that fucking stupid that you see me lose on TV and you think that means I can't fight? You think because you can win a tussle with a drunk nobody that you're better?"

"Hey, *you* decided you can't fight," she says. "Not me. You quit during that fight. You crumbled and you tapped out. I could have told you it wasn't for you sooner, but I didn't. I let you figure it out yourself. All those years we kicked it I never gave you shit for being all talk even though you were."

"I can fight, you ignorant jerk. Yeah, you saved my ass when we were kids, but we're not even in the same league anymore. You barely even train."

"If you're in another league, then why aren't you *in another league*? You're talking about coming to fight for Harlow just like I do, hot shot. And you're going to get chewed up and spit out there too because you're fucking soft. Sorry I tried to save you from it."

"Get the fuck out."

"What's the matter, you want to hit me? I dare you."

"Just go, Vic."

"Set me straight, Moretti." She steps closer and grabs my shirt. "Set me straight."

"Hey!"

It's the loudest I've ever heard Simone speak. We freeze with Vic's fist still twisted in my shirt as I stare into her eyes. I want to grab that fist and twist it so fast her wrist snaps into five pieces. This obnoxious animal. Belligerent but stupid as a fucking stump. Any chance she gets she charges headfirst into a brick wall, but she really has charged into a lot of brick walls for me. For that, she gets to keep her wrist.

"Go," I say.

She glances over my shoulder, I assume at Simone, and drops her arm.

"If you weren't such a bitch you could handle the answers to your questions without being a fucking baby." She slams the front door on her way out. I rub my head before I turn to Simone.

"I'm really sorry about that."

Simone looks me up and down. "Listen, I don't know how to patch drywall."

"What?"

She rolls her eyes and says it again. "I do not know how to patch drywall."

"Me either."

"Okay, so maybe let's not fight in the living room."

I can't help but smile as I process her meaning. "Simone, was that a joke?"

Her eyebrows come together like I'm slow. "No."

She retreats to her room, and my blood simmers in the silence. I did ask Vic questions and then lose it over her answers, but she deserved it, right? That wasn't honesty, that was cruelty. She was trying to hurt me. She wants me to fail, like Eden said.

Or, she could just be right. She could just be saying what I've spent my life afraid to know since I was a skinny kid with a smart mouth.

Do I really know that I could defeat Vic as easily as I should be able to? Or did I not hit her because I don't even know that anymore? There are levels. I might not have made it in the UFC, but I still walk through any random street rat with an attitude problem. Right?

I search for my phone. I throw couch cushions and pillows and papers everywhere until I find it on the floor. I scroll to Harlow's name and hit send before I can second-guess it.

"Hey," she says, a happy familiarity in the greeting that doesn't match the grave urgency I feel.

"I want a fight."

There's a long pause. The kind where people usually ask you to repeat yourself, but she doesn't.

"I want a fight," I say again.

"Laila…" She sighs. "There's a lot to consider."

"Fine, let's consider it. Can we meet? Tomorrow? Today? Now?"

She laughs. "I'm a little busy this we—"

"Harlow, please?"

There's another long pause. "Okay. Tomorrow. I'll send you the address."

"Thank you."

"See you tomorrow, killer."

CHAPTER TWELVE

The slightly manic energy level of my phone call to Harlow yesterday has receded to something closer to nervousness. That and a little embarrassment. If I remember it correctly, and I'm afraid I might, I basically begged her to meet with me today. That would be awkward enough, but to add to it, it was the first I'd spoken to her since she drove me home after the rooftop. The sexy rooftop.

At the time, I could have sworn she was looking at my lips too. Sneaking glances down my body. Finding her way just a little more inside my space. I would have put good money on it or at least felt confident enough to acknowledge to Vic that something more than a temporary employment arrangement was afoot.

But then Harlow drove me home, and nothing happened. No kisses were kissed. No plans were made. No phone call had followed. If I hadn't been so out of my mind mad and frantic after my argument with Vic, I would have put a lot more thought into breaking the silence.

I know the go-to charade is to pretend you have no clue when someone is interested in you. Every woman I've ever dated has played that game. The "I'm too humble to ever assume someone likes me" game. It's a safe pretense. You never get burned, never think someone likes you when they don't, never make a move you shouldn't have made only to look like a moron. Never have to take a chance.

That's never been me. I'm a flirt. I pick up on it when a woman is checking me out and more often than not, I find it fun to play and to pull her into deeper waters. I have good instincts for the difference between barroom fun and true interest, and reading the subtle signals women send is a puzzle I love to turn over. So as nervous as Harlow can make me, and as out of my league as she is, I admit I was surprised when I was forced to consider that I read that night all wrong. Then embarrassed, because in the process of reading it wrong, I definitely sent some signals she couldn't have missed.

Maybe it's for the best that I called her in such a state because I wouldn't have been likely to do so at all otherwise. Or maybe it's all that much more embarrassing. One second, she was just trying to be a nice person, offer me a little quick cash. Next thing she knows I'm making eyes at her and placing desperate, demanding phone calls.

It's a miracle she's even seeing me, and though it never occurred to me that the address she texted was anything other than her house, it's another slapping reality check when I give it to the taxi driver and he responds, "The park?"

"Oh," I say as I click the seat belt. "Yeah, I guess so."

She's having me meet her in a park? Does she think I'm a fucking psycho who shouldn't know where she lives? Did I put off that level of crazy when I bulldozed through her trying to tell me she was too busy to see me? God, I really did do that, didn't I?

The driver completes the easy journey with all the tactless precision you want in a good cab driver, pulling into the park in minutes and throwing his hands up at the congested road and kids running between cars.

"Come on," he says as a seven-year-old dashes right in front of him, followed by a mom who's reaching to retrieve him while clinging to the two-year-old that is sagging off her hip. "Oh good, make sure all three of you die."

They're far from the only ones. There are kids everywhere. Like a bounce castle threw up. Nothing good will come from making him sit through this line of chaos, just a higher bill. I pay him and jump out, estimating myself to be close enough while realizing I don't know exactly where I'm going. The park? Who meets someone at the park without telling them it's a park and where inside said park they're meeting?

I pull my phone out to chastise her only to see I already have a message that says, *Baseball.* I look across the expanse of grass I've landed on. The sun is piercing straight through my eyes into my brain, but I spot what must be a baseball diamond if the gleaming daggers of light are indeed bouncing off silver bleachers like I suspect.

I start toward "baseball," wading through children and soccer balls and discarded Capri Suns. It finally clicks that I'm at a sporting event. Well, thirteen or so of them to be more exact. Why would Harlow want to meet me at a children's sporting event? That's not something you do just because someone is being a creep. That's something you do when you're a creep.

Or a parent...

But that's not possible. I mean, it's possible, but no.

When I get to the baseball diamond and see the field covered in spots of tiny human, my brain swirls with confusion. I wanted something to click by the time I got here, but it's still a children's sporting event.

"Hey!"

I jump and turn. Shield my eyes and take in the image.

It's Harlow, all right, beautiful as ever and not in any apparent need for medication. She's in a baseball shirt and hat, and she's happy. Not that happy is a bad thing, and not that she isn't one to smile. That smile of hers gives me the shyness as often as anything else about her, but I'm not used to seeing her smile like this. No smirk. No hidden thoughts. Just big and free and unguarded.

She puts a hat on my head and pulls it so a slash of shade relieves the sun's assault.

"Oh God, thank you."

"Thought you might not bring one."

"Since you didn't tell me it was a baseball game and all?"

"Exactly that."

My eyes adjust and clear. She's still smiling. It looks good on her. So does the shirt. It's hugging all the right places, and it's a testament to her gorgeous body that it takes me as long as it does to process the team name across her chest.

"The Silly Sluggers?"

"That's us!" Harlow nudges her head toward the bleachers for me to follow. In just a missed beat, I have to jog to catch up to her because she's out of there like nobody's business.

"Uh, Harlow?"

"Yeah?" she says without slowing.

"How do I say this…"

I climb the bleacher steps and follow her down the bench, not sure I have her attention as she manages to step over every single drink, snack, and long-legged parent in her way without taking her eyes off the field.

"Do you have a kid?"

She reaches an opening and stops. It takes me a moment to realize these are our seats because she makes no motion to sit and is scanning the field. Finally, I adjust to this completely different human in Harlow's body and realize it's the cutest thing I've ever seen. I can't help but smile watching her look for her little whoever.

"I told you I was busy today, but you sounded a little…"

"Unhinged?"

She looks over with brilliant sparkling eyes and smiles warmly. "Kind of."

I turn back to the field and consider asking her to clue me in with a number or something, but I'm curious if there's a mini-Harlow out there and if I'd know them when I saw them. There's a mix of genders, all around seven, all adorable and doing their level best to simply manage the equipment with which they've been entrusted with little hope of using it effectively.

Harlow leans closer and points. "Number eight. Short stop. That's Zoey."

I squint at the little girl in her Silly Sluggers jersey, one of the only players on the field in a pose that suggests any level of athletic ability or interest in what she's doing. I smile and start to tell Harlow so, but she points again.

"And number eight, right field. That's Zane."

I take a sharp breath as if the anxiety of two children is mine to deal with, but when I see Zane way farther out than these kids have any hope of hitting, spinning in a circle while he looks up at the sky, I laugh.

"Oh my God, they're so cute. They're both number eight?"

"The coaches tried to get them to pick different numbers, but it was hopeless." She shakes her head while she watches them. So much love is pouring out of her I inexplicably want to hug her.

"Twins," she adds with confidence that it conveys a full explanation.

"I had no idea you had—"

"They're my niece and nephew." A sly smile comes back that makes it clear she was having fun withholding that, but there's still something shining from her I've never seen before, and I want to be in its light.

"You did that on purpose."

She laughs. "I'm considering stealing them so it's all the same."

I would have never pictured Harlow with kids, of her own or anyone else's for that matter. I wouldn't have pictured her liking kids, but she clearly adores these little suckers, and the involved aunt thing is integrating into the way I see her faster than I would have thought it could.

"I'm sorry I'm interrupting your family time," I say. I feel guilty I bothered her with my needs when she has a life that is so much fuller and more, well, normal than I would have ever guessed. My sudden, urgent, bloodlust feels so out of place and unimportant here.

"No worries as long as you cheer loud," she says as the batter strikes out and the Silly Sluggers run toward the dugout. "Good job, Sluggers!"

I whoop for them as they stumble and scramble and wander the wrong way while coaches wrangle them in.

"You picked the right girl," I say. "Being loud, I can do."

"Then you're in."

"So, you're the baseball aunt. Did you play?"

"I took a pitch to the eye my first time ever trying," she says. "Then they decided to let me try pitching instead. The batter hit it and cracked me in the eye again."

"Oh my God." I laugh. "That's tragic."

"It's not my game." She winks. "But Zoey loves it."

"And Zane?"

"Zane loves Zoey." Harlow smiles fondly and I nod my understanding as I remember the little guy spinning in the outfield.

"Got it. And they're your..."

"Sister's kids. The youngest two out of six."

"Six? Good God, is she okay?"

She smiles at the joke but answers seriously, "Not really. Not because of the kids. She loves the kids, of course. But she isn't well."

"I'm sorry."

Harlow shrugs, though it's clearly not the kind of thing she can shake off. "She has a hard time getting to things like this, so I had to give baseball another chance."

"Well, I do think it's your duty as a lesbian anyway."

"Who said I was a lesbian?"

I pause, jolted. I'd never so much as questioned if Harlow was a lesbian, which I suppose is rude and could explain how I got myself overexcited in the first place.

"Vic?" I make a face that conveys I'm trying to pull one over on her.

"Uh-huh," Harlow says.

"Please be fucking with me."

She laughs and nods. "I'm fucking with you."

"Rude and wrong, Harlow—" I want to say her last name and realize I don't know it.

"Hayes."

"Really?"

"Yeah, why? What's wrong with Hayes?"

"Nothing. It's nice. Harlow Hayes. It just sounds…planned."

She laughs. "I mean, yeah? I do believe there was a name planning phase sometime during the pregnancy."

"You know what I mean. It just sounds nice."

"Well, thank you," she says. I feel a warmth flow from her into me. This family thing is contagious. "So, you wanted to talk. Urgently."

"Yeah," I say. I'm still embarrassed but resolved to power through it. "I want a fight."

"I think I did catch that. Let's go, Zoey!" she screams as Zoey comes up to the plate. Zoey bends her knees and takes a practice swing that looks damn good compared to the rest of the ones I've seen.

"I want to fight Katarina."

"Ah," she says. "Of course."

"Is that a problem?"

She waits for Zoey to swing and when she misses, Harlow cups her hands to make a megaphone and yells, "Don't worry about it, Zoey! Be patient!"

Then she looks back to me, that same carefree thing all over her that I've never seen at the fights. It's nice, soothing but from a different source than her usual reserve. Less that you can't get to her because she's such a badass and more that you can't get to her because she's truly happy.

"You know the arrangement," she says. "With Eden."

"I'm not her student anymore. The arrangement doesn't apply."

"You're her favorite. Her personal mentee."

"I made it very clear I was out. She doesn't own me. She knows that."

She looks skeptical but nods. "Remember, everyone fights in the Yard first. I haven't given out a single pass on that. I can't start now."

"I don't want a pass. I'll fight in the Yard."

The corner of Harlow's mouth tugs into a smile. "You sure? Katarina is beyond the Yard. It won't be her. Not your first time."

I won't pretend that isn't irritating, but of course I understand. There's not an organization in the world, not even an underground one, where you get to walk in from the street and demand the exact fight you want without earning it in some fashion.

"That's fine. Whoever, whenever."

"Whoever, whenever, huh?" She elbows me. "What's gotten into you?"

My argument with Vic flies across my mind. My teeth find each other just thinking of her, but I don't know how close she and Harlow really are. What Harlow might already know or think about it.

"I just need to know who I am in there. Even if this game isn't for me, the UFC, the belt, the cameras. The person you saw on TV in a ball on the ground can't be me. That can't be everything."

"Laila." Harlow tilts her head. "That never was everything, but people who have never fought a day in their life are always going to talk shit about real athletes who are actually putting themselves out there. You can't stop that."

"I know, but I can't live the rest of my life as a coward. Do you know what it's like for me to walk down the street around here? You know the way people laugh at me when I pass by?"

"They're idiots," she says. "They'll stop. It'll blow over."

"Or it won't, and I'll always be a fucking joke."

"Everyone loses if they have the guts to really challenge themselves."

"Yeah, but losing a fight isn't like losing a baseball game, Harlow. You know that. Not the way I lost. My own friend doesn't even respect me."

"You mean Vic? Did something happen?"

Zoey swings and misses again, and Harlow and I yell out in unison. "You got it, Zoey!"

Zoey taps the ground with the bat and toes at a clump of dirt.

"Head up, baby, you're okay!" Harlow yells.

"It's really not about Vic," I say. "She just made me realize some things."

"What did she do?" Harlow's eyes flash with something deadly that sends a tingle through me. The idea of her fighting for my honor, I admit, is not something I would change the channel on.

"It's okay, Harlow. Vic did what she does."

"Then why are you friends?" she asks.

"Why are you?"

"We're friendly enough, but nothing I wouldn't put up in flames if she crossed a line," Harlow says.

There's a question on her face that's so endearing, like she's asking if it needs to go up in flames. "You don't have to do anything on my behalf, but thank you. Just give me the fight. That's all I need."

"You don't have to prove anything, Laila."

"I do though. To myself."

She shakes her head like it's against her better judgment. "Okay. If you're sure."

"I'm sure."

"You scared?"

"Yes."

Zoey clocks the next pitch between first and second. She flings her bat to the ground and runs for first while Harlow and I scream and jump. I've never been as invested in a team sport in my entire life as I am in this little girl getting to first. She does effortlessly while the second baseman runs to retrieve the ball that is rolling toward the outfield. Zoey steals second before the short stop realizes he's needed on second.

The throw goes over his head, and pure chaos erupts as damn near every player chases the ball, all of them struggling with the act of actually grabbing it while Zoey steals third and keeps running, turning her hit into a home run.

"Let's go!" Harlow and I scream together, then laugh. Zoey turns to find Harlow as she jumps up and down and Harlow waves wildly. Zane and the rest of the team plow into Zoey's celebration, and it might all be the most wholesome thing I've ever seen.

"I didn't know you had family," I say.

"What?" Harlow asks over the noise.

"Nothing. I just didn't know you had family."

"Of course I do." She smiles. "Don't you?"

"Well sure," I say. "But, you know, not like this."

"Like what?"

"Like..." I pause. "Like with all the warm and fuzzies and stuff."

Her eyebrows come together, and she tilts her head again. She's got a dose of puppy in her.

"Oh, don't do that. Don't feel bad for me."

"Well, don't say pitiful stuff then." She beams.

"They love me and whatever. They're just messy and don't exactly get me." I realize the game is ending soon and she'll want to be with those cuties when it does. "Well, hey, thanks—"

She pulls me into a hug. I'm a hugger, but I fall into it like I've never done it before. She muscles through my stiffness and squeezes me. Really hugs me. Not those bullshit hugs where you barely touch and it's over before it starts.

"You still feel bad for me, huh?"

She laughs. "You know it's also an option not to joke your way through everything. You can just hug me."

I nod and pull her back into the hug, trying not to be so damn awkward about it this time. Her body feels so good, so warm and strong, and it fits against me. Her hair smells like cedar and her arms wrap around me in just the right places.

"Thank you."

"You are not a coward," she says. "Vic has no idea what it is to step out under those lights."

I squeeze her tighter because while I can manage to stop joking long enough to hug her, I'm not prepared to cry. "I won't let you down, okay?"

"Never ran through my mind."

Chapter Thirteen

The air is cool and sharp. The voices on the other side of my mother's townhouse door fire back and forth at each other in a tone and volume that's difficult to distinguish as fun or fight. That makes it festive. Not in the Hallmark, Santa Claus, merry whatever kind of way, but in the more realistic, Thanksgiving kind of way where the men are yelling at the TV about football and the women are yelling at the men about their one responsibility that's gone neglected. Only it's not Thanksgiving.

I knock like I'm trying to break the thing down to cut through it all. Voices erupt into a war about who should answer the door and clomping clumsy thuds lets me know it has fallen to one of the men. The door swings open and my brother Louis fills the frame.

"It's just Laila," he shouts and walks away.

I roll my eyes and step inside. "Awesome."

When I walk into the kitchen, my mom's back is turned as she hovers over the stove. Louis is at the kitchen table with the chair turned out so he can sprawl his giant man legs across as much room as possible while he and Dad stare into the corner where the fifteen-inch TV sits.

"Hey, kiddo," my dad says from the end of the table where he's watching the game. I lean into his one-armed hug and then punch Louis on his splayed thigh.

"Laila!" Mom shouts my name like an accusation.

"Hi, Mom."

She turns and points a spatula at me. "What the hell's the matter with you?"

"Great to see you too, Mom."

"Let the girl eat first, Maria," my dad says.

"Did you quit Tony's Chicken already?" She jabs the spatula at me.

"Uhh, yeah." I bite my lip and brace.

"I don't understand you. I get my brother to give you a job, a good job, and you just up and quit two weeks later? Was it even two weeks? What the hell goes through your head?"

"Uncle Tony was fine with it, Mom. I promise."

"Yeah, that's what you think." She grabs a basket of rolls and holds it out for me to transport to the table. Louis is grabbing at it before I can even set it down.

"He was fine, Mom. He barely noticed."

She follows me out and sets down a bowl of salad. Louis sticks his fingers in it, fishing for a crouton. I slap his hand.

"Gross, don't be a pig."

"Bite me."

"Look, he's my brother. You think I don't know when he's upset? Of course he's nice to you, but you know what happens next? He calls me." Mom slaps Louis's hand this time and he makes a face like he's never been more shocked. "He calls me, and he says Maria, I gave your daughter a job and she quits before she's even done training. What kind of a thing to do is that? How am I supposed to answer him?"

"He did not say that."

"Yeah, well he wanted to."

"It just wasn't for me, I'm sorry."

"How would you know in two weeks?" Mom's volume goes up three notches, and Dad reluctantly turns away from the TV.

"Can't we do this over dinner?"

"It is dinner, Joe. Talk to your daughter."

I smile and sit, intertwine my fingers and meet his eyes. Dad isn't the scolder of the family, he's the perpetually exhausted. He ran out of steam with Mom years ago and she kicked him out soon after, but he still finds his way back for occasions.

"Is there something else you think is for you?" he asks.

"How is she ever going to find out if she quits every two weeks, Joe? You're supposed to give two weeks' notice, not two weeks' employment." She slams the spaghetti in the middle of the table and flops into her seat, cupcake apron still on. Her dark hair falls in loose curls that look as frazzled as her expression. "You have to put in the time, Laila, find your place. Move up. Like your brother." She points to Louis, who smiles with triumph. "You think he liked cleaning the bathrooms and stocking the shelves down at the hardware store? He didn't. But he stuck it out. Now look at him."

All three of them gesture at Louis like his success speaks for itself. Dad looks tired, the skin growing loose around the once strong stubbled jaw Louis inherited.

"Who, him? This guy is your big example of a winner?"

"Hey, be nice," Dad says. "It's his night."

"It took him six fucking years to bump up to assistant manager in a complete shithole."

"Hey, I'm going to have a salary now. You ever had a salary?" Louis leans over the table to shoot the word at me.

"They do that so they can make you work more hours without paying you more, dummy."

"Joke's on you, they are paying me more." He misses my point with so much confidence.

"No." I pinch my forehead. "I mean per hour. Forget it."

"Not everyone is promotion material, Ma. Or Tony's Chicken material."

"Excuse me for wanting more," I snap.

"Oh yeah, like you were ever going to be a real fighter. You just didn't want to get a real job," Louis says.

"You do all realize I had a steady job for years, right? You act like I can't hold down a gig. And I was a real fighter." I kick Louis's leg about as hard as I can, and he kicks me back.

"Hey, knock it off," Mom says. "And, Laila, that fighting place? That is not a job for a young woman."

"Yeah, well, it paid my rent just fine."

"And you quit that too," Louis mutters.

"What are you planning to do now?" my dad asks.

"Thank you for finally asking." I wrestle the tongs from Louis and serve myself a pile of salad. "I actually already got another job. A better job."

"See, you worry too much," Dad says to Mom.

She squints at him, and then me when she asks, "What is it? What's better about it?"

"It pays better, for one."

"Beautiful," Dad says.

"And it's something I'm interested in."

"What does that mean? What is it?" Mom asks. I hate that she's so sure it will be something she doesn't approve of, and I hate it even more that she's right.

I shove spaghetti in my mouth to give myself a second to find the right words. "It's like, an event coordinator position."

"Like weddings and stuff?" Louis asks. I want to kick him again, but I think he might've actually meant that one innocently.

"Uh, no, not weddings."

"Parties?" Dad asks.

"Sort of?" I cringe.

"Laila, what is it?" Mom demands.

"Sporting events."

"Fights," Louis says.

"Laila?" Mom glares at me.

I sigh. "Yes, Mom. Fights."

"Oh, not again. Why?" She drags the word out like she's in pain.

"That's where all my experience is, Mom. I know a lot about it, and I like it."

"You like it? You like being around that with the blood and the sweat and the criminals? Are you trying to give me a heart attack?"

"Oh my God, it's a real sport, Mom. Pretend it's basketball, and you won't get so worked up."

"Maria, just be happy she isn't fighting anymore," Dad says.

Louis and I make eye contact. I shoot him a look that says I will find Darth Vader level dark side capabilities and telekinetically squeeze his fucking throat shut if he suggests to them that I'm fighting again. The non-verbal threat confirms his suspicion, and he smirks, but he stays quiet. It's nothing I can or ever have hidden for long.

When you fight, you start turning up bruised, and when you do that, you have to either come clean or give Dad your hit list. That said, I haven't fought yet, and this night doesn't need to get worse.

"Laila, I don't understand why it always has to be so hard with you," Mom says. "Why do you always have to do things so weird?"

"So weird?" I can't help the sass that infiltrates the word, and Dad gives me a light smack on the back of my head for the attitude.

"I don't know how else to say it, Laila," Mom says. "You're just not happy until there's something dangerous or seedy about it. I don't know why you can't just work at the bank or a bakery or something like a normal girl. I swear to God if you did the next thing out of your mouth would be that it's only open in the middle of the night on the worst corner in the city. Why do you have to do that? Do you have a death wish or something? I thought I was going to have to worry about my boy with that stuff, but it's my little girl who needs to run around in cages getting blood all over her."

I fall silent, the words all tumbling into the sinkhole in my chest that collects such feedback. It's a deep pit. It takes a long time to find the bottom and feel the reverberations of the landing, but down they go.

The table falls silent. Mom has always been a pit bull, and there's always been an understanding that she means well, but she finds people's limits by smashing them. She closes her eyes.

"I'm just saying I want you to be safe, sweetheart. Joe, you talk to her, I don't know." She shakes her head and gets up to find something to add to the table.

Dad stares at his plate as he tries to put something together. He finally looks up. "You know, you're so gorgeous. I don't know why you don't just find a nice guy who wants to take care of you."

I laugh and shake my head as Mom exclaims, "Joe! What is the matter with you, you can't say that!"

"What?" He flings his hands up.

"She likes *women*, Joe. She's told you a hundred times." Mom smacks his head.

"You want her to be safe. I want her to be taken care of. What's so different?" Dad yells.

"It's different, you buffoon. Jesus, Mary, and Joseph."

"You know, this is really a great party," Louis says. "Celebrating my promotion and all."

"Louie, come on," Mom says. "You know we're all very proud of you."

"Hey, they're happy with you. What more do you want?" I ask.

He sits up straight and motions at his chest. "Oh, I don't know, maybe for the dinner for my new job that I worked very hard for not to be about you for five seconds. Maybe that, huh?"

He's actually very handsome when he sits upright. Dark hair, scruffy face, tall and strong, sensitive brown eyes, olive skin. Mom's bone to pick with Louis is that he should start a family, but the girls come too easy for that to be of interest.

"He's right," I say. "Tell us about your new job, Louis."

"Yes, honey, tell us all about it." Mom puts cookies on the table and sits back down.

"Oh, I wouldn't want to bore anyone."

"For Christ's sake, son, tell us about the job," Dad says.

"Are you sure?" He hits each of us with his sassy diva face, then starts yapping about his new benefits package, how he's going to transition from being one of the guys into "the man," and how he thinks suspect hardware purchases that involve rope and shovels should be handled.

I enjoy the best part of these gatherings—Mom's food—in silence and wait for it to be over. I try to remember if either of my parents were ever anything like Harlow was with Zoey and Zane. Maybe when we were young enough. When we hadn't disappointed them yet. Maybe after the divorce, when they weren't so busy hating each other.

I can come up with moments that signal love. Times my dad saw red over boys who tried things with me or when he tried to teach us the importance of changing air filters. Times my mom poured peroxide on our scraped knees or stood up for us when teachers called to say we'd gotten in trouble.

They love us, and that's more than a lot of people can say. I should be grateful. Even Louis isn't half bad as far as little brothers go. He was my dearest pet when he was little, still small and shy and not yet grown into the features that have made him attractive and popular as an adult. We're just a cluster of islands now, ferrying messages across open water. There's no bridge. There's no fuzzy homey feeling when your family love language is worried yelling.

I know why Mom yells when I tell her I want to be a fighter. I know why Dad yells when I tell him I prefer women. I know why Louis yells when they're not yelling at him. It's a funny thing wanting to be enough while also wanting your dead-end job to not be enough. So, I yell at Louis—because the day I don't mock his job is the day he knows we don't think he's capable of more. It's dysfunctional at best, which is a word I thought was always properly paired with family.

If a family doesn't look dysfunctional, it's just not in focus yet. Yet, something about Harlow and those damn kids yesterday. I think they might be functional.

Chapter Fourteen

"Home sweet home." Harlow swings the front door open. I step inside, instinctively looking up as I do as if something is going to come loose and fall on me.

"Did you really ever live here?"

"I really did." She steps in after me and drops her supplies inside. When I turn to look at her, she's silhouetted by the light from the open door. Her faded, torn jeans hang low on her hips, and the sliver of skin showing is tan and smooth. I look back to her face, both soft and strong, the planes and lines playing with the light like a sculpture in a riot. Her steps echo, hard wood and thin walls composing it together.

The house isn't in any better shape than the yard behind it, but I can imagine it was beautiful once.

"Was it…"

"Like this?" She looks up from the bag she's digging in. "Not as far off as you might imagine, but no, not this bad."

"What happened to it?"

"Time. It was my grandmother's. We didn't realize how bad it was getting until it was too late. She never wanted anyone over here. She always came to us for holidays, claimed everything was fine. I don't imagine she really knew all it needed. It got away from her."

Harlow picks up the bags again and moves toward a hallway, passing me as she makes her way to a bedroom and turns inside. I follow her into what clearly serves as an office with a desk in an otherwise empty room save for the random disconnected cable and phone lines. I glance across the hall to the second bedroom where a queen bed sits similarly solo in its space.

"She left it to you?"

Harlow looks up, and I can see her remembering her grandmother. There's that same sweet, uncomplicated love I saw her share with her niece and nephew.

"It would have been my dad's, but once he got a good look at it, he found it more stressful than anything. There was a lien on it from unpaid taxes, and with all the work it would take to make it something you could rent or sell for a decent price, he was ready to let them just take it away."

"Ah, but you saved the day."

She holds up tape and gauze to wrap my hands with a question in her eyes, and I nod.

"Thanks."

She nudges the desk chair my way and sits on the corner of the desk while she pulls my hand onto her leg. My breath gets stuck in my chest feeling her thigh under my palm.

"I don't know if I saved the day," she says. "But I paid the back taxes, and it became mine. I'll fix it up one day. Just doesn't make sense to do it while I'm still using it for fights."

She wraps my hand in a competent, practiced pattern, showing no signs the contact between us is doing to her what it's doing to me.

"Is that your bed in the next room?" I ask.

She locks eyes with me and smiles just a little. "Yes. Why?"

"Why just a bed?"

"Because I don't live here anymore," she says, looking far too amused. "I had to for a little bit when I first bought it, but I saved up and got my apartment as soon as I could."

"So, you own not one but two homes?"

She tilts her head and moves on to wrapping my left hand. "Technically, but you see the state of things. I couldn't really have the kids over when I was here. It wasn't safe. The apartment is my home. This place is more like a long-term pipe dream, and it got to keep the bed."

"What's the dream?"

"Oh, you know. Make it how it was, what it could be. Have a home. A family."

"Harlow." God, it's really not fair to say shit like that to women. Least of all when you look like she does.

She glances up from her work on my hands and smiles. "Cheesy, right?"

"It's beautiful."

"You think?"

I want to run my hands through that soft blond hair. To pull her to my lips and taste her dreams. I want to disappear into them.

"Yes," I say. She looks in my eyes, grays and blues bursting and reaching. In any other world I would lean in. If she was anyone other than who she is I would know that pause and I would be able to grab it, but my heart just beats, holding me still and hypnotized in its rhythm.

"Are you ready for this?"

"Yes," I whisper.

"Who's cornering you tonight?"

I come back into my body in a cool awakening. "Oh. No one."

She straightens. "No one?"

"I don't have anyone. Not that could do this anyway."

"What about Vic?"

"Fuck Vic."

"I get that, but you can't have no one."

"*Fuck Vic.*"

"Laila, I'd do it if I could. But—"

"No, of course you can't do it. You're the boss. I didn't think that. I don't need a corner."

"You do need a corner."

"I mean it's not ideal, but it is what it is."

"I'll get one of the guys to do it."

"You really don't have to."

"Look, the extra guy I have tonight can't fight for a damn, so don't take his advice seriously, but he'll take care of you. Get your stool and water between rounds. Basics. I wish you'd have told me sooner. I would have found someone better."

"I'm not planning to let it go more than one round, Harlow."

Her face changes with amusement, the way everyone's does when I talk like that. I've never inspired fear.

"Okay, but shit happens," she says. "You need someone watching out for you."

I laugh. "In the Yard?"

"Yes, especially in the Yard."

I grab her hand and squeeze. "I'm going to be fine."

"Did you even train?"

"In the one week of notice? No, not really. I went for a run."

"Oh, Jesus. Laila, you do know these are real fighters, right? Maybe not in the same way you're used to, but most of them do train in some way, and they do take this seriously."

"I know, Harlow, but I don't have a gym anymore, or a coach, or a friend. Up until two months ago I trained with the best in the world every single day, though. I like to think I haven't forgotten everything."

It's not like I can't make friends. I used to have more than I could manage, but when my life became fighting my circle got small, and I left my circle at Emerald Tiger. Voices in the front room signal arriving fighters, and I feel Harlow's anxiety spike.

"Okay, listen. I have to go start herding, but use this room to warm up, and warm up for real. Push it. Sweat hard."

"Harlow, I kn—"

"And when they say fight, you go after her like you've never gone after anyone. No dancing, no feeling it out, no touching gloves. The Yard is not for pretty, it's for mean."

Her intensity focuses me, and I nod, holding the eye contact for as long as she wants it.

"I know you can grapple, but this is not the arena for it. The ground has glass and nails and all kinds of shit. Don't do it unless you have to, and if you do, be damn sure you're on top. Don't let her push you on the fence. There are sharp edges in some places, and it's being held by a bunch of drunk idiots who might trip and fall and then boom, no fence and you're on the ground."

I nod again.

"And don't you ever, *ever* take your eyes off her. Not until you're at home in your fucking fuzzy socks, you hear me? Not when the ref says stop, not in between rounds, not after you win, never. Not even when you're in back again. These girls do not like to lose. And if you knock her out, then you watch her team and make sure they don't get any ideas. Understand?"

"Got it."

She puts her hand on my knee and squeezes. "Watch out for yourself, Moretti. And have fun. I'll see you after."

The room feels bigger after she leaves, hollow and a little eerie. I feel alone. Not just because I am but because it's involuntary. There's not a soul in the world I both could and would ask to be here, and that's just fucking sad, isn't it?

I sigh and start moving around, taking a stance and shadowboxing. It feels ridiculous by myself in my shoes in the dusty back room of a dilapidated building on a parcel of untended land owned and operated by an underground fighting ring entrepreneur who happens to be the sexiest woman I've ever seen in person. If Mom thought I was off the script fighting for Eden at Emerald Tiger, God help me if she ever hears about this.

It takes time to shake the self-consciousness away, but I move through it. I forget the house and how ridiculous I must look. How ridiculous my life must look. I cut the air with jabs and hooks and kicks until I'm covered in a layer of sweat and fear.

I'm not as fit as I was just two months ago. That's a really easy way to lose a fight, maybe the most common. They don't always call it that, but it shows its ugly face through a thousand facets. Losing speed, power, and form. Losing discipline. Inactivity. Not being able to escape pins, the list goes on and on. It might be a knockout or a submission on paper, but all too often it's something that wouldn't have happened if you were better conditioned.

True exhaustion is not something you can simply ignore as much as people would like to believe it is. I'm under no illusion my waning cardio isn't a threat. I'm under no illusion that anyone bold enough to fight inside a chain link fence for money isn't a threat. Even though the audience is small and the level lower, in fighting the stakes are always your life, and this endeavor feels as perilous as it ever has. My mind clambers for a way out like it always does. I'm still me, and I'm still not the animal I need to be.

A tap on the door interrupts my urge to hurl. When I turn, a guy is sticking his shaved head into the room.

"Are you Laila?"

"Yes."

"I'm Greg. Harlow sent me to corner you."

"Oh, hey."

"You're up in five. Do you need anything?"

"Just a better life plan."

He laughs. "It always feels like that right before, but if you were in the audience tonight, you'd be jealous of the fighters."

That is true and gives me pause. "So, everyone feels like this?"

"Anyone with half a brain. Just tell it to shut the fuck up and bite your mouthguard. It's not the boss of you."

All this time I've thought the courage was the silly voice and the fear was the real me. I've never considered it was the other way around. I like it. I like it a lot. I retrieve my mouth guard and gloves, all the while telling the clammy, shaky fear to shut the fuck up. Greg runs over to help pull the gloves over my wraps and Velcro them in place.

"That what you're fighting in?" he asks.

"Yeah, is that a problem?"

"No, you can wear whatever you want. Just asking."

"I heard the ground is rough out there, so I figured I'd keep the shirt."

He nods. "Yeah, good call. Shoes too."

It feels nothing short of bizarre to fight in shoes. Just shadowboxing in them felt every kind of wrong, but barefoot is not an option. Gloves are also optional, but not breaking my hands seemed like something that didn't need overthinking.

I almost ask him who I'm fighting, but aside from the fact that I'm not sure he knows, it's hilarious I don't. I guess that's what happens when you say whoever whenever. I'm sure Harlow made a reasonable match, and she can't possibly have the training I do. Whatever she can do, I should be able to overcome it. That's why I'm here. To prove that's true.

Greg stands beside me as I wait by the sliding glass door for my cue, bouncing from foot to foot. When they signal me, I bound through the space toward the cage. The difference between cheering and jeering never felt so narrow. They know who I am. They saw me at my most pathetic. It doesn't matter because they're about to see a different side of me.

The ref meets me by the cage and holds out his hands for my gloves.

"Are you willingly stepping into the cage with the intention of winning tonight?"

"Yes."

"Do you understand you could be seriously injured or killed?"

"Yes."

"There will be no eye gouging, no interference from your corner or the audience, and no weapons of any kind including anything found inside the cage, the cage itself, or the ground. You will stop immediately if I command you to, but you will protect yourself at all times. If you no longer wish to fight you must signal clearly by tap, verbal tap, or both. Do you have any questions?"

"No."

"Step inside, fighter."

The men holding the fence swing a full panel open to let me inside, making faces as they do, some encouraging, some mocking. I circle the cage to measure the space. Small. Smaller than any official cage, but prone to change as it's held by pulsing human bodies. There's a slight mound in the center, clumps of grass and dirt, glints of light shining off things you don't want lodged in your skin.

The voices erupt again, and I realize I have company. She's stockier than I am, but who isn't. One side of her head is shaved while the other has straight hair to her shoulder. I guess the logistics of tying it back could be tricky, but I can't believe she left it loose. Can I grab it? That very short list of rules didn't forbid it.

She shakes out her arms and legs and stares me down. "You ready, girly?"

I walk right up to her hostile foul face. She's thicker but a little shorter. The ref shoots an arm between us as the crowd screams. "Not yet! On my command! Back up!"

I wasn't going to hit her. I just wanted to see her eyes. I want her to see mine, because I'm not afraid anymore.

"Fight!"

I take Harlow's advice as seriously as I've ever taken Eden's or anyone else's. I come at her like it's a ten-second round and swing an absolute haymaker at her on the off chance she doesn't know what she's doing whatsoever and can't spot it the way she should.

She comes at me with the same urgency and ducks my punch, not a testament to her amazing reflexes but evidence she already planned to barrel into me. Her head hits my chest, and she drives forward. She's strong, from her build but also from her level of commitment.

I take a step back to absorb it, turn, and hip toss her over my right leg. She hits the ground hard, and the crowd screams their approval. I drive my knee into her solar plexus. She squirms, bucking, rolling like a rabid animal, showing her back to me, then rolling onto her stomach, then back again, anything to get free and all terrible decisions, but she's doing it so fast I can't quite capitalize before she's doing the next outlandish thing. I move past the notion of pinning her down and just swing for her head.

She eats a shot and dives for my foot. I use the opportunity to punch her in the head again and again, but she seems unaffected, or at least not affected enough to give up on my foot, a prize I'm not sure is worth it until she starts wrenching it away from its natural range of motion in the most rudimentary attempt at a submission.

I stand up and try to tear it free, planning to kick her once I do, but she's latched onto it with every ounce of her strength and has a hold on my shoelaces that's making her grip a real problem. I drop my knee on her ribs as hard as I can, but it's not a big enough motion. She grabs my heel and cranks it toward her, clearly trying to do something in the ballpark of a leg lock but lacking the technical skills. That doesn't mean she can't really fuck something up pulling on my joint like that, though. I rotate to protect the angle, then yank away as hard as I can at the same time she pulls back, and my shoe pops off my foot.

I face her again just as she flings my shoe at my face. It actually clocks me in the mouth pretty good, but I can't help but laugh at the chaos. I step toward her to finish this, but she lunges from the ground straight into my gut and rams forward so hard I can't even put a foot down before the back of my head hits the fence and some guy's knee on the other side of it hits my kidney. I fall. A rock jabs into my back, at least I hope that's all it is. She's on top of me in an instant, swinging both arms in a flurry.

The hits don't land hard enough to knock me out, yet they're overwhelming. Too much to keep up with, too wild to block, too fast to grab. I search for a way to get my legs between us and create space, but she's plowing forward too hard, so I switch strategy and wrap my arms around her, pinning her to me so she can't get a punch off. I trap her knee with my foot and bridge my hips hard enough to yank her off me and take her place on top.

A thrill at my success zings through me. I congratulate myself on the devastating ground and pound I'm about to issue, but her hand cups the back of my neck and she yanks me into a nasty elbow strike that lands in a clean, focused point. I know the second it connects it means blood, and soon the drops are falling on her chest, but it doesn't faze me.

I force my posture straight, breaking her hold on my neck, and drop my right hand on her as hard as I can. Her lip splits, but as I pull back to do it again the ref's hand wraps around me and pulls me off her.

"Stop! That's round one! To your corners, you have one minute!"

Shit, so much for not going past one round.

It takes me a minute to get oriented enough to both spot Greg and remember he's my corner. He slaps down a stool and waves me over.

"Good round, good round." He hands me water and my shoe. He wipes my face as I put the shoe back on. The white towel comes away stained red. "She shouldn't have thrown it at you. That's technically a weapon."

"Whatever, it's fine."

"Try kicking her knee out."

"What, Cobra Kai style?"

He shrugs. "She tried to rip your foot off. Watch out for that."

"Fighters, ready!" the ref screams.

"Thanks, Greg." I jump up, and he disappears with the stool.

"Fight!"

I launch forward with an attack to start the round again, but this time it's tailored just for her. I'm counting on her to come barreling in headfirst one more time. She does, and the flying knee I'm throwing at the space I expect her to fill lands full and perfect. The crowd collectively reacts to the crack of impact, and she falls face forward, unconscious.

I put my hand in the air as the ref lunges to stop the fight. The crowd screams and cheers as I do a lap around the cage with my fist up. I turn back to check on the girl, but she's still out. The doctor and ref work together to bring her back, and soon she sits up to polite applause.

I watch my back as I exit the cage like Harlow warned, but I'm too buried in congratulations for anyone to try to attack me. More relief than I know what to do with floods my body. Something went right. Finally. I look through all the faces for Harlow. My need to share this with her feels urgent, but I don't see her.

I step through the sliding door to the house. The noise falls away like a weight, and I take inventory of my body. A cut over my brow, a deep bruise and maybe a scrape on my back. An ankle that feels okay now but will probably be swollen tomorrow. A raw patch of skin on my chin. And that delicious ache in every muscle. In the relative terms of combat, unscathed.

I check the main room for Harlow, but she isn't there, just the rest of the fighters yet to go out, looking nervous. God, it's euphoric to be on the other side of that, and not the easy way. I sigh and head for my bag in the back, disappointed I can't find her. Even eye contact across the crowd would do.

I make a sharp right for her office and smack into her. Right into her gorgeous, long, hard body. With the jeans and the sleeveless shirt and backwards hat and the arms. Good God, how dare she.

"Whoa, sorry," she says.

"Did you see it?"

She smiles and reaches to hug me. "Of course, I saw. Congr—"

I grab her shirt and pull her to me while I go on my toes to capture her mouth. She stiffens, but it makes her fingers press into my sides, which only sends another surge of lust through my body. I commit to the kiss, uncertainty be damned. I switch from balling her shirt in my fist like a threat and run my hand up her gorgeous neck, feeling her soft skin against my fingertips.

It feels like it takes a month, but her body finally reacts, and she grabs me. Her palms move to my hips and pull me against her in a powerful motion. She steps backward into her office, towing me with her. I kick the door closed behind me and tumble into her as she backs into her desk. Her lips part, and she kisses me back. The heat of her mouth moves through my body slamming into my core. I'm falling into something with no rules and no sanity.

I run my hands up her back, throw her hat to the floor and plunge my fingers into her hair. I press my body against hers, against the desk as I feel the fullness of her lips and sink deeper into her. I want to touch everything. I want to drop to my knees and taste her right here and now, but her fingers glide into my hair and tighten, and her tongue slides into my mouth. Her energy changes as she catches up. She touches and kisses me like she owns me.

Her hands slide down my back to grab my ass, and she picks me up. I wrap my legs around her waist as she pins me to the wall. She pushes her hips into me, and I gasp as the ache slams into my stomach. Her arms flex as she pulls my hips and presses against me again. I whimper in her ear as my arms tighten around her. I kiss her warm neck, tug just a little with my teeth until I feel her tremble.

"I want you," I whisper in her ear.

Her hand finds my jaw, and her eyes meet mine. They're locked onto me and burning with intensity that makes me feel like I've never been seen before this moment. Her eyes drop to my lips, but a bang on the door makes us both jump.

"Harlow?"

The doorknob turns, and she sets me down just as Vic comes in. My feet are on the floor. I think we're even disentangled, but Vic rolls her eyes the second she sees us.

"Wow. Really?"

"What is it?" Harlow asks.

"They're looking for you." Vic gestures over her shoulder.

"I'll be right out."

"They've been looking for you."

Harlow pauses and meets my eyes. I try to give her permission to go, not that she needs it. "Fine," she finally says. She squeezes my arm. "Good fight."

"Yep," I say. "Thank you."

Harlow leaves and Vic crosses her arms before looking me up and down.

"What?" I snap.

"Don't fuck with her, Laila. She has a good thing going here."

I thought I couldn't be madder at Vic, but I was wrong.

"I know she does. I'm not fucking with her. Why would you even think that?"

"She's together. You're not, and you're already making her do not together things. Fooling around in the middle of an event with a competitor? Do you know how bad that looks?"

"Oh, so now you're a saint and just want what's best for everyone?"

"I do, actually."

"Go away, Vic. If you really care all you have to do is keep your mouth shut."

She shakes her head and says, "Good fight," before she closes the door again.

I slide down the wall, my body full of aches and fire. I try not to smile, but it's impossible. Vic can't ruin this. Kissing Harlow here, now, was not among my greatest acts of discretion, but I can't pretend I regret it.

Chapter Fifteen

Harlow's text is both direct and not. An address and the words, *Come train.*

Come train. I do know she's taken it personally that I don't have a gym or training partners or even a decent friend who watches enough UFC to pretend to know how to corner me, but she doesn't really mean come train, does she? After that kiss? That world-tilting, axis-changing, gravity-defying kiss? Surely come train is code, right?

"I'm going to go, obviously," I say to Simone, who has been doing her level best to pretend to listen to this dilemma for fifteen minutes while she clicks away on her computer screen. "What I need to know from you—" I hold the pause ungodly long until she finally breaks.

"What?"

"Do I wear gym clothes?"

"Yes."

"Okay, but you didn't even think about it."

"What's there to think about? She told you what you're doing, so yes, dress appropriately."

"But you're kind of super literal."

"Why did you ask me then?"

"Because I need your help."

"Then listen to me."

"Okay, but could you at least pretend to think about it? She gave me an apartment address. So maybe we're doing apartment things. Not gym things."

Simone rolls her eyes and pauses her game. "Or she's driving you to the gym when you get there. Even if you are doing apartment things, don't ruin the game. What else are you going to do anyway, show up in lingerie and just hope you don't embarrass yourself?"

"Okay. Good point, but gym clothes aren't sexy. What if we are doing apartment things?"

"Wear those shorts that barely cover your ass and the racerback tank with the see-through mesh or whatever. You look good in that."

"Simone." I put my hand to my chest. "Yes, I will marry you."

"This is why I can't help you."

"Seriously, be my friend. I have a vacancy. Several actually."

"If I say yes, will you go on your date?"

"I don't know if it's a date, but yes."

"Okay, we're friends. Now go, and don't do anything weird."

"Impossible."

I put on exactly what she told me to, and not just as a gesture of friendship but because it really is probably the hottest I can get while still calling it gym attire.

"Makeup?" I shout.

"No."

"But—"

"Sweat."

I roll my eyes and nod, then grab my keys and throw on a hoodie. "See ya."

"Happy ho-ing."

The ten-minute journey is easy. The building is identifiable as outside of my financial bracket but still nondescript. I buzz her apartment, which is on the seventh floor. She buzzes me in without asking who it is. I can't sit still as I take the elevator up. Why should I be nervous around Harlow? I've had my tongue in her mouth. You'd think that would put me past nerves, but it's worse than ever.

She's so warm and natural and not nervous when she answers the door.

"Hey," she says. "Come in."

She steps aside. Her warmth soothes me. The outside may be nondescript, but the inside is gorgeous, expansive with windows that overlook a better view than I would've expected. There's a bar separating the modern kitchen from the ample living room, which consists of two parts, an area gathered around a TV and fireplace, and an open space with martial arts mats on the floor. There's a shelf against the wall with all the gear you could want.

"You live here?"

"I do," she says.

"Your apartment is a gym."

"Well, it's an apartment too, but yes. What do you think?"

"What do I think?" I smile at her suspense. "Two things. One, it's amazing. Two, I didn't realize you train like that."

"I told you I was a fighter."

"Right, you said you were a fighter. This looks like you are a fighter."

"Well, I do run a fight promotion. It comes in handy. Like when I have a new fighter who doesn't have anywhere to train, for instance." She winks.

"Right, so I'm meant to believe you have this entire setup on the off chance some weirdo who fights for a living but doesn't have a place to train comes along?"

She smiles like she's been busted. It's adorable. She looks so comfortable here, leaning against her bar top. She should in her own home, but she really, really does. I don't think I feel that at home anywhere.

"I find uses for it." She turns to her kitchen counter and grabs an envelope, then walks it to me. "For your fight."

I glance at the envelope, then her face, searching it for a clue.

"Go on."

I take it and notice the weight right off. I flip open the envelope and pull the cash out. When I look at her, she just smiles.

"How much is this?"

"Ten."

"Thousand?" I practically yell.

She laughs. "Yes, ten thousand."

"Harlow." I lock eyes on her. "Is this really a normal rate?"

"As opposed to what?"

"A favor."

She looks genuinely surprised.

"It's on the high end for a first fight, but you're a highly trained, UFC level athlete. I'm planning to make you a star. I know an underground star is a weird concept, but we have them. I would still pay you this if I didn't know you, and it's just a starting point. It's going to go up. A lot. I told you I pay my fighters what they're worth."

"So, this is what I'm worth to you?"

She tilts her head and cracks a smile at the trick question. "It's the first installment, trouble. Don't try to woman me."

"Don't tell me you're impervious to women."

"No one is impervious to women, that's why they're feared far and wide. Now, did I motivate you enough to train?"

I catch myself biting my lip and have to get a grip.

"You going to train me?"

"Someone has to."

She pulls off her jacket and tosses it on the couch, leaving her in a tank top with those gorgeous strong arms visible. She ties her hair up and steps onto the mat, a space that's easily twelve by twelve. She does the Bruce Lee come get me motion. I kick my shoes off.

"You sure you want to do this, Hayes?" I tease her.

"I can't have my new premier fighter not training. You're good, but if you don't stay sharp, you're going to run into the wrong gutter scrapper sooner than later."

"So, what're we doing?"

"We're going to warm up for a round, and then you're going to show me what you got."

"How does one even practice a Yard fight? Do I just pull my finger breaks and fishhooks?"

She shakes her head and tosses MMA gloves at me. "You dork."

I put on the gloves, trying not to be weird about how much I don't mind getting my hands on her.

"I don't even know how good you are," I say.

"Well, you're about to find out, I guess."

To say I find out is an understatement. Even in the warmup round, Harlow is way faster, way sharper, way more efficient, than I would have ever predicted, and don't get me wrong, I expected her to be good. She moves like a pro. Not like a once upon a time pro, like a right fucking now pro.

The timer she set beeps, letting us know a new three-minute round has begun, and I'm already winded. Harlow nods at me and holds out her glove to let me know it's about to crank up a notch. I take a deep breath, not loving how tired I am or how tired she isn't, but I touch gloves.

She moves in and throws a couple jabs, then moves out. Her footwork is effortless, her posture casual but engaged. She reaches out and pops me with a cross to the body and follows with a hook to the head. She doesn't hit hard but also doesn't throw it sloppy, just lets me know she's there. Good sparring partners are hard to come by, people who will challenge you without egos flaring. Harlow is excellent. She's also kicking my ass.

I can feel my time away from the gym, my waning familiarity with this level of precision and discipline. Harlow has the grit of a street fighter and the technique of a professional one, and it's a mix I'm obsessed with.

I push a front kick at her, trying to close the extra distance her height advantage gives her. I blitz in and throw a flurry of punches. She absorbs some, slips others, then counters to the open space below my elbow. I stand my ground and exchange with her, our punches climbing in intensity. She's aggressive yet manages to stay responsible defensively. She doesn't throw it all away on a shot the way the girls in the Yard do. She's hard to hit, and even when you do it's never clean.

I've pushed through two exhaustion barriers by the time she breaks a sweat. I don't care what she claims, this woman still trains like a pro. I don't know where, and I don't know with whom, but there is nothing casual about having this setup in your house and there's nothing casual about the way she's fighting. She could easily be champion of her own promotion, and it makes me wonder if the way Katarina shrank before her is because Harlow controls the money or because she's been on the other side of this imposing assault before.

The timer beeps again. I spend the full minute break sucking in as much oxygen as possible, too tired even to speak. When the next round starts, I suck it up and put it on her. She's taller and stronger and fitter, but this is far from the first time I've had to deal with that, and I'll be damned if I can't be a real pain in the ass when I want to be.

I get lighter on my toes and move more, throw more, throw crisper. I want her to know what I can do even if it kills me. I mix up my attacks, change my tempo. I get my cracks, but she's maddeningly calm, and I can feel her unspent power in every controlled impact. I want her flustered.

Just before I've punched myself out, it finally dawns on me this is MMA and I shoot, fully committed to a double leg takedown. My left shoulder finds her left hip. I drive my head into her ribs, turn the corner, and drive through. She tries to sprawl, but I bring her to the mat before she can find leverage. I can only hope the level of her striking means she can't grapple for shit, but of course she quickly proves that isn't true.

In striking, using your full strength means injuries. In Jiu Jitsu, that isn't the case, and it's one of its best aspects that you can spar at full power and still walk away intact. Feeling Harlow's full power is sobering. She escapes my most earnest attempts to pin her, defends my trickiest submissions, and hustles me in the scrambles until I'm so exhausted I'm seeing spots. I defend her submission attempts too, but the moment I get too fixated, she reminds me she can punch me instead at any time. She's a true mixed martial artist and never forgets all her weapons, never gets stuck in one mindset or another. She also remembers all the illegal tactics available to her, showing me the moments where I'd be in danger of getting kicked while I'm down or having my grips peeled off by individual fingers.

Finally, the timer buzzes, and she releases me from my crunched position. My limbs flop to the mat, my shirt soaked in sweat. Harlow turns off the timer and lies down beside me.

"You get enough work in?"

I laugh. "You are not funny."

"Just making sure. Good stuff, Moretti."

I shake my head and turn onto my side. "Please. That was not my best work. And who the fuck are you?"

"You did great. You're just a little out of shape. You'll be kicking my ass before you know it. And everyone else's."

"Do you still want to fight, Harlow?"

"Professionally? No. My days have passed, and I'm too busy. I'm not sure it ever really leaves you, though."

"How old are you?" She doesn't look or fight like "her days have passed."

"It's not that. I'm thirty, but I had my shot. I've moved on."

"But you know you could, right?"

She shrugs. "That ship has sailed. It didn't get very far."

"I can't believe that. You're so good."

"Doesn't always matter," she says. "A lot of chips have to fall your way to really make it. Even if you do everything right, you'll always need a little luck, and I've always been a little short on it."

"That's not fair, and that's not how it's supposed to work."

She shrugs. "Maybe not, but it's worked out all right for me. You just have to make your own luck."

"With illegal enterprise?" I tease her, and she smiles shyly.

Her chest glistens with sweat as it rises and falls. I can't help but scan her body, knowing better than ever how perfect it is now that I've just spent an hour struggling against it. I want to roll around with it in another way. I want to fix whatever injustices have put that quiet sad look in her eyes. I want her to know how talented she is. And I want to know what she sounds like when I touch her the way I want to touch her.

I shake myself back to the moment, remind myself I'm covered in sweat and probably look like a damn mess. I was invited here to train, and train we did. Maybe that's really all she wants.

"You know, for training me, you really didn't give me any instruction."

She smiles. "Oh, Laila, I would never presume. I'm just helping you get back in practice."

"Presume."

She shakes her head. "No way."

"What, are you scared?" I laugh.

"Absolutely."

I smack her arm. "Come on, tell me what you saw."

"Really?"

I roll my eyes. "Yes, really."

She makes a skeptical face but relents. "Okay, you're very technical. You do everything the way it's supposed to be done. You're fast. Your kicks are beautiful. You're well rounded, great on the feet, great on the ground."

"But…"

"I didn't say but."

"Okay, but there has to be a but. What do I need to work on?"

She sighs. "Well, I think it's going to take you some practice to embrace the world of anarchy that is now open to you. This style of fighting favors the aggressive and the wild. If I was worried about anything it would be that. People are going to come at you with a lot of energy and some fucked up ideas and you tend to…"

"What?"

"Shut down."

It's not that drastic of a criticism, but I feel myself retract. "I do not."

"Maybe it's not the right word," she says. "You get overwhelmed. You're a little reserved."

"What do you mean?"

"Your personality is so free and impulsive. It's one of the things I love about you. It makes you who you are, and it should make you perfect for this, but sometimes it just doesn't show up in your fighting, and I'm not sure why."

"Because being impulsive and reckless is dangerous in a fight," I say it too fast, too hot. I've worked for years at mastering control in a fight, and now she thinks it's a weakness.

"I'm not saying you should be sloppy. You already have technique. You're never going to be that. You just get, I don't know, intimidated or something. You shrink. When you're feeling good you don't do it. You're spectacular. Like that knee the other night. It's just when you think someone is really good you kind of…"

"What?" I snap.

"It's not a big deal, Laila. Experience will—"

"You think I give up?"

"I didn't say that."

"Then finish the sentence."

She sighs, and I hate how I'm reacting. Like a toddler.

"I'm sorry," I say. How she doesn't tell me this is why she didn't want to talk about it I do not know.

"Laila, the last thing I'm trying to do is break you down."

"Just tell me the truth. Am I a quitter?"

Vic accused me of not being able to receive the truth, and of being a quitter. What if she's spot-on? Harlow grabs my hand.

"Hey. You are incredibly skilled, and you are an animal when you believe in yourself. You just underestimate yourself sometimes. You decided I was better than you too soon, and it changed how you fought. You accepted positions you could have challenged. You waited for me to slow down. When you look at someone like they're your lunch, you're unstoppable. We just need to get you seeing everyone that way. We will."

"I tapped out."

"Is that what's bothering you?"

"I quit."

"You didn't quit, you lost."

I scoff. "Much better."

"It is," she says. "Everyone loses, Laila. Tapping out is about knowing when you've lost and saving your body. It's not about quitting. It's about coming back tomorrow."

I exhale away the ache. I squeeze her hand, hoping she takes it as a sign I've passed my urge to act with abandon.

"See, you should be my trainer."

"I'm here for whatever you need."

"And that won't cause problems for you?" I ask.

"What do you mean?"

I shrug, wrestling with the fact that I selfishly don't want to give her an out.

"Vic said a thing," I finally say.

"Ah."

"About the kiss. About how it would look bad. How it could fuck you over."

She smiles and looks away, then flashes back with those gorgeous blue eyes. She looks so genuinely amused.

"Hey, you had just won a fight. You were on a high." She shrugs. "You had a moment. No big deal."

My heart sinks.

"Right. Okay. And this, being here with you, training. It's not going to look bad or whatever?"

"I'm not planning to advertise it, but no, it's not a problem."

"I don't want to fuck up your life, Harlow. I can find someplace else to train."

I'd rather not find someone else to kiss, but apparently, we just had a moment. *I* just had a moment.

"I wouldn't have invited you here if it was a problem, Laila."

"Right. Okay. Great."

"You're mad." She says it as a statement, but very real confusion is all over her face.

"Nope, I'm good. I should just get going."

"Laila."

"I'm good, thank you for the session." I get up and shove my feet into my shoes, trying to shake off the embarrassment.

"Moretti."

"Harlow, you've done nothing wrong. You've been ridiculously perfect, actually. I just need to go."

"Okay, well—"

"I'll call you for another training session. Or you'll call me when you have another fight for me."

"Sure."

"Good night, Harlow."

I dash out of her apartment without looking back. I can't look at her again. She'll see it all if I do. This is why women wait to be kissed. So that they don't end up this asshole thinking something is happening when it isn't. So they don't ask their roommate what to wear only to come back home a couple hours later dodging eye contact. This feeling is a very convincing reason to never make the first move again.

Chapter Sixteen

I'm not someone who requires a night of hard drinking to sleep until noon. I'm also not someone who gets a lot of drop-in visits other than Vic from time to time, who sleeps later than I do and isn't expected to turn up with an apology for another two weeks. Yet someone is knocking.

"Simone, door," I call toward the hallway, but there's no answer or movement. I lift my head. I can't really see into her room, but there's usually a shadow on her back wall when she's in her chair, and there isn't one. She actually left the house. Figures.

Another gentle knock sounds, and I realize the best guess might be Simone herself. Did she lock herself out? I force myself out of bed and run my hand through my hair. I stumble down my hall and put my face to the peephole.

My heart launches through the ceiling.

It's Harlow. I jolt up and knock over the candle on the side table.

"Laila?"

"Uh, yeah. One sec."

I sprint to my room, or do the closest thing to it that I can without sounding like a stampede. I yank off my sweatpants and the shirt I'm wearing that's so oversized it's giving my knees a run for their money. I yank on jeans and a T-shirt that isn't anything special but is at least intended to be worn in public. I brush my teeth at Mach 3, wet my hands, and run them through my hair, then dash back to the door, flinging it open and pretending not to be out of breath.

"Harlow?"

"Did you just wake up?"

"Ah come on, I tried so hard."

She smiles and runs her hand through her long hair, looking a little sheepish. I didn't think she had that particular emotion in her.

"Sorry," she says. "I should have called. I did call, actually, but you didn't answer, which should have been my clue not to come bother you, but I was passing by and just thought…"

"It's okay. Come on in."

She steps inside and looks around. She's dropped me off a few times now, made sure I got to my door safely, but she's never been inside. I feel naked letting her see it. We couldn't fit her martial arts mats in here even if they were the only thing in the room.

"Nice place."

I scoff. "Yeah, okay."

"It is," she says, looking a little too concerned she offended me. I laugh. "It's nothing special, but it does the job. Are you okay?"

"Yeah, sure." She leans to look around the corner. "Of course."

"Looking for something?"

"No, I just thought you had a roommate."

"I do. She isn't here."

"Got it."

"You want her number or something?"

She smiles. "No, I was just wondering if we were alone."

"We are. What's up?"

Her busy body language settles down. It must be fight business. Vic did say how careful she is about keeping it secret. I figured she would expect my roommate to know. I don't know how I can keep it from her, but I guess I can try. She's lucky Simone is the way she is.

"Do you have something for me?" I ask. "Another fight already?"

"Oh, no," she says. "I wouldn't ask you to get back in there this soon. Heal up. Take your time."

"Okay. So then…"

"I didn't sleep very well last night."

I laugh. "And you came for some pointers from the master?"

"I came to fix what kept me up."

She steps closer while I forget to breathe. She's in shorts today, and her long, toned, tan legs are assaulting my self-control, but I'll throw myself out the window before I read her wrong again. Even though I think I know what she's saying. Even though her ocean eyes are flashing with intent. Even though the neck of her shirt falls under the gorgeous lines of her collarbones, and I want to press my lips to them.

She steps closer, her lips parted, her eyes heavy on me. I want to say something, but I can't. I can't think or move or breathe with her locked on me like that. She's so sexy it's debilitating. I'm afraid to touch her, to find out she's a dream or forever just past my fingertips. But I would touch her. Even if it was only for a night. Even if I'm afraid of how helpless I'll be when she's done. I still want her to do it. I need her to.

"Harlow." Her name finally comes out in a whisper. In a plea to wield her powers gently.

She steps closer and pulls me into her arms, against her body. She takes the kiss from me slowly. Her lips are full and soft and claim mine with controlled conviction. The warmth of her mouth takes over as my body shapes to hers, as she holds me where she wants me and my cool fingers find the back of her warm neck. Her tongue slips into my mouth. A shiver ripples through me as longing floods my body.

My head clouds, and to say the room disappears isn't enough. The world disappears. Gravity disappears. Life disappears. Somehow even my body disappears, and this symphony of sensation exists without it. Her hands move over me, running up my sides as she kisses me deeper until a quiet moan vibrates in my chest. She reacts to the sound with a sharp inhale that sparks energy and awakens something rebellious in me that wants to see her undone.

I slip my hand under her shirt and feel the contours of her stomach, the lines of her abs and the soft glow of her skin. Her breath goes choppy as she lets my fingers explore, and I trace them upward slowly, wandering, but making no secret of my intent. Kissing her is a full body experience, and I want more of her gorgeous form. Her hands slide up my back, pulling my shirt up with them. Cool air touches my skin and brings me back to what's happening, but I let it swallow me again. Just as I'm about to lose my mind, demand she pull my shirt and everything else from my body, there's a knock on the door.

I freeze, not sure if I'm more confused or annoyed.

"Your other wakeup call?" she asks.

"I don't know," I say. "I wasn't expecting one knock today, let alone two."

I glance at the door, more than a little tempted to ignore it, but another knock sounds.

"Go on," Harlow says. "It's fine."

She drops her hands, and my shirt falls back in place. I smile at her hair that I've tousled and kiss her one more time before I go look out the peephole a second time. My heart falls onto the floor.

"It's Eden," I whisper.

"Of course it is."

It might be the first time I've ever seen Harlow irritated, maybe even nervous, so I figure it isn't the time to tell her there's nothing "of course" about it. I haven't seen or heard from Eden since I got my last check.

"I don't have to—"

"Yeah, you do. Go on. Do you want me to go?" She gestures over her shoulder toward my bedroom like she's going to hide in the closet or crawl out the window.

"Harlow, of course not."

I open the door just as Eden was turning away. The thought of almost missing her, of her giving up, causes a little bolt of alarm that surprises me. I want to see her. Even with Harlow here. Even with her mad at me.

"Hey," I say.

"Hi."

I wave her in, and she steps inside. She pauses when she sees Harlow. "Ah. Yeah, that tracks."

"It's not what you think," Harlow says.

"That's a tough sell at the moment, Hayes."

Neither of them has the disposition to get into a fight in my living room, but I feel the need to put myself between them anyway.

"Eden, please. She hasn't done anything wrong."

"I can think of a thing or two."

"Okay, well who hasn't, but I'm not your student anymore, Eden. She can be here."

"Is that all you have to say to me?"

"I told you I'm sorry, Eden. I don't know what else I can do."

"You told me you didn't want to fight anymore is what you told me. That it just wasn't in you. That you didn't have it. You said you couldn't waste any more of your life or body on it."

The realization that she must know I'm fighting again settles in slowly. Fuck. I imagine Eden's world so different from my own I sometimes forget she's from this neighborhood just like I am. Being the biggest thing to happen to MMA within a thousand miles I should have known nothing remotely fighting related slips by her. I guess I assumed Eden is busy with bigger things and let myself believe we'd never have to have this conversation.

"I meant it when I said it." It comes out in a pitiful whisper.

She looks like I've smacked her in the face. Eden believed in me when no one else did, like no one else has. Now she's just standing there looking betrayed, and I don't know how to fix it. I have betrayed her. Not only her gym, but everything she ever taught me. I've been weak when she gave so much to make me strong.

"So, what?" Eden shrugs. "The money?"

"No," I burst. The money is nice, but God, I need her to believe. "No."

"What then? Her?" She nods at Harlow.

"Give her a break, Bauer. She's finding her way back," Harlow says.

"She's more lost than ever," Eden says. I glimpse the pain and anger she's restraining just long enough to swallow a new mouthful of guilt.

"I do want to come back to Emerald Tiger," I say. It sprays out of me uncontrollably, my feelings unfolding in front of me as much as either of them. I feel Harlow and Eden both lock onto me, and I'm not sure which is more surprised. I catch a glimpse of Harlow's furrowed brow and want to scream at them both to end this stupid rivalry or whatever the fuck it is. They're cut from the same cloth.

"I do want you to be my coach, Eden. I want to come back to the gym. I even want to fight again. I just want to do it for Harlow. I'm not UFC material. That hasn't changed, and that's why I haven't come back. But it doesn't mean I have to give up everything. It doesn't mean I can't make a living at it."

I search Eden's eyes desperately for signs of happiness, of something mended, but she shakes her head.

"You know I can't do that, Laila."

"Eden, please."

"And what about when all the kids want to be like you? When the up-and-comers want to know where your money comes from? When half my school is trying to make ends meet with underground fights?"

"They don't have to know," Harlow says. "I'll still honor our agreement, stay clear of your students. Just make an exception for Laila."

Eden scoffs and shakes her head before sharply extinguishing my hope with a brutal, "No."

"But—"

"It's *illegal*. Or have you two conveniently forgotten that? It's illegal and dangerous and irresponsible and someone is going to die one day."

"She has medical staff," I say. If I can just open her mind. Harlow isn't who she thinks.

"Yeah? And what are they going to do when someone gets kicked off of a roof? Or soccer kicked in the face so hard their neck breaks? Or slammed on a rock that breaks their skull? Or gets HIV from someone bleeding all over them?"

"We take precautions," Harlow says. "More than you think, and we do ask about bloodborne diseases."

"You ask?" Eden's incredulous expression is sharp as a knife. "And you think none of the people fighting for you are doing it because they got turned away from real promotions who actually test? You think no one's ever lied to you?"

"It's not perfect, but I'm trying," Harlow says. "It's been a long time since you've seen it. Every event is safer than the last. You know what I want to do with the promotion."

She shakes her head again. "You've been saying you want to go legit for years, Harlow. If you really wanted to, it would be done."

"It's not that simple."

I feel like I can't breathe watching them talk, realizing how much they've talked before, how much I haven't thought about and how much I don't know. Eden dismantles my hopes with ruthless rationality. Like she can feel me crumbling, she turns away from Harlow and looks at me again.

"You know what I'm about. What Emerald Tiger is about. I'm trying to give my students a way forward. Everything I teach is about character, discipline, perseverance. I'm trying to show these kids that when you give everything to your dream and you refuse to stop, when you refuse to stay down, you can make it out and you can do it without selling drugs or stealing or lying. I'm trying to show the world that this sport is beautiful and the people who do it are artists and athletes, not meatheads and criminals. I won't compromise that, Laila. I wouldn't be helping you if I did, and I'm not going to live with secrets. I'm sorry, but this *good enough* thing you're trying to do is not good enough."

She comes over and hugs me, and I can't explain why it feels good even though she just smashed the feeble beginnings of my new life.

"Please be careful," she says before she lets me go. All I can do is nod. She squeezes my shoulder and heads for the door.

"Hey," Harlow calls before Eden leaves. "I care about my fighters too. I really care about Laila."

Eden nods. "Good. I'll honor the agreement, Harlow, but I think you know there will be hell to pay if anything happens to her."

She leaves without waiting for an answer, and the room falls silent. The space between Harlow and me feels like a canyon filling with dark matter. It's like a train just ripped between us, and we're still spinning in the wind.

"I'm really sorry," I say. "I knew she wouldn't love finding you here, but I didn't know she knew I fought."

"It's okay. She's trying to watch out for you." Her eyes look dark and resigned. "Is that it, then? Are you done with this now?"

"What?"

"You said you want to go back to the gym. I'm not trying to get in your way if that's what you want."

"I also said I want to fight for you."

"Do you still?" she asks.

I can't pretend I don't feel naive after Eden's evisceration. She shined a very ugly light on the darker possibilities of what Harlow does. Of what we're doing. Any one of the things she mentioned could happen, and not one would be worth the cash or even the glory.

"What did she mean you've been wanting to go legit for years?"

"Do you want me to go?"

I shake my head, confused and jostled. "Are we having the same conversation?"

"If you want out just say so, Laila. I'll understand."

"I want you to answer the question, Harlow." It comes out snappier than I intended, but it seems to have the effect I wanted of shaking her out of her assumptions.

"Back when Eden and I made our arrangement to stay out of each other's way, part of why we were able to get there was because I had the intention to transition the Yard into a legitimate, sanctioned promotion. She's obviously lost patience with that goal."

"Were you really going to? Or was that just a way to stop her from reporting you?"

The way her expression softens with pain and her posture pulls away is subtle, but it makes me regret the question.

"Of course, I really wanted to."

"So, what happened?"

She turns away like she's looking for her jacket or maybe a weak wall to kick through to escape. Anger swells in my chest. I want to tie her to a chair and force her to deal with me. Stop pushing me away. Stop assuming I can't handle it.

"Harlow, can't you give me a chance to understand?"

"Will you come with me?" she asks, her voice so much softer and more level than just five seconds ago. Her eyes are open wells, and the pull they have on me is a riptide strong enough to make me realize with enthralling fear that I'm falling for this woman. I don't know if she means to the mall or the Yard or Egypt, and I don't need to ask.

"Yes."

CHAPTER SEVENTEEN

We drive without music and without talking. The dull roar coming from Harlow's mind is noise enough. I can feel her reliving everything Eden said. Everything I said. I can feel it piercing her armor, her mind scrambling to patch the vulnerabilities.

"It isn't far," she says.

I want to hold her hand or touch her leg, stroke her hair. I want to kiss her neck and pretend none of this happened, but those touches are out of place while we're still on this side of whatever we're driving toward.

It takes fifteen silent minutes for her to pull onto a road and slow down to a pace that tells me we're getting close. It's a neighborhood. Rundown. Not to the level of Harlow's grandmother's house, but a no-collar type of energy. More mailboxes are broken than standing, rain gutters sit at random, disembodied from their homes. Kid toys and trash combine to litter the yards and street. An old blue mustang sits on cinderblocks without tires, and garden level windows are barred.

I want to ask her if she's showing me her third house, but it doesn't seem like the time for jokes. She pulls over to the right and turns the car off. I take in the structure. It's like others on the block, standing but old. Peeling, sagging, small, very lived in. It's a bright blue color an HOA would never approve of with pink trim that makes it look like it specializes in gender reveals. There's a collection of bicycles on the front porch and a baseball bat in the yard beside a driveway that's in the middle of its transformation from concrete to gravel.

"Where are we?" I ask.

"This is my sister's house," Harlow says.

I spin to look at her, both flattered and trying to work out where six children could possibly fit in this little home that can't be more than nine hundred square feet.

"The one with all the kids?"

She nods. "The only one I've got."

"Wow. Are we going in?"

"It's a lot of chaos in there, but yes. If you're willing, I'd like to."

"Of course I'm willing."

She opens the car door, then leads me to the front. There's the sound of that chaos she mentioned coming through the door.

"My family's house sounds like that too," I say and smile at the familiarity. "Only they're not children, just immature adults."

"Ah good. Then you'll hold your own." She smiles, and I feel her relax just a little. The feeling is contagious and soothing.

The door opens at the hands of a teenage boy who lights up at the sight of Harlow. He throws his arms around her without an ounce of teenage reserve.

"Aunt Harlow's here!" He shouts into the house, and a stampede of feet and giggles charges us.

"Dylan, this is my friend Laila. Laila, this is my sister's oldest. He's the one who gives me such a good workout training. He's really talented and getting too strong for me."

Dylan smiles but adopts a shyness at her compliment, giving a little awkward wave. He's tall and strong and beautiful with Harlow's body style and blue eyes.

"Well, then he's definitely too strong for me. Nice to meet you, Dylan."

A rush of little people surrounds Harlow, hugging her and competing for attention. The shouts are incomprehensible as she absorbs the excitement and promises to look at all the things they want to show her. She lets them sweep her inside, and Dylan motions for me to come in.

"Thanks," I say. "How long have you been training?"

"Forever, I think," he says.

I laugh because with Harlow in his life, that makes perfect sense. I've known many martial artists who started so early they don't know what it is not to train, and they always end up with a different level of fluidity than the rest of us.

"I wish I could say that. I'm sure you're amazing."

He shrugs, and I take in the living room. There's a maze of toys on well-worn wood floors that are covered in scratches and marker streaks. The bare walls are wearing a lot of art from the hands of children too, and though better thought out and resembling something like an attempt at a meadow, they were likely unauthorized projects.

There's a couch on the back wall where Zane is jumping between the back and the cushions on repeat, and a recliner in the corner where a young woman who must be Harlow's sister sits looking completely immune to the noise. When she sees me, she straightens out of her exhausted slump and smiles.

"Oh, hello." She starts to get up though it's clearly a laborious act.

"Hi there." I rush over. "I'm Laila. I hope you don't mind—"

"Oh, Laila. I wanted to meet you." She reaches out to hug me while I stammer at the fact that Harlow has apparently mentioned me. Harlow walks over with Zoey in her arms, who's getting a little too big for it but clearly loves the way Harlow is jostling her around while she giggles.

"Sorry." Harlow smiles at me. "Laila, this is my sister, Blair. And this is Logan, Eli, Zane, and Zoey."

She points at each of the boys before jostling Zoey in her arms again. Logan and Eli look like they must be around ten, while I already know Zoey and Zane are seven. "You met Dylan," she says. "Where's Aspen?"

Blair shakes her head discreetly. "She's not having a good day. She's resting in my room."

"Oh no." Harlow looks sad but not surprised. "I'll just check on her real quick." She sets Zoey down and touches my shoulder as she goes for the hallway.

Blair smiles at me and retreats to her recliner. Her resemblance to Harlow isn't glaring, but the longer I look at her the more I see it. They have the same beautiful eyes, and it seems like most of the kids got them too. She's tall like Harlow, but frail while Harlow's athleticism is obvious. They share blond hair, but Blair's is shorter and tied back in a ponytail I doubt it often leaves. She looks sick, drained, and I remember Harlow's vague statement that she isn't well.

"My daughter Aspen has epilepsy," Blair says once the kids go back to their horseplay.

"Oh, I'm sorry. That must be hard for her. And you."

"It's well managed, for the most part, but she has her days."

"How old is she?"

"Fourteen," Blair says, looking both happy and sad to remember it. "She loves training with Harlow and Dylan, but she hates that she can't compete. That's the worst of it. The things she can't do."

Dylan falls onto the couch beside us to listen in, his eyes sharp despite his brothers wrestling beside him.

"I'm sure Harlow shows her the best of it," I say.

Blair smiles and nods. "That's true. She's amazing with them. I'm sure you can tell they adore her."

"Just a little."

"Well, everyone does when they get to spend time with her. Not too many people do, though."

She takes a survey of me that isn't antagonistic but is a far cry from subtle. For some reason I didn't predict her sister would be protective. I guess sisters usually are, but I assumed it was Harlow who did the protecting around here.

"That doesn't surprise me." Harlow has always struck me as a heartbreaker, but maybe I have it wrong. Maybe Harlow has been hurt. "I adore her, too."

Harlow comes back in the room and catches Zane as he leaps off the couch at her. She zooms him back to his feet and comes to stand beside me.

"Is Dad still coming by?" Harlow asks her sister.

She shakes her head. "He picked up extra hours."

"Okay, well I just wanted to swing by and see everyone. Do you need anything?"

"No, we're okay. I'm glad we got to meet your friend though."
Blair winks at me to let me know how seriously she takes the word
friend, and Dylan rolls his eyes to let his mom know she isn't smooth.

Harlow pops him on the arm. "See you tomorrow, bud. One
o'clock?"

He nods, and she makes her rounds of goodbyes before backing
out the front door with me in tow.

"Are you sure you're ready?" I ask on the way back to the car.
"You don't have to rush on my account."

"No, it's fine. I see them all the time."

We slide into the car before she continues.

"I drop in on them three to four times a week, train Dylan and
sometimes Aspen twice a week, do Zane and Zoey's baseball three
times a week, and drive Logan and Eli around to friends."

"Wow. I see my family when my brother gets a promotion. So,
every six to twenty years."

"Really?"

I shake my head. "No, he's only ever gotten one, and I doubt it
will happen again."

I love that she laughs at my stupid jokes. Even with all the love
that obviously exists in her life, I feel like she could use more laughter.

"Got it, so I won't be meeting your family any time soon."

"I'm kidding. We see each other. But not like that."

When Harlow pulls up in front of her apartment building, she
looks over. "Can you come up? There's more I want to show you."

"Sure."

A little tingle of excitement fizzles. I try to remind myself of the
adventure we're on. I'm supposed to be getting answers, not going
all soft for her eyes or hot for her body. She asks me to wait in the
hallway when we get to her apartment, probably prudent if confusing.

I'm staring from side to side down her hallway trying not to look
out of place when she reappears with a bottle of wine, a blanket, and
a folder.

"Oh wow, what's going on here?"

"Let's go." She guides me back to the elevator.

"Are we getting drunk in your car?"

She rolls her eyes and hits the top button.

"No. I seem to remember you're a fan of rooftops, and this one happens to be why I bought in this building."

"Oh really?"

The elevator opens to a dazzling cityscape. We're not as high up as we were on the night of the fights, but the view rivals it anyway. It's a beautiful angle of the skyline, and sunset is approaching full of pinks and oranges.

"It's gorgeous," I say as she guides me to a couch that sits beside a firepit. "Isn't it open to the whole building?"

She kneels to start the firepit and nods. "It is, but you'd be surprised how often I have it to myself. I was hoping it would be one of those nights."

"Looks like it is. People don't come up here?"

"They do sometimes, but mostly just when they first move in. I guess like anything else people lose interest."

"Dang, Hayes. That's bleak."

She laughs. "I didn't mean for it to sound sad."

"No, you're right. People live just off the beach and never go. It's a thing."

She gets the firepit going and sits beside me. "I've lived here all my life and I've never been to the Statue of Liberty. Or the Empire State Building or any of that shit."

"Me either. So, we're just as bad as the rest of them."

"Maybe," she says. "But I have been known to lock the rooftop door from time to time to soak in this view."

"Naughty."

"I guess it's just a matter of what moves you." She opens the bottle of wine and grabs the blanket.

"Are you romancing me?"

"What, this?" Harlow holds the wine up. "No, this is for me."

She drapes the blanket across herself and leans back with the bottle. "This is for you." She hands me the folder.

"Of course."

She smiles while she fishes two wine glasses out of the cabinet on the wall behind us. She pours the wine and hands me a glass, then spreads the blanket over me too. The air is just getting cool enough to need it as the sun goes down. I nod and smile. "Okay. Okay, you're smooth."

She takes a sip of her wine and shakes her head. "Nah, I just come up here a lot. I know the drill. The folder really is for you."

I take the yellow folder she's holding out for me, but I can't seem to open it. "Harlow, whatever this is, you don't have to prove anything to me. It's not my place to judge you."

"No, but you're worried. You have doubts about fighting for me, and you have doubts about what kind of person I am."

"I don't."

"You do. I wanted to be offended, but I can't. You said you were trying to know me and that I wasn't making it easy. So, here you go. Know me. If you still want to."

Her expression is so sincere, so open, that I can hardly respond. I just want to hold her, but she nods at the folder. I open it, taking a second to understand what I'm seeing.

"Gladiator Combat League?"

I flip through the pages and slowly process that these are all business documents. To establish a corporation, to acquire a promoter's license, athletic commission licensing, a full business plan, anti-doping compliance, streaming licenses, it goes on and on.

"Harlow," I say a little too loud. "Harlow, these are all filled out. There's so much here. This is your plan to make the Yard legit?"

She nods and sips her wine.

"This is everything. You're done. Why haven't you filed these? What are you waiting for? What happened?"

She laughs at the rapid-fire questions. "I wanted you to see how serious I was about it. I didn't just say that to pull one over on Eden."

"But what happened?" I hold up the papers as if she doesn't already understand the extent of how hard she worked.

She puts her feet up on the edge of the fire pit and looks out over the skyline. "A lot of things happened, but the fast way to say it is family."

"Your sister." I put our trip to the house together.

She nods. "My sister."

"You said she isn't well?"

"She got pregnant young, had Dylan when she was seventeen. Then Aspen when she was nineteen. It was never going to be easy, but she was in love with her boyfriend. They were going to figure it out, young and broke or not. Then they found out Aspen has epilepsy, but they were okay. They got married. She busted her ass and became a nurse. He was a mechanic. They had Logan and then Eli, and things got tight. You could tell they weren't the same. Too much work. Too much struggle. She got pregnant again. When they found out it was twins Jimmy just lost it and left. Said he couldn't do it."

"Jeez. A little late to decide that."

"I always thought he was just having a breakdown and would get a grip. In the meantime, my sister started working even harder to take care of the bills. I helped with the kids as much as I could, but the truth is Dylan did way too much. Then one night on a double Blair was so exhausted and out of it she stuck herself with a needle. She ended up with hep C."

"Fuck."

"They were able to manage her symptoms at first, but she hasn't done well. She has a severe case, and her job was demanding. She didn't feel it was right to treat patients while she was dealing with the brain fog, and she was missing so much work, eventually she had to leave. I'm sure you noticed she's lost a lot of weight and has a hard time doing things."

I nod again.

"Well, if her sorry husband was ever going to come back, he definitely wasn't after that. My parents tried to help her, but my dad has been a bus driver for thirty years and has never had much to spare. He's worked his ass off his whole life and has nothing to show for it. He's working overtime as we speak just to keep his lights on. I help him when he lets me, but he hates it."

"What does your mom do?"

Harlow bites her lip. "Well, she's in jail at the moment."

My heart squeezes. "Harlow."

"Yeah, it sucks. She got busted selling counterfeit handbags."

"What do you mean counterfeit?"

"Like Louis Vuitton, Gucci, Fendi. Only not."

"So, knockoffs? What's wrong with that?"

"Well, she wasn't selling them as knockoffs. She bought knockoffs and made them better by hand and sold them as real. She was pretty incredible at it, actually, but she got cocky. Took it off the corners and onto the internet. Made a fortune for a minute but got caught the next."

"Wow."

"It's okay, you can laugh. It's kind of funny."

"I wasn't going to laugh. I was going to ask if you had any laying around."

Now she laughs and bumps my shoulder with hers. "I do not, but my sister might. Didn't know you were a handbag girl."

"Well, there's a lot you don't know about me."

"Oh yeah?"

"Sure, I'm very mysterious, but that's for another night. Go on."

"That's about it. Everything was falling apart. My sister was sick, the kids didn't have a dad. She was home with them, but she was so exhausted and in so much pain she couldn't manage six young kids by herself. My mom tried to do something to change their lives, and did for a minute, but now she's ruined her own. Dad means well and checks on them as much as he can, but he can barely take care of himself and wouldn't see a way to make better money if it smacked him in the face. He's a worker bee through and through. I was signed with the UFC at the time and thought I was going to make it all okay. I was two and one and up for renewal, but they dropped me."

"They dropped you with a winning record?"

"They did. I wasn't compelling enough."

"What?"

She nods. "They do that sometimes. Maybe they had too many fighters or wanted to cut the budget, or they just didn't believe in me, but they let me go. I was devastated. And furious. And worried about my family, and the only one who could do anything about it."

"So, you did something."

"I started the Yard. I admit I was pissed at the UFC and everything that wanted to be like it. I was pissed at my dad for not being able to think bigger and at my mom for being reckless and at my sister for being broken and at her husband for being weak. I had a lot of blame to go around, and I was going to show them how it was done."

I laugh. "Yeah, that sounds about right. You kind of did, though."

"No, I created a monster, and I can't tame it. I went after big investors. I got them, and everyone got paid. It was all fun and games, but when people throw that kind of money around, you sell a piece of your control whether it's on paper or not."

"Sam?"

"Yeah, he's one of them, but there are more. Don't get me wrong, I'm grateful. They love what I made, and they bring in big bets and real money. It means my sister's mortgage is paid and my nieces and nephews have what they need. I have the freedom to take them to baseball and the movies and they get to have a real Christmas. It means my dad's fridge is always full and if the day comes that he can't work, I can make sure he's okay. Hopefully, one day it means I can fix up my grandma's house and my nieces and nephews can stop living three to a room. I can pay my fighters a fair contract so they can do the same thing for their families. I owe everything to Sam and the others who believed in the Yard, but they don't want to see it change. If they wanted to invest in a legit promotion they would have. They like rough and chaotic and secret and exclusive. That's the whole point for them. I know it looks like I've done nothing, but getting a doctor at the events, getting people off of concrete when they fight, getting competent refs, screening to make sure people have some kind of experience, no one wanted any of that except me, not even the fighters. I do care about people."

"I know you do."

It doesn't feel like enough. I hate that I ever made her feel otherwise. I squeeze her hand.

"Can't you still do this, though?" I hold up the folder. "I mean, you've already done all the work, and you deserve to do it the way you want to do it. It's your business."

"I could, but I'd be starting over. I'd have to rebrand. That's why there's a different name on the paperwork. My big money supporters would disappear. Even if I could weather the gap until I could get things rolling, my fighters couldn't. They're used to a real paycheck. I'd lose most of my talent. I don't know how many would follow me to a legitimate promotion even if they could afford the pay cut. They don't all want that. Vic doesn't. I could try to rebuild. Maybe I'd make it, but maybe I wouldn't, and then what? How do I risk that? I pay my sister's mortgage. What do I do if it doesn't work? Move all seven of them into my apartment?"

I've never wanted to be rich and capable of making problems disappear with money so badly in my entire life. I imagine it's the exact feeling that drove Harlow to make the choices she's made.

"I can't imagine taking care of my entire family. That's so much for you to take on."

She nods. "I know. I know they're not my kids and it's not my fault and it's not my responsibility, but when people you love aren't going to make it without you, what else can you do?"

I'm not sure what to say because this heroic effort Harlow is making is just that, but she shouldn't be shackled. What kind of young person just decides it's their job to support six kids that aren't theirs? And her sister and likely her father in more ways than she's saying. Most wouldn't even be capable, and that would be the end of it.

"I don't know," I say. "But, Harlow, if you did it once you can do it again."

"It's a different thing."

"I know, but with everything you've done for so many people they're going to want to support you."

"I want to believe that, but the truth is I've never seen anyone get anywhere the legit way. My dad and my sister did things the way they thought they were supposed to. Got a steady job and put their head down, and they're both fucked. I tried to do things the real way and I ended up fucked. You tried too, and here we all are. I'm not sure the world is built for a nobody to climb out."

"Your mom is fucked too, though, Harlow. How risky is what you do, really? For you. Legally."

She takes a deep breath and puts her arm around me, pulls me against her. Only when I feel the warmth of her body do I realize I'm shivering, but as soon as I do I melt against her, and she wraps the blanket around me better.

"It's a risk," she says. "But mostly if something happens. If people start reporting and complaining or if someone gets seriously hurt. As long as we don't put ourselves on the radar, it's not a priority for the cops. They know everyone is participating willingly, and we're not a public nuisance or involved in other kinds of crime."

"So, you feel safe?"

"Safe enough."

I rest my head on her chest, smell her warm cologne.

"So, what do you think?" she asks.

"I think you're beautiful."

The sound of her laugh against my ear makes me smile.

"Not what I meant but thank you."

"I'm not leaving." I kiss her chest and pull my arm tighter across her waist. She squeezes me back, and while that feels warm and safe enough to drift off to sleep, my view of her long, strong stomach and perfect legs is sending other messages through my body.

I run my hand over her stomach and down her leg to her knee, then trace back up inside her thigh.

"What are you doing?" she whispers.

"Touching you."

I lift her shirt and kiss her stomach, tracing my lips across her hips soft and slow until she shifts and runs her hand through my hair.

"Is tonight one of those nights where you locked the roof door?" I ask.

"Coincidentally, it is."

"How fortunate." I unbutton her pants and open them, pulling them down to make room for one more kiss, then pull a little farther for another. She laughs and tugs on my hair playfully until I come up and kiss her mouth.

"What's the matter, tough guy? Don't know how to let me take care of you?"

"I want to touch you too, you know," she whispers.

"Mmm, maybe I'll let you when I'm done with you."

She smiles, but I kiss her again, swinging my leg over to straddle her and parting her lips with my tongue. Her hands land on my hips as

I push my body into her. Our kiss heats to a thousand in an instant as I disappear into a rhythm against her tongue. Her hands move up my back and into my hair as she pushes her hips into me. I shudder, and the pressure makes me wet instantly.

She grabs my shirt and pulls it over my head slowly before tossing it aside and kissing down my neck. The feel of nightfall, cool against my skin, mixing with her hot tongue across my chest makes me quaver as I plunge my fingers into her hair. She pulls my bra out of her way and takes my nipple in her mouth, her tongue sliding over it lightly. I gasp and cling to her, as she adds pressure, and her fingertips press into my back.

My body has never reacted like this, not with this kind of intensity, not this fast. For fuck's sake, I could get there just like this, from her playing with my nipples while I grind on top of her, and it wouldn't be hard.

I pull her head back by her hair and kiss her again, then pull off her shirt. Her body is beyond gorgeous. The kind of thing you see in a magazine, and though I've been around many a fitness-obsessed athlete, Harlow has the kind of body that brings people to their knees, which is exactly where I want to be. Her shoulders are strong and wide, her waist long and trim, her abs gently etched, and her breasts full and perfect, covered in a black bra that while flattering needs to leave her body immediately. I release the clasp and throw it to the ground while I kiss her. I feel her laugh just a little in appreciation of the move while she duplicates it with ease and cups my breasts as she kisses me deeper.

I move down her body, kiss my way down her neck, along the crevice between her exquisite breasts, down her stomach, until I slide off her to my knees and part her thighs.

"God, you're gorgeous," I whisper.

I grab her waistband and pull, stripping everything, yanking her shoes from her feet so I can rip her pants and underwear down until she's naked.

When I look up, she's watching me, eyes flashing with anticipation. There's not an ounce of self-consciousness in her expression, which only turns me on more. I separate her thighs with my palms, press my bare waist between them as I kiss her, penetrating her mouth with my tongue as I slide my hips against her wet center rhythmically. She takes in a sharp breath and moves beneath me in sync. I feel her losing track of the kiss, losing control of her body as it trembles and pulls at me, as her breath goes choppy and she finally whimpers the smallest helpless sound in my ear.

I slide my hand between us and trace down to her pussy, barely touching her as she writhes. When I feel how wet she is we both come undone just a little.

"Fuck, Harlow. You know the things I want to do to you?"

"Show me," she whispers.

I slide my fingers inside her and let her moan slam through me. I fuck her slow, sliding into her deep and firm, watching her breasts rise as her back arches. I circle her clit with my thumb while I caress her inner walls until I feel her tightening around me and her moans come at my command. Her hand pulls my hair, and not gently as she rides my hand. I press my free hand up her body, finding her nipple and pinching. She moans and squirms, and the pulse beating inside me intensifies as I watch her.

"Fuck, Laila."

I bite my lip and try to keep myself from getting lost in how turned on I am. In how much I want to push my hips into her and come on her. But I want to feel her come even more, and I drive my fingers into her in the rhythm her body is telling me she wants. I lower myself onto my heels and take her clit in my mouth, pressing my tongue against it before sucking on it gently.

"Oh my God," Harlow moans in the most feminine sound I've ever heard her make. It sets me on fire. I push inside her again and suck on her clit. Her body tenses and tightens and her head falls back. Her grip pulls my hair, and she moans as she comes, pressing hard against my mouth and holding me there as she pulses. When she releases me she goes limp and takes a shaky breath. I kiss her stomach and feel her breath rise, my fingers still inside her feeling her pulse.

"Fuck I'm a mess for you," I say.

She smiles and lightly pulls my hair again. I start to come to sit beside her on the couch, but she stops me with an outstretched hand.

"Oh no," she says. "You stay right there."

I wait, amused and curious. "Okay."

"Take off your pants."

"Hey, if you're thinking your turn is over, I was just getting started."

"Take off your pants," she says again. There is mischief in her sexy, darkened eyes that makes my mouth go dry. I take off my pants, letting the cool air hit my skin and remembering we're outside, on a roof that's all our own.

"Walk over to the rail," she says. I look over my shoulder to the rail that's ten feet away.

"You want me way over there?"

She doesn't even answer me. Just does that ridiculously sexy smirk that drives me nuts like she's daring me to defy her. I smirk back and go to the rail, lean back against it. The cold metal bites my elbows, but I'm so in my body I like every sensation offered to it. Harlow slowly stands up and walks over. She presses her warm body against mine and leans down, kissing me slowly.

"You're sexy looking at me like that," she whispers. "But I meant this way."

She grabs my arm and turns me around so that I'm looking over the rail at the twinkling city lights. "I brought you here so you could take in the view."

She kisses my neck, her warm breath seeping through my body while her hands move down and slide my underwear off.

"While you take me in."

My breath comes out all ragged as her fingertips trace up the backs of my thighs. Her arms wrap around me and her body presses against my back. She traces across my hips and touches me, sliding down and feeling my wetness. My head falls back onto her shoulder and her other palm slides up my throat, then down to play with my nipples.

I push my ass back into her hips, and she returns the pressure, then nudges my feet apart with her foot. She runs her hand through my hair and down my spine. I push back into her again, and she grabs my hips, then pulls me even farther. My pulse picks up, and I have to suppress a moan at the mere realization that Harlow is about to fuck me from behind on a roof. Her hand grabs the back of my neck, and she slowly but decisively lowers my head as she pulls my hips farther back into her still. I accept her command, anticipation flooding my body as her hands move over my skin.

Her palm on my neck somehow keeps my entire body warm while also making me feel like a possession, and I've never wanted to be possessed so much in my life. Her other hand moves up my leg, sending shivers through me as she caresses my inner thighs until she gets to my center. She doesn't hesitate or fumble or waver as she pushes inside me and tightens her grasp on my neck. I cry out from the unbelievable surge of pleasure, as much from the way she's filling me as her command on my body.

"Fucking God," I moan. She grabs my hair and thrusts inside again, her hips following her hand until they press against my ass and my chest presses on the rail. The sea of brake lights and headlights and window lights and streetlights all blend into a glimmering reflection of ecstasy.

Her fingers find all the right places, and I feel myself quaking around her as waves of pleasure crash through me. She moves faster. Her fingertips press into the front of my thigh as she uses it to hold me while she fucks me, her teeth finding the back of my shoulder.

I lose track of the string of profanities she's tearing from my throat as she plays with me. Takes me. Fills me. She grabs my hair again, and I know this time she means for me to come. Knowing someone wants me to come is usually enough to make it virtually impossible, but not with Harlow. Just feeling her demand it takes me over the edge, and when she pumps into me harder I feel it come from my toes and my fingers, through my arms and calves, into a slow-motion explosion through my core, an energy field that swallows us both. I reach back and seize her hair as she kisses my neck, holding her against me as the orgasm clamps me in a hypnosis, as it peaks and slows and somehow peaks again. She holds me tight, her arm fastening me together while I tremble. When it finally subsides, I feel like I haven't had a real breath in an hour and like I'm returning from another place.

Harlow's grasp on me softens, and I turn to face her.

"Jesus," I whisper and kiss her softly.

"Hey, if you're thinking your turn is over, I was just getting started." She winks before she descends to her knees.

"Wait." My whisper is pathetic and unconvincing. I have a long list of things I still want to do to her and every intention of carrying them out. But Harlow. With those incredible eyes and the silky hair and the perfect body, the ridiculously hot way about her. On her knees with that beautiful mouth kissing me, her tongue caressing me. I'm helpless. She's as relentless as I am, which means this is going to take all night.

Chapter Eighteen

I wake up slung across Harlow's body. My arm is draped over her chest. My leg is across her naked waist as her hand holds it there. It takes me a second to recognize her room. Last night I wasn't paying as much attention to the décor as I was to the way her body tastes and the notes of her orgasms.

The room is already light, but it's the incoming warmth that lets me know we've slept in. I reach for my phone and see that it's eleven. Given that it took us until three to give it a rest, that doesn't seem unreasonable. When I set my phone back down on the nightstand, Harlow stirs. I squeeze her and kiss her shoulder, waiting for her to fall back asleep, but her eyes flutter open. I smile as I see memories fill her eyes.

"Mmm. Hey you," she whispers.

"Hey, beautiful." I trace my fingers down her arm, thinking about how they felt around me. When they were soft. When they were rough. I drag my fingers down her stomach, barely touching her until I go under the blanket that covers her, biting my lip as I confirm she still has nothing on.

She laughs. "You need more, Moretti?"

I smile and get on top of her. "Mmhmm." I kiss her neck and press my hips slowly against her until I feel her body wake up. It's almost imperceptible at first, but I put her hands on my breasts as she starts to squirm and ride her until she's pushing her hips into me. She matches my rhythm, satisfying my aching body more and more as she pushes into me harder. She sits up so we're chest to chest, wraps those arms around me again, and crushes me against her. I whimper with pleasure, feeling helpless in her grasp.

"You trying to fuck me to death?" she whispers.

"What's the matter, Hayes? Too much for you?"

A fire comes into her eyes, and I smirk as she takes the bait and flips me onto my back. She pushes between my legs hard and a little mean and utterly sexy. I moan in her ear as she drives inside me.

"You going to set me straight?" I whisper.

She grabs my throat, moving up so her fingertips are on my jaw holding me firmly but gently. I move my thigh between her legs and press up into her. Her breath breaks, and she takes the invitation, grinding against my thigh as she fucks me with her fingers in a single rhythm. I weave my fingers into her long hair, feeling the soft ends of it tickle my naked chest until she starts sucking my nipple. I arch into her. I feel like an instrument she's an expert at playing. Her thumb rubs across my lower lip and I bite the tip until she thrusts deeper inside me. My head falls back as I cry out.

"Come with me," I say, breathless and helpless. She moves up my body just a little to give herself more contact, and then she moves on top of me in the most intoxicating, reckless, greedy way, taking me, touching me, fucking me. My orgasm builds and tumbles over like a river overflowing. I go weak and rigid at the same time. She drives into me and tenses as she comes. Her energy pulses from her body and engulfs mine as she holds me in her thrall.

When her body relaxes, she rests her head on my chest, floating on my chaotic breath. I kiss the top of her head and hold her.

"Listen, you can't have this much sex with me *and* hold me like this unless you want me to get attached. Everyone knows that."

I laugh. "Oh, God forbid we get attached." She laughs, but I feel something inside her that's serious and afraid, and I hold her tighter. "I told you I'm not going anywhere."

Her fingers tighten. If Harlow is just now worrying about attachment, I was early to the party. I'm not someone who can resist feelings or even wants to. Then again, what I usually experience are flares of passion. There and then gone. Whatever Harlow is doing to me is burning hotter and deeper, and she's underestimating her hold on me if she thinks I'm going to just float away. I bury my face in her hair and breathe in the smell of her shampoo. She kisses my chest and sits up.

"I have to shower. Dylan and Aspen are coming over soon. We have a training session today."

"Oh, yeah. You said something about that at their house."

"I'm sorry. Timing could be better."

"That's okay. I'll go."

"You don't have to," she says. "I mean you can, but you can also stay in here and relax. Or join us."

"Join you?"

"Of course." She shrugs. "They'll love it."

"Are you sure?"

"Dylan will even give you a run for your money. Kid is getting really good."

Somehow spending time with Harlow's family, with the kids she treasures like her own, feels every bit as intimate as all the things we just did with each other's bodies.

"Okay." I barely speak, like the word is going to bite me.

"Okay, then. Shower?" When she checks the time and sees how soon they'll arrive, we manage to rein ourselves in enough to actually complete the process before the knock on the door.

When Harlow answers, Dylan and Aspen light up. I can't get enough of how excited they are to see her even though it happens so often. Dylan looks surprised but unbothered to see me. Harlow puts her hand on Aspen's shoulder. She's younger and shorter, but otherwise a female version of Dylan, beautiful with light eyes and dark hair and a vaguely mature look to her young face.

"Aspen, this is my friend Laila. Laila, this is the last of the clan, Aspen."

Harlow guides both kids inside as Aspen smiles at me shyly. They both start winding their wraps through their fingers in a well-practiced routine while I stretch on the mat.

"So, you're the one who used to train at Emerald Tiger, right?" Dylan asks.

I glance at Harlow because I would love to know when she did all this talking about me, but I look back and answer him.

"Yes, for a very long time."

"So, did you get to train with Eden Bauer? And Brooklyn Shaw?"

I smile. "Yes, Eden taught me most everything I know. She gave me my black belt. I've trained a lot with Brooklyn too. And her brothers."

"Did you roll with Théo Shaw?"

The question tunes me into how much of a fan Dylan really is. Anyone with even a peripheral knowledge knows about Eden and Brooklyn, both of them dominant UFC champions whose rivalry turned romantic relationship captured the zeitgeist. Brooklyn's brother Théo, however, is a legendary Brazilian Jiu Jitsu champion. He's just as deserving of Dylan's awe, but the number of people who follow BJJ closely is a fraction of those who follow MMA.

"Yes, I did a few times. He's incredible. Leandro too."

"No way. He's so big." Dylan laughs at the notion of me rolling with Brooklyn's other very famous brother, and he's not wrong.

"Yeah, he crushed me, but he's very nice."

"What about Parker Collins?"

Now he's referring to one of the newest signed UFC fighters to join the team. The kid knows exactly who trains at Emerald Tiger. I would venture he knows their records and styles and anything else worth knowing.

"I think she's trained with them all, bud," Harlow says.

"Yes, he almost dropped me on my head the first day, but he caught me."

"Cool." Dylan laughs and lines up in front of me. I realize whatever it is they usually do during these sessions, he's planning to do it with me. I can't help but feel a little giddy about it. Harlow stands across from Aspen and starts calling out combos for her to execute, holding out her gloves to catch the blows.

"Is that what you want to do?" I ask.

"Sure, but you'll need real pads for that."

"Ah, of course."

I laugh as I take off my gloves and trade them in for mitts. His assurance I'll need them is one and the same as telling me he's about to be hitting me with some real power, which doesn't surprise me at all. I've given intro classes to countless new Emerald Tiger students who all wanted to stand out and earn respect the fast way. I tend to be the first one they try to murder but not the last. I slap the mitts together and hold them up.

"All right, let's see what you got. One, two."

He cracks a jab, cross.

"Three, two." Hook, cross.

"One, one, four." Jab, jab, uppercut.

"Duck, four." I swing for his head. He ducks and throws the uppercut on his way up. I step to the right and watch him step to circle with me. I call combos at him in rapid-fire, adding movement and throwing strikes back for him to block, slip, or duck. He responds fast and throws everything as hard as he can. His gloves land with powerful slaps that penetrate through to my palm and ring a crisp sound. When he's in a rhythm, I start calling for kicks too, then throwing them back for him to block or catch. Soon I don't have to call and can just show the pads while he identifies the hits needed.

His pupils are big and black, and he has the look strikers get when they're looking center mass but taking in their entire field of vision for signs of incoming strikes. He's good. Really good, and I offer nods and "yeses" to make sure he knows it for a solid fifteen minutes before I finally motion at him to bring his elbows in a little. He does it without any hint of resentment. If he's this good and also receptive, he could have something.

"Step for the angle before you throw the next combo."

The step is clunky.

"Again."

He steps. I hold my right mitt over the left side of my face so he can see the shot better. His posture corrects itself as he cracks the punch into the mitt so hard it takes a little jolt of adrenaline to keep the mitt from smacking me in the face.

"Good, angle out."

He steps.

"Other way. Away from the power hand."

He nods, his eyes lighting up as he digests the reason. I throw a light low kick.

"Stay light on that front leg."

He nods, but when I throw a kick at it again, it's still heavy.

"I want you to imagine that you might have to sprawl out of a takedown at any time. That's how light you want it."

"Are we adding takedowns?"

I can't help but laugh because he would clearly love nothing more.

"Maybe not with all four of us on the mat, but you want to be light on that front leg even if you're just striking. It's going to make your footwork faster. You'll be able to get that leg up in time to check my kicks, and you can get your kicks off faster. It'll even make your punches stronger."

"Really?"

"Yep. We're transferring weight and energy. What's stronger, a jab or a cross?"

"A cross."

"Because?"

"Because it's the hand in back."

"There you go. Weight on the back leg does the same thing. It's also going to keep you from overextending and make your counters faster. Trust me. You'll like it."

It finally occurs to me his consent isn't the only one I should have felt out before I started spouting off advice. I look over my shoulder at Harlow a little nervous I'm stomping through her territory. She and Aspen are sitting on the edge of the mat watching us, and Harlow is smiling.

"Well, go on. Try it," she says.

I hold up the mitts and put Dylan through another thirty combos or so, offering only micro adjustments as he trains his body to do what his mind is asking. I don't think he means to or notices, but as he starts to get it, a smile spreads across his face. When he finally looks exhausted and soaked with sweat, I drop my arms and slap him on the side.

"Good job. It's looking great."

He beams, and we go sit beside Harlow and Aspen, who had a much easier session and have been giggling about something for five minutes.

"What'd you think?" Harlow asks Dylan.

"It was awesome," he says. "Can we do it again?"

Harlow looks over to me, and it takes me a second to realize she's trying to ask me.

"Oh, of course," I say too loudly, and they all laugh.

"And in return you can help Laila get ready for her next fight," Harlow says. "He's an animal on the ground too."

"When's your next fight?" Aspen asks.

"I'm not sure yet."

Harlow smiles discreetly.

"Am I?"

"It can be in six weeks if you want it."

"Of course I want it. Who is it?"

"Her name is Sierra Waters. Mid-level. She's six and three. Mostly a striker."

"Great."

"Something wrong?" Harlow asks, looking amused.

"No, it's fine. I know I have to climb the ranks. I can do it sooner, though. I don't need six weeks. I want to get through whoever I need to get through and get to Katarina."

Harlow laughs and the way it lights her face up smolders in my chest. I can't help but smile too. "What?"

"Nothing, I'm sorry. It's just fun hearing you talk like that. Like the entire roster is just a nuisance on the way to Katarina. I'm glad you're feeling good."

"She's really good, Harlow," Dylan says.

Harlow punches him on the arm lightly. "I know, kid." She looks back to me. "I'll get you Katarina as soon as I can, but she's already slated to fight Vic next. They fight in two months."

"That's really happening?"

Harlow shrugs. "Vic earned her shot, and she says she wants it."

"Can I have her next?"

She laughs again, and it melts me again. Damn, it's hard to focus.

"It depends," she says. "On what happens in your fight. On what happens in theirs. And a few others. It probably wouldn't hurt for you to get a couple more under your belt anyway, but I promise I'll do my best, okay?"

I have to shake myself out of looking at her like I want to take her clothes off again. "Deal."

"When are you going to get me a fight, Harlow?" Dylan asks.

"Uh, never, buddy. Nice try."

"Come on. I could totally do it."

"Mom would never let you," Aspen says.

"Mom doesn't have to know."

"Absolutely not," Harlow says. "And I would never let you either."

"Why not? You're letting Laila do it."

"That's different."

"Why?"

"Well, she's an adult for one."

"So, when I'm eighteen?" Dylan asks.

"No. And it's time for you two to get home."

"That's not fair. I'm a good fighter."

I want to help out by saying that he's a *really* good fighter. His skill at his age means he could be making a run at the real thing in a real gym if he wanted to, but I'm not sure if Harlow just opposes him fighting in her organization or if she opposes it in general, so I hold myself back. It seems obvious that he would pursue it given his natural talent and all the hours they've clearly put in, but it also doesn't take much brain power to imagine all the reasons they might want something different for him. Something that doesn't involve broken bones and torn ligaments and blood.

I want to tell him he should go train at Emerald Tiger, explain how generous Eden is with scholarships and custom pay plans when money comes up, and how much safer the environment is when worry comes up, but I don't know that Harlow wants that either. He'd likely be there already if she did, so I say nothing, and he leaves with only the promise that we'll train again soon.

CHAPTER NINETEEN

Six weeks sounded like an eternity when Harlow first said it. When she told me Sierra needed the time even if I didn't, I took the news as if six weeks isn't a perfectly normal and reasonable amount of prep time. The urgency isn't about Katarina. My loss with the UFC, absence from Emerald Tiger, and full-on break has left me feeling behind and wasteful even though it hasn't been all that long. In a career that is often over by thirty-five, where you can expect to be interrupted by injuries and setbacks, there's little time for personal meltdowns or distractions.

The worry and impatience faded as the weeks dropped away. Alternating between helping Harlow with events, training full time, and falling into bed with her for the hottest sex I've ever had has made time illusory. Finding training partners who can put in enough hours and truly push me has remained a full-on pain in the ass even with Harlow trying her best to connect me with people in the underground world, but that's meant extra time for cardio and weight training. What I've lost in technical training I've gained in pure fitness.

I was a member of other gyms before Eden converted Emerald Tiger from a Taekwondo dojang to offer a full MMA program. I had Muay Thai and BJJ gyms I was part of for years, both of which would welcome me back. I didn't have the personal relationship with them that I do with Eden, and they would never know or care about my fighting habits outside the gym. It would give me a formal environment and as many training partners as I can handle. Yet, I haven't done that.

Something about training in Harlow's apartment with whatever yard scrapper has a spare hour makes me feel alive. I like the way they bring gloves with the padding ripped out. I like the chaotic, wrong way they move. I like the way they succumb to ego and emotion when they're losing and risk it all on a hail Mary. I like that they aren't looking out for me. I'm no one's little sister, and if I take it too lightly, I'll end up crashing into Harlow's coffee table or watching a joint go the wrong way.

I like that I can feel their shitty family and childhood trauma and fast-food side job and unreturned calls on the mat with us. I like the way all that wrong somehow adds up to something right. It's vicious and heartless and real, and every time I survive it, I feel a little piece of me resurrect.

Harlow peeks around the corner. "Will you be good to go in about fifteen?"

I nod and give her a thumbs up in between shadowboxing, but she comes over anyway.

"You're super ready," she says.

I nod. "I know."

"Don't forget to be careful."

"Harlow, I'm going to be fine."

"There's a pole in the middle of the room, don't forget. And it's carpet, but it's thin and there's concrete under it. Treat it like concrete."

I smile because I saw it myself before I came to the back, and she's reminded me at least five times since already. I squeeze her hand. "I know. I got it."

Forgetting to be careful isn't a bad way to describe the journey I'm on, but she's right. Overcoming the urge to cower under pressure isn't just abandoning caution, it's refusing to find safety through submission. It's finding it another way.

This is my first time at this venue. It's a basement strip club and the oddest blend of luxury and busted. The seating is all VIP, and the bar has a crystal top. The stages, lights, and stereo are all high-end production, yet in this case "exclusive" means it's hidden underneath a liquor store on a grungy street corner where not even the highest rollers want to be caught wearing their Rolexes and diamonds.

The pole she warned me about isn't a stripper pole, though those are around too, elevated on stages with black, easy to miss stairs. The one she's worried about is one of those thick structural ones you find in basements that could mean lights out if you let someone plow your head into it. It's a strange space, at a glance big and open, but a small clearing before it becomes an obstacle course.

"Where's Matt?"

I cringe because she's asking about my corner, one of the guys I've been training with, and he isn't here.

"You're kidding," she says.

"He'll be here."

"We have ten minutes."

I shrug.

"We've discussed this."

"Well, Harlow, I don't know what to tell you. I have no friends fit for the job."

Dylan begged for the job, but Harlow wouldn't let him do it. She thought it would only exacerbate his determination to get a fight for himself.

"You know, Vic is here."

"No."

"Laila, she's by far the best person to—"

"She called me a bitch. Like a weak, pussy, can't fight bitch, not a crabby bitch. Vic can suck a—"

Vic rounds the corner. Her eyes meet mine like she wasn't expecting to see me even though she must know I'm fighting.

"How sweet, talking about me."

Harlow gives me an intense look practically begging me to ask Vic to corner for me, but after the things Vic said there's no way I'm asking her for help. She steps closer and looks me up and down. I'm in a sports bra that does a bang-up job at showcasing the abs and arms I've built and sculpted. I hope she's measuring their capacity to strangle her.

"You look great," Vic says. "Ready to go."

"Of course."

"Look, Laila, I know things got a little heated between us, but I really was just trying to be a friend in my way. I thought you wanted out and were too worried about what everyone thought to walk away. I was trying to make that okay for you."

"By trying to fight me?"

She rolls her eyes. "You know I get carried away. You're my girl, though. I would never hurt you."

"You wouldn't get very far if you tried, Vic."

I expect it to set her off, but she smiles and eats it. "Well, I see you're all in again. I'm happy for you. You know I'm pulling for you, right?" She punches my arm and walks away. Harlow makes a desperate face at me to accept the peace offering.

I roll my eyes. Vic always gets away with this kind of shit because everyone treats her like she's emotionally stunted, and I hate it, but she has a way with timing.

"Ugh. Vic?"

She turns back.

"Will you be my corner tonight?"

Her eyebrows shoot up, and she comes back. "Really? Sure."

"Okay, well good, because you're on in two." Harlow squeezes my wrist and looks into my eyes.

"Oh Jesus, just kiss." Vic covers her eyes. Harlow slaps her arm and disappears into the main room.

"What was that?" Vic asks. "No kiss?"

"We don't do that around here," I say in a low voice.

"But you are doing it, right?" she asks. I can't help but smile even though I haven't completely warmed back up to Vic. She nudges me. "Yeah, you are."

"Shh."

"Okay, but is it amazing? She's so hot."

I can't help that ridiculous giddy thing that happens, and I finally nod. "It's amazing."

"Head in the game, Moretti," she says, becoming mock serious in a snap. "You've got a fight in two minutes."

"You're ridiculous."

"Yeah, but you really do."

"You think I don't know that?"

Part of me wonders if I do truly know. Just a few months ago, being moments before my *Contender Series* fight had me in a ball on the ground. This is arguably more dangerous, but I'm steady. There are still nerves but not like before. It's different. I'm different. The Yard freed something.

"Let's go, fighter." The coordinator waves at me. I start my walk out at a fast pace.

"You got this. No sweat, baby. She's got nothing on this ass." Vic slaps my ass as she follows. It's embarrassing to admit and not always worth it, but Vic is fun.

There's no cage, just the open room and a ring of people gathered to see violence. The ref checks my gloves and confirms I understand the very simple rules, then waves me to join Sierra in the open space.

It's not often I enjoy a size advantage. I'm five foot five and naturally lanky, but I've packed on some muscle, and looking at Sierra, I'm feeling like I'll be able to have my way with her. I've never felt so confident. Not even against new students in the gym because I don't have to take care of Sierra. When you're responsible for another person's safety, you don't just have to be better than they are, you have to be much better. You have to be able to beat them at partial effort. Here, I don't have to be safe.

"Ready?" the ref asks. I nod, and he starts the fight.

Sierra charges me. I hook under her arms and throw her past me, letting her momentum take her straight into the crowd. She trips, and her face goes straight into some guy's hip, but he also halfway catches her. She pushes back to her feet and comes at me slower. She steps into the pocket, where we can reach each other, and throws a hard cross. I raise my hand to block and take it mostly on my shoulder, rolling with it so it has no effect.

Her shots are nice and long, well distanced with full extension. We trade punches as I feel out the rhythm. Her power is tolerable. A five-year-old can water your eyes if they get you in the nose, but she's not throwing anything that feels like a knockout threat. I slap her jab aside with my right hand and follow it through with an elbow that cracks her in the cheek. She doesn't react. No stumble, no running, no swinging for the fences, but I see that look in her eyes, like an animal in danger, and a tingle of excitement goes up my spine.

I walk her down, back her into the crowd and cut off her angle. I blast a right hook to her body. It slaps so hard the whole crowd reacts to the sound as her posture crunches over. I follow with a jab to her face. Shuffle to cut her off as she tries to circle out again and slam another hook to the body. She crunches down again, covering her side and grimacing.

The thrill of winning zings through me, clutching my entire body like something sour as I commit to a flurry of punches. I fire them off fast, a blast of aggression taking up all the air in the room. I want to overwhelm and dwarf her. I want to blitz her until she crumbles. I want her to give me her soul. I want her to shrink, and she is. The crowd is roaring. Vic is screaming at me to finish it. I've got her.

And then there's a crack. A crash of thunder. Blood flows down my face. I look down, stunned as the drops fall red on the floor, on my hands. It rolls down my face. She hits me again. I stumble, almost regain my footing, then take a hard push to the chest that puts me on the ground.

She's rushing over and there's no time to stand up. She swings at me as hard as she can. She starts a mile away. I see it a mile away, but I can't react. Her fist comes down on my face. At the last second, I stiffen my body, especially my neck, and save myself from hitting the back of my head on the floor, but it still dizzies me.

She's on top of me and trying to ground and pound this to a finish. I beg my cloudy thoughts to clear, beg my body to come back to me. I've never been covered in so much blood. Not from brow cuts or nose bleeds or anything else, and to make it worse she's bleeding on me too. She swings for the rafters again, her fist shamelessly as far back as she can pull it even though every striker knows that's no way to punch.

My mind clears. The signals my brain is trying to send catch fire in my limbs, and I lift my hips and slam the back of my thigh over her shoulder. I lock my calf down onto her back. My weight breaks her posture down and throws her off balance so badly that loaded fist falls pathetically to my stomach. I shift, still on my back, angling the leg on her shoulder against her neck, trapping the arm she just tried to punch me with against my body, and lock my other leg over my ankle into a powerful choke called a triangle.

She tries to straighten her back and posture up, but my legs are strong, and she has no hope of muscling out. I pull her in and make the small adjustments needed to perfect the lock. With one of her arms trapped in my grasp and the other stuck on the far side of my leg where it can't reach me with any effect, she's helpless.

Once I have the submission locked up to my satisfaction, I tighten it, pulling her in as I constrict my legs. She tries hard not to tap out. I can feel her neck angling and bending. I grimace at the idea of it breaking and choose to just hold the submission instead of continuing to tighten it. She tries to endure it, but she goes limp.

"She's out," I yell at the ref, who confirms it by lifting her unconscious arm, then commands me to let go. I release the submission, and the ref rolls her onto her back and lifts her legs to wake her.

Vic flies out of the crowd and pushes me before picking me up, shouting.

Sierra is back on her feet in no time and actually shakes my hand, never a guarantee. After the ref raises my hand, Vic guides me to the back. It takes me half the distance to realize her palms are on my shoulders as she marches me forward because I'm not exactly walking straight. When we get to the back, Harlow is pulling me onto a chair before I even see her. She kneels in front of me and waves the doctor over as she inspects my forehead. She wipes my face down with a towel, but I feel fresh blood flow.

"Hey," I say.

She finally makes eye contact and sees my smile. "Hey, you." She smiles back, against her wishes, I think.

"I won."

"You did." She shakes her head.

"I'm okay."

"You need stitches," she says. "That was a nasty headbutt."

"She headbutted me?"

The headbutts I've taken before have all been accidental and agonizing, but nothing like this, which makes a lot of sense since the lunatic actually grabbed me and did it on purpose.

"Yes."

I nod, considering it, then let it go. "You're really pretty."

"You're concussed."

"And really pretty?"

She finally laughs and kisses me on the cheek. "Yes, and really pretty."

She trades places with the doctor, and I let her stitch me up, but all I want is to look into Harlow's eyes again. The pain of this cut has nothing on the pain of losing. This cut is no problem. I can look people in the eye with this cut.

CHAPTER TWENTY

I'm about two weeks overdue for a haircut, but as I pull my spikes down over my forehead, I confirm that even if I was willing to look this stupid, it's not long enough to cover the two-inch horizontal cut across my forehead.

"You think they'll buy it if I say I fell down the stairs?"

Harlow appears behind me, looking at me through the bathroom mirror.

"I think if you're going to lie, you can do better than the oldest domestic violence excuse in the book."

"Fine, I saved a baby. From a fiery…runaway…bike messenger."

"That was you?"

She kisses me on the cheek and steps up beside me to start messing with her own hair in the mirror even though it's already beautiful. I grab the wax and try to convince my hair to return to its usual messy spikes.

"You know, you'd think at some point hair would achieve some kind of memory," I say.

"It does," Harlow says.

"So it's being a pain in the ass on purpose?"

"Well, it is you."

"Are you trying to say I'm a pain in the ass?"

She leans in to examine her skin. I'm overly fascinated by Harlow's beauty rituals. She can go through all the feminine motions even though she hardly ever touches a product. It's endlessly amusing to me trying to figure out what exactly she's doing.

"Not a pain in the ass. Just, you know, lippy."

"My hair is lippy?"

"Yes." She turns and kisses me. "And super-hot no matter what it does."

"Nice save."

"I thought I was supposed to be the nervous one. Meeting the parents. You get to just sit back and get birthday presents."

"Hah. They'll love you," I say. "You're beautiful and successful and a patron saint. You'll pass inspection in five minutes and the rest of the time will be spent grilling me."

"On your birthday?"

"Oh, sweet girl. Yes, on my birthday. You ready?"

She pulls me into her arms and kisses me. Her lips are so soft that for just a second, I almost forget all the stress.

"I'm ready if you are," she says. "Unless you need a naked birthday present first."

She pushes me onto the bathroom counter. I laugh even though the surge of arousal she's sending through me is very real. She's already given me several naked birthday presents.

"If you give me any more, we'll just have to be in for the night." I run my hands down her body. "To be clear, I'm not saying no."

She laughs and kisses me. "I do want to meet your family though."

"It's really not all it's cracked up to be."

"Is it too soon? I don't have to go if it is."

"Oh, Harlow, no. I'm not hiding you; I'm sparing you. But come on, we'll go."

I stop trying to wiggle out of this. I can't have her thinking I don't want it to happen because of her. The truth is I can't wait to show her off. I just know what the wound on my head will produce in Mom.

She drives, handing me the bottle of wine and gourmet chocolates she's bringing as a gift.

"They're going to trade me in for you."

She smiles. "They will not, but I'm glad you think they'll like it."

When we get to the door, the typical chaos inside is scaled back from an eight to a four.

"They're already on their best behavior for you," I say.

"That's cute. They don't have to be."

When Louis opens the door, he does a poor job of hiding his reaction to Harlow. I can't tell who he admires more, Harlow or me. He's such a big, scruffy, man-slab these days I often forget he's my little brother, but when he stares at me like I'm a god for getting Harlow's attention long enough to bring her home, he looks the way he used to when I showed him how to prank Mom with fake spiders and snakes.

"Hey, bro."

"Hey. Happy birthday." He hugs me, which is the first time he's done that in God knows how long.

"This is Harlow."

"I'm Louis." He hugs her too, managing to be less weird about it. When we get inside, Mom is cooking as usual and Dad is at the table, but it looks like she muscled him into a collared shirt. I can't help but share a private smile with him, and he gestures at it like it's unbelievable.

When Mom turns around, Harlow gives her the wine and chocolates. Mom looks at them like she's about to cry.

"Oh my God, that's so sweet!"

"It's really nice to meet you, ma'am. I'm Harlow."

"Call me Maria. Joe, did you see?" she asks Dad, then turns and smacks Louis on the back of the head. "Why can't you two ever do anything like this?"

"And there it is," I say.

Harlow laughs. "It's the least I could do."

"Oh, stop it, she's going to throw us on the curb," I say.

Mom nods like she might and pulls Harlow into a hug.

"Oh my God!" Mom yells as she spots me over Harlow's shoulder. Her hands cup her face. "Oh my God, what happened to you? Joe! Look at your daughter's head." Mom runs over and reaches out to touch me but pulls back. "What happened?"

Dad squints like he can't quite see it, which is hilarious since his eyes are fine and it's massive. He's a man's man. The real deal version of a dude who wouldn't notice if you cut a foot of hair off.

"It's nothing. I'm fine. The doctor saw it. I'm all good."

"What happened?" she asks again.

Louis's eyes dart to meet mine because he already knows. For how much I call him an idiot, he's really the most astute of the bunch.

"It's nothing. Look, I took a fight. Just a local thing, nothing big. We bumped heads. I wouldn't have a scratch otherwise. It's no big deal."

"That's more than a scratch, Laila. What are you talking about? You said you were done fighting." She throws her hands up.

"I know, I know. But, Mom, you know I love it, and you know how much time I've put into this."

"I don't understand it, Laila. Why would you want to do that to yourself? Don't you care about yourself?"

"You know I do."

"How can you say that and then go into a cage and let someone do this to you?"

"Well, I didn't *let* her. It was an accident."

"An accident is falling down the stairs. It isn't a cage fight."

I shoot Harlow a look that says we should have gone with the stairs lie, and she tries to cover her laugh. Dad motions at me to come closer so he can examine the cut, then sighs.

"Your mother's right."

She holds up her hands. "You heard him? When's the last time he said that? Now you know it's true."

I descend into my chair and pull out the one beside me for Harlow.

"Yes, yes, parental unity noted. Can we please move on? We have a guest."

I shamelessly gesture at Harlow, and Mom sits down with us.

"Don't think we're not going to pick this back up, but you're right. Harlow, what do you do?"

Harlow hesitates. I put my hand on her back.

"Don't worry, it's totally fine for you to work around fights, just not me."

"Are you a fighter too?" Dad actually lights up without understanding the hypocrisy in the least.

"Oh, no, not anymore," Harlow says. "I dabbled for a while, but it didn't pan out."

If Harlow dabbled, there isn't even a word for what I've done, but I don't contradict her.

"Harlow is starting her own promotion," I say. "Like a new UFC."

"Like for pros or amateurs?" Louis asks.

"A mixture," Harlow says. "I'm hoping to create something where up-and-comers can develop their skills, get used to the pressures of competing, and start developing a following in a promotion that offers them a lot of support and fair pay. Down the road of course I hope we can compete at the highest levels, but I'll offer amateur matches too. It's an important part of the process, figuring out if they even want to go pro and getting those early experiences. What's most important to me is just creating more options for these athletes so they don't get exploited fighting for practically nothing in front of no one."

It still sends a flutter through me watching Harlow talk about her business.

"That's wonderful," my mom says, only she really means it. "Wouldn't that be wonderful, Laila? I mean she's been talking about the UFC since she was barely a teenager and I know those kids get rich, some of them, but wouldn't it have been nice if you could have made a living all this time?"

I fight the urge to tell her I did make a living. I love Harlow's vision, and it is true I never made enough money fighting to be able to stop working at the gym too. I don't recall ever calling her from a cardboard box, either, but I don't need to ruin what is actually an effort to be nice to Harlow.

Next thing I know they're going on and on about Gladiator Combat League, Harlow's future empire. Dad wants to know all about the business structure, Mom to know if the fighters can get some kind of pass for free massages, and Louis wants to know how many people Harlow knocked out before she quit fighting. They love that Harlow is who she is, and the mixture of joy watching them accept her and confusion they see no dissonance in their reaction exhausts me without my saying a word.

It's the obvious explanation to say it's because I'm family. They're not responsible for Harlow and can enjoy her choices. There's more, though. A little voice reminding me of what Vic said when we argued in my living room. Would my family support me if they believed in me? Is the reason they're so against it that they feel the way Vic does? That I'm not suited? If I was built like Harlow, would they feel differently? If I could get through a confrontation without calling someone a butt nugget, would they be my biggest fans?

Eventually, they serve dinner, remember it's my birthday. My twenty-sixth. I vowed to be in the UFC by twenty-five. It sucked when that date came and went, but I figured it still counted if I squeaked it out by the end of twenty-five. Now that's gone too.

They give me cake and presents. They forget about the cut on my head. They drink wine and tell Harlow their favorite family stories. It's probably the best family outing I've had in five years, yet in the car I feel deflated.

"You okay?" Harlow asks after a silent mile.

"Is it just impossible to take me seriously?"

"No. You're very serious."

I roll my eyes. "I'm—"

"Serious. I know." Harlow looks over and tries to make me smile, but I fight it. "Okay, what do you mean?"

"Everyone just assumes you can do anything you want. If you wanted to fight, great. Start the next UFC, no problem, amazing. Don't get me wrong you can, and I totally love that they love you. It's just, they weren't sure if my uncle should trust me around fried chicken."

Harlow smiles and squeezes my leg. "Well, I do believe there was a comment about having the cooks spit on Vic's food at one point."

"Not helping. And I didn't really do that."

"Babe, I'm just playing. Parents are always going to be more worried about what their kids are doing than a stranger. Even if they thought I was completely stupid and wasting my life, they're not going to say that to me, and you wouldn't want them to."

"It was more than that though. It wasn't fake."

"Well, I'm glad. But don't forget they weren't super excited about the real me, they were excited about the dream version of me. If you want to go back and tell them I run an illegal underground fighting ring, I'm sure they'd be happy to hate me."

"You know I don't want that. And it's not the dream version of you, it's just the slightly distant future you. It's not a pipe dream, it's a real thing that you're really doing."

She sighs and shifts.

"You know that was a compliment, right?" I ask.

"It might be a pipe dream. I told you I don't know how to actually get it done."

"You do, though. You've already done most of it. You just have to pull the trigger."

"But I can't," she says. "Pull the trigger."

"You will. Someday."

Silence fills the car until she finally says, "What if I don't?"

"Harlow, you will. You're going to find a way to do this that you're comfortable with, where you know your family will be okay. Even if you just save up a pile of money until you can afford the time gap to set things up, you'll do it."

"Assuming it will only be a gap is a really big assumption. It could fail."

"It won't."

"It could, Laila. I appreciate the confidence, I really do, but I can't just risk everything based on 'you got this.' It's more complicated than that."

The silence settles like snow. I feel like that scolded idiot again. The one who doesn't know how the world works and needs to be ushered to the safety of a nine to five.

"I know it's complicated." I hate how sheepish it comes out.

She sighs. "I'm sorry. I didn't mean it like that. I guess I just don't know how to make it work or if it will ever work, and I'm afraid you're waiting for me to be more than I can promise I'll ever be."

I let her words settle, wait for the ache to subside. I look at her face, lit up in the red of brake lights, and I see the fear enough to reach out and brush her hair out of her face.

"I love the way you are now, Harlow. I'm not fantasizing about a different you. It's because of who you are now that I know you can do it."

She looks over, her eyes full and powerful. "I believe in you too."

"Well, thank you."

The light ahead of us turns red. When she comes to a stop, she puts the car in park and leans across the center console to kiss me. If putting it in park didn't tell me she means business, the passion of her kiss does. She grabs my jacket and pulls me into her lips, kissing me so fully I'm dazed and lose the world. The car behind us honks but goes around before either of us can be bothered. She kisses me until the kiss is complete, and then she says, "And I love the way you are too."

Chapter Twenty-one

Harlow grabs the bottom of the loading dock door, then heaves it over her head hard enough it continues on the track and locks open. She turns toward me and waves at the inside of the warehouse with a proud smile.

"Ta-da!"

At least eight people are inside scurrying around, transporting chairs and tables and cords. I step inside and absorb the octagon in the middle of the open industrial space. It's a full-size regulation octagon, raised a good five feet so the whole crowd will be able to see the fighters inside it. The space around it is open and much bigger than any area I've seen Harlow fill so far.

"Wow. May I?" I gesture at the octagon, and she follows me over to usher me up the stairs. I open the cage door, noting it has a lock to make sure the door doesn't accidentally fly open if the fighters slam into it.

"Very nice." I step onto the canvas. It has the slight spring and airiness that helps absorb impact. The poles that support the cage are covered in padding. It's indistinguishable from an octagon you'd find in a professional promotion. "You got the real deal," I say.

"Well, it's a championship fight. The problem isn't coming up with the octagon, it's getting it set up and torn down. It can't be done at most of our venues, but I rented the warehouse for two days for this."

"This is so fucking cool, Harlow."

"You haven't seen anything yet. These guys will be setting up the bar in back there, a betting table over there, and we're going to make walkout tunnels for the fighters, have each corner in different spaces so they're not on top of each other while they're trying to get their heads right."

I spring around on the canvas and throw playful punches at her. I can't help but geek out seeing her event come together like this. So professional, so real. Maybe it really is just because it's a championship. Maybe she's done other events like it before and this is just the first time I've gotten to see it, but I can't help but think about our last conversation. I don't want to spoil it by bringing it up, but I don't know how she could possibly doubt that she could create a successful, legitimate promotion when she's already doing everything but the paperwork.

"Now I wish I was fighting tonight," I say.

She smiles. "Don't worry, I'll find a way to make it even better when it's your championship fight."

"Against Katarina." I grin.

"Or Vic," Harlow says. "It will be her if she wins tonight, you know?"

"I'd rather fight Katarina even if she does."

"I'm sure I can arrange that, but don't you want the belt?"

"Do you really see Vic coming away with the belt tonight?" I ask, muscling through the guilt I feel saying it out loud. Harlow's lack of surprise says a lot, but I still wait for her answer.

"Vic has won a lot of fights I didn't see her winning, so I can never say anymore."

I've seen Vic dog fight her way out of a dozen hard spots too, but this feels different.

"She doesn't have the training for this," I say. "Katarina is a brawler, but she also knows what she's doing. Vic thinks she can just gut her way through anything, and I guess that stupid brave thing works for her, but she doesn't take this seriously enough."

"Well, she asked you to be in her corner. I think that's the closest thing to admitting she needs help I've ever seen her do. And they had two months to prepare. Maybe she took it more seriously than you think."

"You know I can't do much for her from her corner. I should have trained with her more, but she never wants to."

Harlow kisses my forehead. "You've done everything you could. The rest is up to her."

"Yeah, but this wasn't your idea or hers. It was Sam's. I know you're grateful to him, Harlow, but the guy gives me the creeps. He's not after the best matchup, he's after blood and drama. I don't think he's exactly looking out for her best interest."

Harlow's lip tugs at the corner in surprise, and I remember it was Vic who told me this was Sam's idea, not Harlow. I see her processing, and it looks like she's coming to terms with an accusation more than a revelation.

"Yeah, Sam wanted to see it, but Vic had been asking for it for ages before that. He just suggested with her last win that it was time, and if I thought I was just feeding her to the wolves I wouldn't have agreed. She's my friend too, Laila, and she put together an impressive win streak. She might surprise you."

"I know, I'm sorry. I just don't like it."

"Why didn't you say so sooner?"

I throw my hands up. "Because I didn't want to fuck up her big opportunity. And then I started fighting and I thought it would look petty and like I wanted it for myself. Plus, I knew she'd do it anyway and then I would have just undermined her confidence which is the only fucking thing she has going for her. And then we weren't even speaking, and it was really none of my business."

Harlow laughs. "Who knew you were carrying all this."

I take an exaggerated breath and exhale. "Maybe I just needed to say it out loud. You're right. I've seen Vic win a fight by pulling a girl's ear so hard it started to rip. She's an animal. She might be the perfect person to give Katarina her own medicine."

"There you go. That's the spirit. She just walked in. Stay away from Katarina and try to keep Vic away. No prefight bullshit. That's Kat's favorite stunt, but I told her not tonight. She should keep her distance. If Vic gets her going though…"

"Yeah, I get it. Two loose cannons. I got her. Do you need help with the rest of this?"

"If you can control Vic, we'll be golden."

"So, the hardest job in the house, thanks."

"Exactly." She kisses me on the cheek, and we climb out of the octagon as more people start to show.

They're still working on setting up, but the tents that will serve as the scaffolding for our warmup area are up, so I meet eyes with Vic and nod to the one she's assigned. She follows me into the tent and slings her bag to the ground. Her hair is braided for the fight, and she's in sweats and a hoodie for now.

"How are we feeling?" I ask.

"Like someone's face is about to get busted."

"Okay, not an emotion."

"Sure, it is."

"Do we know whose face?"

Vic scowls. "I'm going to fuck this chick up."

"Okay, that's what I want to hear. You want to relax or you want to move?"

"Let's move."

I hold pads for her. Dylan's technique is already crisper than Vic's, but she's strong, and this isn't the time to try to teach. She's never been receptive to my advice anyway. She imagines herself as being able to kick my ass in a "real" fight, and I've never shown her otherwise. It does stick with me though, what Harlow said about her asking me to corner her. When she did, I just took it as reciprocity after she cornered for me, not a bid for assistance, but maybe not.

"She's a mean bitch," I say to test the waters in her language.

"Yeah, she is."

"Don't let her get her hands on you. I know you like to throw people around, but she does that too, and she's big, Vic. Don't risk it. Keep your distance and look to land the right."

She meets my eyes for a long second. I wait for her to blow me off, but she finally nods.

Anticipation builds. Other blue corner fighters fill the tent and warm up with their coaches. The chatter in the warehouse builds from a hum to a buzz to a roar as the drinks flow and the first fight starts.

I peek outside the tent and smile as I realize Harlow has filled the warehouse. There are at least five times the amount of people I've seen before. I know Harlow's focus is always a select, high roller audience over a big one, but I imagine this must be her true following represented, and it's impressive.

Blue lights blast from somewhere behind our tent, and the fighter from our corner who's up raises his fist before starting his walk as his song plays at concert volume. The tunnel the guys built is an aisle that keeps the crowd off the fighter without blocking the view. Everything about this setup is working and exciting. I don't know if I'd rather be experiencing it as a fighter or an audience member, but something tells me I can't slip away to watch, that I need to stay with Vic.

When her fight is finally next, I warm her up again, pushing her hard. It feels wrong when you're about to fight, like you're wasting precious energy, but being truly warm and loose is essential for injuries and nerves.

They finally cue me, and I cue Vic. "You ready?"

"Born ready."

"Let's go then, Champ."

"DNA" by Kendrick Lamar comes on, and she starts her walk. I follow just behind her and take my place in her corner by the cage.

The lights darken and Katarina walks out from the other side of the warehouse, backlit by red. When she steps into the cage, she locks eyes with me and makes the throat slitting motion until the ref yells at her to come to the center. I can't hear what he's telling them, but I imagine it has something to do with clean fighting. What a laugh. The only consolation is that Vic isn't married to clean either.

The ref motions them back to their corners, and Vic backs up to where I sit on the other side of the cage.

"You fucking got this, Vic. She's going to charge you like a big dumb bull. Don't let her grab you. Step and strike."

"Fight!"

Katarina charges forward like I thought she would but doesn't try for the takedown. She just pushes Vic into the cage and swings for her head. Vic ducks and swings back with a wild hook. Kat hits her with a combo that ends with a knee to Vic's gut. Vic alternates between trying to cover up and swinging for the fences, but she makes no attempt whatsoever at footwork or distance management. She's just there to stand and bang, and it's ugly.

"Circle out!" I yell to pierce the crowd roar. They're screaming their heads off at the action to open the fight, and I can't blame them. This kind of chaos is a dream come true for viewers, two people holding their ground and hitting as hard as they can, but it's a nightmare for Vic as the smaller fighter. To make matters worse, Katarina is also more technical and able to land three for every one she takes.

She slams her forearms down on Vic's chest and holds her against the cage as she knees her in the body and legs. Vic tries to throw an upward elbow at Katarina's chin, but Kat pulls back and throws her own elbow at Vic that lands with a snap. Blood pours from Vic's broken nose, and she pushes Katarina off as hard as she can, only to follow her with a wide haymaker that misses.

Katarina takes advantage of Vic's momentum and trips her. Vic crashes to the canvas, and Katarina takes a second to wag her finger at Vic before leaping on top and raining down punches while the audience loses its mind at her taunting. Katarina's strikes slow down as she becomes more calculated, choosing her shots and landing them. I scream at Vic to use her legs, but I doubt she can hear me. She's shutting down, but before the ref can call it, the buzzer sounds, and the round is over.

I jump into the octagon and wave her over, slamming the stool on the canvas and grabbing her arm as I guide her to it.

"Breathe."

I wipe her face with the towel and try to control her broken nose. There is no official, licensed cutman. It's not that I can't handle the crude act of putting the cotton up her nose, but a real cutman would be able to use coagulants to stop the bleeding. Pressure alone isn't likely to do much in one minute, but I do my job and press ice under her eyes too. She asks for water, but when I pour it in her mouth, she chokes on it. Her eyes are vacant.

"Hey." I snap at her, and she looks at me. "You cannot stand there and take those punches. You have to circle and move. She's fucking big and strong which means you have to be small and fast. You can't just bite your mouth guard and go with this girl. Victoria. Do you hear me?"

She nods, but I don't like the look in her eyes. Whatever she's thinking about, it isn't winning.

"Vic, do you want to call it?"

That snaps her back. "Fuck you."

"Okay, well give me something then."

The break expires, and she stands. She looks a fucking mess with the blood from her nose falling onto her chest. I leave the cage and round two starts. It's even uglier than the first. Katarina manhandles her, and if Vic is trying to be more elusive like I asked, I can't tell. She keeps chasing the game changer, the one shot that can turn the fight, putting everything into every attempt even though loading up is making her way too slow to actually land anything.

It's like I can see Katarina stealing her energy as her dominance makes her sharper. She shoots a double leg takedown and lifts Vic, standing with her on her shoulder for an extra second just to show off her control, and then she slams Vic to the canvas. The ref is hovering beside them ready to end the fight, and I wish he would already, but the clock is winding down from twenty seconds, and I know he'll likely let her ride it out.

When the buzzer sounds, I jump into the cage again. Vic is staggering, looking around the octagon confused about where she's meant to go. I go get her and guide her to the stool. Her face is scratched and swollen and bleeding. The black and blue under her eyes is darkening by the second. I'm ready to see exhaustion, pain, fear, embarrassment, determination. I'd take anything, really, but she's a zombie.

"Vic, we need to call this."

"No," she says, snapping back to her body the way she did before.

"Vic, this is not going to turn around in the next five minutes. You're just going to get hurt. Badly. Please trust me. It's over. You're down two rounds with one to go. You'd have to finish her."

"I'm not quitting."

"Fine, I'm calling it for you. You don't have to quit."

She grabs my arm, her fingers pressing into me so hard I think her nails might break the skin. "Don't you fucking dare, Laila. Don't you dare. This is my fight. You're not my fucking coach. You're my friend with a towel."

"I'm your corner which means I'm here to watch out for you, and I'm telling you this is too far gone. You are too far gone."

"Bullshit." She shoves my arm away. "Quit being a pussy. If I go down, I go down swinging. No one threw the towel in on you when you got your ass handed to you in the UFC, did they?"

"That's different, their refs are highly trained to know when it's enough. This guy should've stopped it already. And the shit that's legal here will change your life, Vic. It's not worth it."

"I said no."

I lock eyes with her, my mind screaming trying to decide whether or not to override her. She'll hate me if I do, possibly forever, and she's with it enough to call me a pussy. I squirt water in her mouth just as the buzzer sounds and the ref waves at Vic to stand up like he thinks she might not, but she does. I take the stool and leave the cage, my gut in a knot.

Round three starts, and Vic finally tries to stay on the outside. She shuffles to her right, her footsteps landing hard and tired. Katarina takes the middle of the octagon and rotates with Vic's steps, making no move to chase her. She lets it go on for twenty seconds before she raises her hands and taunts Vic. She waves at her to come on, to step back into the pocket and swing like cavemen.

"Don't take the bait, Vic. Fuck her, she can learn how to move her feet if she wants you."

Katarina hears me and flips me off. The crowd yells, and Vic throws a bomb at Katarina to take advantage of the distraction. Katarina eats it on the chin and locks her arms around Vic's body, then throws her weight back and drags Vic to the ground over her right shoulder.

Vic tries to turn into her, but Katarina climbs on top, digging her shin into Vic's rib and slamming hammer fists into the side of her face. Vic's head hits the canvas, and she's dazed. I stand up, leaning against the cage waiting for it to end, watching the ref. He makes tiny little moves forward but keeps restraining himself.

"Come on, ref!" I scream, but Katarina abandons the ground and pound and even her dominant position to fall back and scoop up Vic's leg for a leg lock. It slows the action down enough for the ref to give Vic a chance to compose herself and fight back. Only she can't. Her face is covered in blood, and she's too stunned to move, showing no reaction as Katarina's legs slither around hers and find Vic's hip, which she'll need to lock down to complete the submission.

It's Katarina's last fight all over again. She deliberately prolongs fights, aiming to do damage beyond what's necessary to win. She wants to send Vic home with long lasting damage just like she tried to with Sophie.

She brings Vic's foot to the outside, setting up a heel hook, a nasty submission that holds the hip in place while turning the foot. It can rip a knee to shreds in an instant with minimal force. It's a dangerous submission even in the gym against people who don't want to hurt you. In Katarina's hands it will damage Vic in a way that means she's never the same, and it will happen faster than the ref can stop it. I grab the towel by my foot, leap to the top of the cage, and throw it in.

"Stop the fight! We're done, stop the fight!"

The ref makes eye contact, processing the information too slowly. I scream at him again. "Stop the fight!"

He turns back and lunges toward them, but Katarina's forearm slides into place on Vic's heel, and she rips it to her left as hard as she can.

Vic screams in agony, and I climb the cage.

I land inside the octagon and kick at Katarina's head as hard as I can. She turns just enough I catch mostly her shoulder, but it sends her scrambling away trying to get to her feet. The ref tries to restrain me, but he's not in front of me enough to put any weight behind it and I cast him off. I reach Katarina just as she's putting her hands up in an innocent motion, but I ignore it and swing. She tries to block, but her arm folds and my knuckles connect with her cheek, splitting open instantly because I don't have gloves.

She gives up the innocent act and swings back. I duck and slam into her chest, pushing her against the fence and swinging an elbow at her head to spare my hands. She gets her glove between my elbow and her ear, but I know it rings her anyway. I pull back to swing again, but then there are arms all over me. A pair around my waist, another around my shoulders. They pull me away. I fight to get free even though I know it's hopeless now.

"Fuck you, Katarina! You think I don't know what you did?"

"I didn't see the towel." She shrugs through the laziest lie I've ever seen.

"You saw the fucking towel, and you heard me too. You're going to pay for this."

She makes the talking motion with her hand and flips me off. The crowd is in chaos, and I don't even know who's grabbing me. I see Vic still on the canvas holding her knee and writhing.

"Let me go," I say, but they drag me out of the cage. "She needs a hospital."

"We got her. You need to calm down."

"Fuck you, you saw what she did. You should have let me put her down."

"You got a couple shots off, okay? Now cool off so you can go with your friend."

They drag me all the way back to the blue corner tent before they release me, standing in front of the exit like linebackers. I finally process the guys and realize they're fighters from earlier in the night, which means they do know exactly how egregious what they just saw was.

An eruption sounds from the crowd. The sound of a fight. I've heard it enough times to know. Someone else is going at it now, probably related to a bet. I move toward the door to look.

"I just want to see," I say when the guys react like they might have to grab me again. A fight in a crowd looks like a people whirlpool, a dramatic center that drags more and more bodies in. It's growing. People try to stop it but only manage to feed it. A bloodcurdling scream splits the air, and my blood chills. I've heard that scream on the street. It's the scream of a fight taking a turn. Of someone getting stabbed or shot or bleeding from the head after a hard fall. It's the shock of something becoming real.

"Where's Harlow?" I yell, but the guys shrug. Of course they don't know. They try to stop me from leaving, but I push their hands away.

"I need to find Harlow and Vic. Let me go."

The crowd scatters in a panic. The dock doors fly open, and most people disappear into the night while others stay and scuffle and yell. I run back to the octagon, but it's empty, a pool of blood left behind where Vic used to be. I scan the crowd for a familiar face, but there are none. Katarina is gone. Harlow is gone. Vic is gone.

I spot one of the guys who was setting up earlier with blood on his hands. I sprint to reach him before he disappears too. People reach out for me, some trying to pat my shoulder, others trying to grab me, but I fling them all away until I reach him.

"Where are they?"

"They're loading into the back of a truck in the side lot."

I sprint outside, circling the building until I find something you could call a side lot. They're gathered around the tailgate of a black Dodge. The doctor, two of the other guys who helped set up, someone I've never seen before, and thank God, Harlow. The guys are talking and gesturing furiously, locked in a state of chaos while Harlow and the doctor, Davina, look controlled but urgent.

"Harlow!"

She turns, and my heart jumps. She's covered in blood. She comes over to meet me away from others and grabs my arms.

"You should leave, Laila."

"What are you talking about? I'm not leaving. Where's Vic? Is this all from her?" Just as I ask, I see the slash across her forearm and process that this is Harlow's blood. At least a lot of it is.

"Vic is in the bed of the truck to keep her leg straight. We're about to take her to the hospital. Davina is taking care of her. Laila, these are not cop people, but I can't promise anything at this point. You should get out of here just in case."

"Harlow, what happened? What the fuck?" I grab her arm and pull it toward me. It's a long, deep gash that's bleeding furiously, pulled apart, exposing layers and colors beneath the blood that fills and spills from her.

"Laila, I can't do this right now. I have to get Vic and Tom to the hospital."

"Who the fuck is Tom? What happened?"

"I'll call you when I can."

She takes a step back toward the truck. The guys jump inside and Davina hops in the back.

"Harlow, what the fuck?" I yell, not sure if I'm more worried or furious. "I'm coming with you."

"No. I'll call you. Go, Laila. Get away from here now. Take my car."

She puts her keys in my hand and runs to jump into the truck's driver's seat, then pulls away, leaving me choking on dust and fury.

CHAPTER TWENTY-TWO

My hands are still shaking as I let myself into my apartment. I can see my breath in the air and jam the rattling key in the lock. I close myself inside, then look at the two sets of keys in my hands. It's worse than the rush of jumping into the cage. The fear at seeing Harlow covered in blood, seeing her drive off with two sets of feet just showing from the end of the pickup. It's sunk its poison teeth into me.

I check my phone, but there's no call or text. I knew there wouldn't be. Not this soon. They'll just be getting to the hospital, but it already feels like torture trying to wait. I set her keys down and pace.

The minutes turn into hours. Vic will likely need emergency surgery on that leg, and who knows what the hell is wrong with Tom or who that even is. Harlow's injury was bad too, the kind of cut that would have gotten the hell out of my attention, but she was treating it like it didn't matter at all. I wouldn't be surprised if she tries to get Davina to stitch her up in the parking lot. So why can't she find a second to call me? I call her even though I know she won't answer and get mad when she doesn't.

I try to muscle my mind under control, and I do for ten-minute intervals between reaching her voicemail directly. She turned her phone off. Or it died, but either way it's off and for some reason that's worse. I look out the window and see the sun coming up.

I snatch up both sets of keys and go back to her Mercedes. I want to go to the hospital and find her. I'd be guessing which one. With a couple of tries I'd figure it out, but she didn't want me there. She sent me away. I'm not sure she'd even be there anymore anyway.

I drive to her apartment, thinking I'm an idiot most of the way there because I won't be able to tell if she's home or not since I have her car. Then I realize I'm actually an idiot because I have her apartment key too. I let myself in, but no Harlow. I knew there wouldn't be, but my heart still sinks. How long am I supposed to wait for her to call me?

I'm aware I'm acting like a nut job, but the wait is cruel. Hours. Why couldn't she tell me what happened before she left? At what point am I supposed to call her sister?

Maybe the cut was even more serious than I thought. She could have needed surgery too. Maybe that's where she is. I burn a hole through Harlow's floors next, pacing as the hours melt away. As morning becomes day and day becomes evening. And then, all at once, it's too much. I can't take one more second, and I can't make it end. I grab the keys once more.

I drive by the hospital, but I don't go in. Shocker, she isn't just standing in the lot looking for me. I drive by her sister's house, but another shocker, she isn't standing in the yard, and I pass without knowing what I'm doing there or slowing down. I drive by the warehouse again, but it looks quiet and empty. No black Dodge. No cops. No Harlow.

And then, finally, I park in front of Eden's apartment building. I look at my phone, and it still sits silent and dark.

I've mostly ignored the fact that I've been crying off and on, but I look in the rearview mirror and at least attempt to pull myself together before buzzing Eden's apartment. It's Sunday now, the one day I stand a chance of finding her at home.

"Hello?" Her voice answers through the buzz box and my resolve shakes. What am I doing here? Eden can't do anything about this other than serve me up a well-earned dish of I told you so. Yet I can't make myself go back to the car.

"Hello?"

"Eden, it's Laila."

There's a pause, and the door buzzes. I take the elevator up to her ridiculously amazing apartment on the twenty-fourth floor that she shares with her fiancé, Brooklyn. I've become good friends and training partners with Brooklyn too. I'm sure Eden has told her all about what's going on with me and what she thinks of it, but I'd still prefer she isn't here so I don't have to face her just this second.

Eden answers right away. She's in sweatpants and a muscle shirt, holding a glass of wine which is a rare occurrence for her and must mean she's enjoying a night in. She opens the door and motions me in. Brooklyn is on the couch behind her in front of the fireplace looking all happy and at peace.

I groan. "God, I'm sorry."

Eden grabs my wrist and pulls me inside. "It's okay, come on."

Brooklyn gets up and pours a glass for me, then comes over and hugs me. "You're always welcome, Laila." She hands me the wine.

I take a sip, wondering just how much of a trainwreck I look like. Car light can be deceiving, and I was barely pulling off stable there.

"I'll let you two talk," Brooklyn says.

"You don't have to do that."

"It's fine, really."

Brooklyn disappears into their bedroom, which I've seen before and is anything but exile, so I don't feel too awful. Eden takes another sip of wine and gestures at the balcony.

"Want to sit outside?"

"Sure. Yeah. That would be nice."

Her view is stunning and sports a view of the East River.

"I'd literally rent your balcony and live out here," I say.

She smiles. "It gets cold, but you can try."

She leans back into one of the wood Adirondack chairs.

"Smart not to go with metal. The whole cold thing." I sink into the chair beside her. She nods.

"What's up, Laila? What happened?"

I lean forward, putting my head in my palms. I check my phone one more time. Nothing. "I don't know where Harlow is."

Eden takes a deep breath, then a deep sip of wine. "For how long?"

"Eighteen hours." I don't bother pretending I don't know the exact answer.

"Did you argue?"

"No. It's worse. I was cornering Vic in a fight last night."

"If it was Vic's fight, why are your knuckles banged up?"

I look down. I'd forgotten about that, but of course Eden would notice.

"It's a long story."

"I'm sorry, is that *not* why you're here?"

"Of course it is."

"Okay, so?"

I pull my hair and groan. "I'm going to tell you, okay? It's just not easy. You're not exactly going to love it."

"I haven't loved any of this for quite a while."

"I know that," I say. "You think I like disappointing you?"

Eden takes another sip of wine, and I see the tension fall away as she considers what I said.

"I'm still your friend, Laila. Just tell me what's going on."

"Will you try not to gloat if—"

"I'm not going to gloat. Go."

"There was a big championship event last night and this evil bitch tore Vic's knee to pieces on purpose even after I threw in the towel, so I jumped in the cage and hit her. Then things got out of hand and some kind of fight or something happened in the crowd and someone got hurt and everyone scattered. When I found Harlow, she was about to take Vic and whoever got hurt to the hospital, and she was cut really bad on her arm, but she wouldn't let me come with or tell me what happened, and now I can't reach her and have no idea if any of them are okay or what's going on. I have her car and her keys and her apartment is empty and her phone is off and I don't know when I'm supposed to call her sister or what I'm supposed to be doing or why she isn't calling. She said she would fucking call."

"Whoa, whoa, okay. Let me process."

"Okay." I nod. "Process. Please."

I down the wine, trying to still my bouncing leg. "Have you processed?"

"It's been three seconds, but yeah, I'm getting there. Are you okay?"

"Fucking no, E—"

"Physically."

"Yes, I'm fine."

"And Vic, her leg is bad, but she's okay?"

"I don't know. It was bad. I didn't want her to go back out for the last round, but she insisted."

"Okay." She falls silent as she thinks again.

"I have no fucking idea about the other person. Harlow wouldn't tell me. She wouldn't let me come with. It was so fucked up."

"She was protecting you," Eden says.

"Excuse me?"

"Laila, I don't want to freak you out worse, but this is bad. She's showing up at the hospital with two seriously injured people. There are going to be questions. And if she's hurt too, she can't exactly pretend she had nothing to do with it. She was doing right by you."

"Doing right by me?" I stand up again because there's too much energy in my body.

"Yes. You walk in there with her you get connected to all of this. Do it with bloody knuckles and maybe you get hauled off to jail. She did the right thing."

"This is all my fucking fault."

Eden raises her eyebrows and shakes her head like the comment is making her dizzy. "How do you figure that one?"

"Because I shouldn't have jumped in the cage. Katarina had it coming, don't get me wrong, but I turned it into a shitshow. That's why the crowd went nuts. That's why someone else got hurt. I'm sure it's why Harlow got hurt." I sit back down and feel tears spill onto my cheeks. "She could just be mad at me for all I know."

Eden puts her hand on my knee. "I don't think so."

"Why couldn't I just keep it together? Wait for my own fight with Katarina. Why do I have to be like this? How long have you been teaching me how to discipline my emotions and I still pull something like this?"

"Laila, I'm not going to pretend you're not impulsive." She laughs. "But I understand. Someone did something awful and dirty to your friend and you reacted. It might not have been the best reaction, but it does not make you responsible for the fact that Harlow makes her living in an illegal way. She's done it for a long time, and she's been careful and smart, but she knew there were risks."

"She was fine until I came along. I ruin everything I touch."

"That is not true."

"It is. You're just being nice because you love me and hate her, but I fucked up."

Eden sighs. "I do love you, but this is not about hating her. My problem with Harlow has always been that I think she puts people at risk. Legally and physically. I know they sign up voluntarily, but something like this was inevitable and overdo. It would have happened with or without you."

"Yeah, you hate her."

She shakes her head again. "I understand her intention, Laila. I don't agree with her methods, but I'll say this for Harlow: she did the right thing tonight. She took those people to the hospital to get real medical help knowing it would put her promotion at risk. She did it herself even with an injury knowing it would put her at risk. She kept you away from it even though I'm sure you begged her not to. She wouldn't even tell you what happened so you wouldn't know in case a cop showed up at your door, I'm guessing. I know you wish she'd handled it differently, but she wouldn't be who you think she is if she had."

"What, do you want her fucking number now?"

She laughs. "Okay, you are unhinged."

I try to smile, but it won't come. I pull my hair and check my phone. Nothing.

"I don't think I can do this," I say. "You were right. It's everything you said. What if she goes to jail? What if *I* go to jail? I wanted to fucking kill Katarina, Eden. I really did. I don't even know how I jumped the fence like that or why I thought that was okay. It's just like this other world where it feels like things don't work the same way, but it's not. Vic is never going to be the same after this. It just…"

"What?"

"It made me feel like a god. Not tonight, the whole thing. It made everything go away. It made me someone else. It made me, hard."

"And you felt soft before?"

I nod, my eyes watering. "I was soft, Eden. You said it yourself. One loss shouldn't have broken me, but it did. That girl shouldn't have beaten me in the first place, but she did. Your school is the best thing that ever happened to me, but I needed to be somewhere that didn't give a fuck about me. I needed to survive something real."

"And now?"

I laugh and shrug. "God, I don't know. I don't know if the Yard even exists after tonight."

"Do you want it to?"

"I want Harlow to be okay, and I know she needs the Yard. She thinks she does at least. And I know now I still want to fight. Tonight was really fucked up, though." I shake my head. "I never want to feel like this again."

Eden finishes her glass of wine and leans forward onto her knees.

"Laila, I know this is the least of your concerns right now, but I can get you in front of the UFC again. When you're ready. If you want it."

"Like, in theory?"

"Like I talked to them."

"You did?"

She nods. "Losses happen, Laila. They know that. When I talk about someone the way I've always talked about you, they know there's something worth seeing, and they know they haven't seen it yet. I would have told you, but things were too fucked up by then. You didn't want it. I don't know if you want it now. I just need you to know you're not stuck."

"What about Harlow?"

"You will hear from Harlow soon. And if she really cares about you, she'll be the first to tell you you're capable of more."

I leave Eden's drained and exhausted. I get Harlow's voicemail again while I drive to her apartment. I just want to be around her things, and to be there in case she tries to come home. I've been awake a full day and night and day again. I go upstairs and find it dark and glittering from her view. I sit on the couch and turn the volume on my phone all the way up in case I doze, but I can't imagine sleeping knowing she's not in her bed tonight.

Chapter Twenty-three

Coming back to my body feels like interdimensional travel. I'm so exhausted it's best described as delirium, and it takes so long to recognize my surroundings as Harlow's living room that I'm about to consider I've been abducted. The night finally comes back to me as I process Harlow's floor to ceiling windows and the fact that the sky is showing the first glow of sunrise. I hear a tap. The same tap that woke me.

The air is cool but stagnant. I jolt, first with fear, then eagerness. I run to the door, fling it open, and throw my arms around Harlow.

"Did you even check who it was first?" She tightens her arms around me and lets me drag her inside.

"No. I've been losing my mind. You said you'd call."

"I'm sorry."

She kisses my forehead and holds me until my heels settle back to the floor. She pours herself a glass of water, comes back to the living room. She sinks into the couch, her head falling back. I sit beside her and pull her arm into my lap, fingering the edges of her bandages.

I try to wait for her to speak. She must know all my questions, but after a cubic eternity, I lose it.

"Harlow, you've got to tell me what happened. I'm dying. I almost had to be committed."

"I'm sorry. I couldn't help it."

"Where were you?"

"With the police."

It takes me back even though I should've been braced for that possibility. "Is that a nice way of saying in jail?"

"It's a nice way of saying held for questioning." She puts her feet on her table, the thuds splitting the gray air, and rubs her face.

"But you're here now. That's good. Right?"

She nods. "Yes, that's good."

"Okay, Harlow, I need more."

"I know, I know." She squeezes my hand, and as simple as that is, it calms me. The stress is strung through her taut body.

"Is Vic—"

"She's okay. She's fucked, but she's okay. Her knee has basically nothing left. Her ACL and MCL were full tears, and her meniscus and PCL were partially torn. It's totally unstable. They did a CT to check her head and make sure she's okay to go into surgery, and she is. It'll happen tomorrow."

I'm not surprised by the extent of the damage, yet it still lands heavy in my heart. It's not life threatening. I guess that should be something, but I've been around enough fighters and enough injuries to know the toll required. It won't be fast, and it won't be small.

"And your arm?"

"Cleaned, stitched, bandaged."

"Okay, but are you all right?"

"It hurts, and there's some nerve stuff involved, but I will be."

I run my fingers over hers. They're swollen and dusky, curled into a tender surrender. I kiss her on the cheek. "You can make this easier any time, you know?"

She looks in my eyes without picking her head off the back of the couch. She looks exhausted. "Am I not being easy?"

I sigh. She is. She's answering my questions, and I don't detect any bullshit, but I feel like anything I don't ask directly might not get conveyed.

"I want to know what happened, Harlow. Can you just tell me?"

She takes a deep breath and sits forward. "Yeah. I can do that." She says the words, but silence settles. Her eyes glaze over.

"Who's Tom?"

"You know, I don't think I was more than ten feet from you when you threw the towel. You didn't see me, but I was right there."

She tests the fingers on her injured arm and grimaces. "That was a good call, but I knew it wasn't going to go well. I knew Katarina wouldn't stop until the ref made her, and I knew he would be slow. No one's ever thrown in the towel in the Yard. Next thing I knew you were in there." She laughs lightly. "That I did not see coming. I should have."

"Why would you? It's not every day a hellion jumps in the cage." I try to joke, but feel the shame swell up.

"Hey, it's not the first time I've seen it. Just the first time at my event. After the guys dragged you out, we lost control. I sent people in to make sure Katarina went to her corner and got Davina checking on Vic. I told the betting tables to hold everything while we sorted it out. We had so many big bets, so much money on how the fight would end."

"What did you rule it?"

"We never got to it. I thought it should be a TKO because you threw in the towel, and that's when it should have ended. One of the judges thought it should be a submission because the ref didn't acknowledge the towel in time, and it was the heel hook that actually ended it. Some people were yelling it should be a DQ because Kat ignored the towel or a no contest because you jumped in the cage. It was a fucking mess. We weren't going to win no matter what we said. People tried to rush the betting table for their money, but the money was locked up, so they came to me."

My stomach turns picturing Harlow at the center of an angry mob.

"I should have been with you. I heard something breaking out, but the guys wouldn't let me out of the tent."

"Good."

"Harlow. I could have helped. You needed hands."

"Laila, the guys keeping you out of it was the only fucking thing that went right. One of our big betters, Tom, was coming unglued. He had a half mil on Katarina by submission, and he wanted to collect."

"Half a million dollars?" I can't help but nearly shout the number even as my brain is locked into Tom's appearance in the story.

"Yeah, like I said, he's a big better. He was screaming at me that it was a submission and demanding I announce it. I was still leaning TKO, but I didn't even tell him that. I just said we were still deliberating to make sure we made the right call. He accused me of setting it all up and being a crook and pulled a knife on me."

Ice slithers down my spine. I don't know why, but I assumed Harlow got cut intervening in someone else's fight. It didn't even occur to me that someone had come after her on purpose.

"Tom is the one who cut you? The same Tom you took to the fucking hospital?"

She rubs her face again, wiping away tears she won't tolerate. "Yeah. I think he was just trying to threaten me, get his money by force, but people saw the knife and freaked. Someone tried to grab him, and he slashed at me. I saw it coming and backed away. I was shocked he got me. I guess I let my arm trail. It was so sharp and clean. I didn't understand the blood pouring down. And then I felt it."

"God, Harlow. What if he'd stabbed you?" I want to wrap my arms around her, but her posture is tight and self-contained.

She sighs. "I've spent some time thinking about that, but he ended up stabbing himself. The guys were trying to hold him and wrestle the knife away. They slipped on the blood and dragged him down. He fell on the blade. Got himself between the ribs."

"Fuck. Is he okay?" I'm not sure if I care.

"I've known Tom for a couple years now. He's always been a nice guy. I've even seen him take big losses before and not make a fuss. He must have thought we planned to throw in the towel to make sure it couldn't end by submission. I don't know. Money does weird things to people, I guess."

"So..."

"I think he'll be okay. They're keeping him in the hospital. They called the cops, of course. They have to. If it was just Vic's leg, we could have said it was from training. I could have gone somewhere else for my arm. A stabbing, though, there was no way around it, so we all picked a story and went in together."

"What was the story?"

Harlow's body practically goes limp as she gives in to exhaustion. I pull her toward me, and she lays in my lap. I play with her hair as she melts against me.

"That we got jumped."

"Ah, a classic. Heel hooking muggers."

"There's more than one way to destroy a knee," she says, ignoring my humor. "Given the blade we needed random faceless violence."

"Did they buy it?"

She sighs. "Well, I'm here."

"So, yes?"

"After they used every one of the twenty-four hours they're allowed to hold me without pressing charges."

"So, no."

"But no charges."

"So, kind of."

"Kind of," she says.

"But you're cut. You're clearly a victim, not a suspect. Why did they hold you?"

"They tend to want to know what actually happened with a stabbing, and we didn't come up with a full-fledged, cross examination proof, reenactable story. We had basics, but they had a lot more questions than we did answers, and I'm sure over the course of all those hours we said plenty of shit that didn't line up with each other."

"Vic would never, ever break though."

Harlow nods. "I know, and Tom doesn't exactly want the truth out there. I'm sure they know we were lying, but there wasn't much they could do for now."

"For now? Isn't it over?"

"I don't know," she says. "I hope so. Maybe they'll drop it when Tom is okay and sticks to his story. If they decide it's something they want to dig into, I don't know what they'll find. There were a lot of people there."

"But you didn't stab him. There's nothing for them to find out about you."

"I organized illegal fights." She sits back up. "God, I'm such an idiot. I always thought even if I do get caught it will just be for that. Permit violations and petty shit. But they can say I'm responsible for the environment that created this. Negligence or reckless endangerment or whatever. I don't know the language."

"How much trouble could you be in?"

"I don't know." She puts her face in her hands again, and I've never seen her broken down. Scared.

"Okay, we'll figure it out tomorrow. Your people are loyal, and this wasn't your fault. There wasn't even really a stabbing. A guy fell on his own knife. It's more like an accident. It'll be okay. And as long as you don't do any more there's nothing to find."

She looks up, a surprised expression on her face that's completely confusing me.

"Harlow, you know you can't do any more, right?"

"Well, I'm not planning to set anything up for tomorrow, but nothing about my life has changed."

"*Everything* about your life has changed. You're afraid you could end up in jail. You almost got stabbed. What more do you need?"

She stands up and runs her hand through her hair. "I mean my family. They don't need that money any less than they did yesterday."

"They're never going to, Harlow, but you can't give it to them from jail. It's time. Launch Gladiator Combat if you still want to do fights. Just do it."

"We've been over this."

"Yeah, it's not that simple. I know. But at some point, you have to figure it out. This is it. This is the perfect time. The Yard is in ruins. You'd be risking everything going back to it, so you might as well risk everything to go legit."

"It's not in ruins. I can smooth it over. I can call it a no contest and give everyone their money back."

"I'm talking about the cops, Harlow, not keeping your betters happy."

"Me too," she snaps. "Who do you think is more likely to snitch, someone who just lost a hundred grand or someone who didn't?"

"Okay, fine, then do it. Then walk the fuck away. Cut ties with this bullshit."

"Why is it suddenly bullshit? You were all about this before."

"Do you really need me to answer that? You were there."

"Yeah, and so were you," she says. "You saw it. The venue, the octagon, the production, the people. Up until the shit hit the fan it was amazing."

"Yes, it was until it wasn't. Your premier fighter is a psychopath, your entire audience ended up in a brawl, your big money better stabbed himself, you have to give all the money back, and the police may or may not be investigating you. You're better than this, Harlow. This is trashy. I did see what you were trying to do, and it's all the more reason you need to go legit. You obviously can, and it's obviously what you want to do. The sooner you get some balls and do it the sooner it will be done."

"Excuse me?" A fire lights in her eyes, and I wish I hadn't phrased it that exact way, but it's too late. "As soon as I get some balls?"

I sigh. "Okay, I'm sorry, but you're afraid, Harlow. You said so yourself. Afraid it won't work out. I'm sorry for the ball comment, but more or less, yes."

"Jesus, you ask me to let you in, to let you know me, and I did, which isn't easy for me, and after everything I show you that's what you come away with? I just need some balls."

"Look, I know your reasons. They're all perfectly admirable excuses to stay in your cage, but that's what they are."

"My family is not an excuse."

"It is. You know you'll always figure out how to help them. That's not what you're afraid of. You're afraid the real world will spit you out again, so you tell yourself it's out to get you and you have to live like this, but you don't."

Outrage flares across her face. "Like how you tell yourself you're only good enough to fight in the Yard even though the only reason you can stand to step in there is because you know they don't have your talent?"

"Maybe a little like that, yeah." I refuse to be mortally wounded. I can take her best if that's what will make her see it. I feel like I can see steam coming off her, but she's still rigid.

"My family is not an excuse. They're people."

"Of course they are, but they wouldn't want to be the reason you never do anything real with yourself."

"They wouldn't, but they don't have a choice. Some of us can't just do what we want all the time. We can't just walk away from opportunities when shit gets hard or jump into cages when we get pissed."

"Nice," I say.

"You can't call me a coward and my business trashy then play victim." Her posture changes, all the energy drains, and she sighs. "I'm sorry."

"No…" I curl my fingers into my hand. "Just be mad at me. I know you are. It's fine. I shouldn't have jumped in the cage."

"I'm not mad you jumped in the cage. I'm mad you jumped in the cage one second and are acting like all this is beneath you the next like you don't remember how this shit started."

I deserve that, but it still sucks. "I really am sorry I did that, Harlow. I never would have if I'd known what was going to happen."

"That's because you just do things, Laila. I'm sure sometimes it's great and sometimes it sucks, but I'm not like that. Especially where my family is concerned. I have to think about what could go wrong."

"Fine, but try thinking about what could go right sometime too. Or what could go wrong if you don't try. How are you still more afraid of going legit than staying with the Yard after this?"

When she lifts her wrapped arm to massage away the headache I'm giving her, I feel a pang of guilt I'm doing this to her now, but we're in too deep.

"Look, I don't know what I'm going to do," she finally says. "I just need a minute."

"Okay. I'm sorry. I should have let you process. I just didn't expect you to be torn."

I spent hours wishing she was here, wanting nothing more than to simply know she was okay, yet the second she walks in I manage to start a fight. Our first fight. I look at the space she left behind on the couch, then at her.

"Come back?"

She sighs and does, wrapping her arm around me and pulling me against her.

"I'm sorry. It's been a long couple of nights."

"Tell me about it." I kiss her on the cheek, then the lips. She's slow to ease into the kiss, but when she does, she sends my world spinning like she always does.

"You know I think you're amazing, right?" I whisper. "I don't think you're a coward. Or trashy. I think you can do anything."

She smiles in between kissing me. "So can you."

"I guess we'll see. Eden said she can get me another shot at the UFC if I want it. She could probably get you one too. I swear to God, Harlow, you could do it. I don't know what they were thinking when they let you go, but you're an incredible fighter. You're still young enough. You have so many options. I hate that you feel so trapped."

She pulls away, straightens out of my arms.

"When did that happen?"

I want to kick myself when I see that look on her face. Like she's been betrayed. She's never loved Eden, but it's never been a problem to merely bring up her name either. I should have waited. For fuck's sake, I should have just let the woman sleep.

"Last night. When I couldn't reach you. I talked to her. I was freaking out."

"You couldn't reach me, and your first thought was well, I guess I'd better give the UFC another go then?"

"Harlow." I look at her like she knows better, and, Jesus, I hope she does. "No. That's not what happened. Come on, you don't think that."

"I don't know what I think, Laila. I mean, how fucking long was I gone? I come back and you have all these demands for me about the Yard and you're going back to Eden to get another shot at the UFC? When you said you were worried, I thought you meant about me, not your career."

"I did. Harlow. Look, she just threw it out there. We barely talked about it."

"Is that what you want?"

I just want this awful momentum to stop, and my answer isn't going to do that, but I can't lie to her.

"I don't know. Maybe."

She goes back to her pacing. "Well, I'm really glad you could get your life together while I was away. I thought it would take you more than twenty-four hours to write me off, but whatever."

"Hey, I didn't know it was going to be twenty-four hours, I just knew you were gone without a fucking word, and I was terrified. I went to Eden's because I was falling apart, not to get my life together. What is wrong with you?"

"You were falling apart?"

"Yes."

"About me?"

"Harlow, yes. Of course I was."

"So you go see the one person who hates me? What did you expect her to say?"

"I went to my best friend knowing she would put that aside, and she did. Where was I supposed to go? What was I supposed to think? You tell me you'll call me and then you never do and you don't come home?"

"Oh yeah right, she put it aside. She put it aside so much I come home, and you want the Yard dismantled and you're making a new run at the UFC? I'm not an idiot, Laila. She got to you."

"Going all night not knowing what happened to you got to me."

"Yeah, but I'm here now, and all I'm hearing is how I need to change everything and apparently you do too, and you've worked it all out with Eden."

"What is so sinister about me talking to my friend? Are you jealous?"

"Of course, I'm jealous. You just going to go back to your old life now? You done slumming with me? Got what you needed?"

That one sends a jab of pain into my chest. I stand up and try to walk over to her, but there's a steel wall in her body language.

"I'm here," I say. "Don't you see me here? With you."

"Yeah, laying out what I need to do if I want you to stay. Right?"

I look at my feet and let the question settle. I didn't have an ultimatum in mind, and I don't want to lose Harlow. I haven't even thought about what it would mean if she decided to keep her life the same.

"I didn't say that. What you do about your business and what we do as a couple are two separate issues."

"Are they?"

"Yes. I think so."

"You think so?" She shakes her head, and her eyes get even farther away.

"This is a lot, okay? I haven't thought about it."

"You need Eden to tell you what to think about it?"

"Well, she wasn't exactly wrong, was she?" I snap.

The silence is deep in an instant. A hollow space explodes between us. I want to take it back, but I know it won't matter. I want to get closer, but I know she'll back away. She's a thousand miles away now.

"You should go," she says.

"Don't do this. I didn't mean that."

"Yes, you did."

"Harlow, please. This wasn't supposed to go this way. We shouldn't have talked about this yet. It was too soon. We just need to process."

"I need to process about my business and the cops and Vic and Tom and this whole fucked up thing, but I didn't need to think about you. I was in, Laila. I was in when you didn't want to fight anymore. I was in when you wanted to fight for me. I was in when you jumped in the cage and wrecked the biggest night I've ever had, and I would have been in if you wanted to try for the UFC. I hope you do. But for all that chasing me you did you've never been in. I've run myself around trying to give you a job and fights and training partners, introduced you to my family and met yours trying to prove to you that I'm a good person, but if you don't see that by now, I can't keep trying to convince you."

"Harlow, it isn't like that. I know you're a good person."

"But you don't know if you want this. Right?"

"It's not that simple."

"It really is, Laila."

Everything in me is screaming at me to just tell her what she's asking to hear. I want to be with her. I know it for sure. I want it whether she ever changes her life or not. Fuck, I do want her. So why won't it fucking come out?

"Harlow…" And nothing comes out.

"You should go, Laila. Go back to your life. Be who you're supposed to be."

There are so many things I want to say to her, but they're all fragments. None of them are enough. Not right now with her eyes hard and her heart on fire. I grab my keys from the table, my eyes filling. I want to fix it. I want to beg. I want to scream that I didn't wait through all these torturous hours to lose her now. And yet, my feet move. And I'm at her door. And I'm in the hallway. And I'm crying in her elevator.

CHAPTER TWENTY-FOUR

Emerald Tiger is unchanged. It has the same look, the same fighters, the same energy. The athletes welcome me back without judgment.

Some people had a fight while I was gone, but many haven't. There are some new faces, but only in the way there always are. The core crew is intact. When you miss time at your school, you don't feel it when you walk in the building; you feel it when someone walks up with a new belt and a new confidence.

Belts are symbolic. Most fighters will tell you they don't matter yet still get emotional when theirs finally turns black. In Jiu Jitsu especially, a system that averages ten years to black belt while having only five belts total, you spend enough time at each color it becomes part of your personality and style. On the Taekwondo side of the gym, belts move faster. MMA doesn't have a colored belt system at all. Those achievements are measured in fight records and the gold and black of championship belts.

In some ways, coming back and seeing everyone's progress makes me feel behind. In others, it's like coming home. Not the home feeling of childhood. It's the feeling when you come back for Christmas after your first year away. All the decorations are still there, the same music and movies and treats. No one's died. No one even looks different, and they've left your room the same for now. You wander around all night trying to figure out what changed, and then you finally realize it was you, and you wonder if you'll ever feel safe again.

Now, my favorite part of the night is when I get to clean the floors. When it's all quiet and empty and the lights are low. When I don't have to pretend there isn't a cannon-ball-sized hole in the middle of my chest.

"Shutting down already?" Eden's voice comes from the edge of the mat as she steps onto the floor. Getting hired back on was a grace I didn't dare to expect, but it's cozier even than returning to training was. I split my old responsibilities with the girl Eden hired while I was gone. I guess it's only fair they don't fire poor Ashley just because I'm giving everyone whiplash.

"I thought the last class ended at 9:30. Did you add something to the schedule?"

"Yeah." She tosses gloves at me. "You."

"Me? I did three hours earlier."

"Of class. You telling me you don't want a private?"

I look at my feet because of course I want a private. I don't deserve a private. Or my job back. Or any of this. It doesn't feel right to be so back, so normal, when Harlow's life is in shambles, which is a complete assumption because I haven't heard from her since I left her apartment two weeks ago.

"You don't have to spoil me. I'm not going anywhere. I'm really back."

She smiles and puts on her gloves. "I'm glad to hear it, but I'm not spoiling you, I'm doing my job. Since you're back and all." She winks and jabs me in the stomach.

I put on the gloves she threw at me, and she jabs me in the gut again.

"You're going to need more energy than that," she says.

I try to smile and put up my hands, but her arms drop.

"Laila, I don't know what happened between you and Harlow, but I know you're hurt, and I know it's hard to do this hurt. It takes everything you have, and you might not feel like you have much."

The sulky part of me wants to write this off as a thing she can't possibly understand, but I like to think I graduated from the teenage belief that no one has ever loved a love like yours before. Don't get me wrong, losing Harlow has caused every symptom of heartbreak in the book, but it's still standard-issue heartbreak. As much as I feel like I'm going to die, as all-encompassing as the aching is, I know I can put my hands up and fight Eden with some semblance of effort.

"Do you want to talk about it?" she asks. "We can. I'll be nice, I promise."

I shake my head. "I don't think I can."

"I get that, and I've been there."

I remember when she was there. She wasn't herself. That much you couldn't miss, but it didn't stop her from doing what she needed to do, and I can't let it stop me. Crying is for bedtime.

"When it hurts, we train harder," she says. "Now show me what you've been doing out there."

I smile and put my hands up. I step forward and throw a combo that she evades before she tosses back a jab that is casual perfection. It comes in so straight and clean you can't see it, and lands so light and controlled on my cheek I can barely feel it. I've sparred with Eden more times than I can possibly count, and everything about this is familiar, yet there's no denying the gap between remembering and experiencing.

I duck to escape a follow-up, but it doesn't come, and I step out to find an angle before punching again. She slips my hands and blocks the knee I follow with, then sinks a leg kick into my thigh and follows with a hook. Every fighter has a flavor. Even if they're excellent at switching up their attacks and habits, there's a certain feeling to sparring them. Fighting with Eden feels like she got the script ahead of time. Fighting with Vic feels like being drunk. Fighting with Harlow was like a riddle, the mirage of an answer tickling the edge of your mind just out of reach.

I imagine every fighter would love to know what it feels like to fight themselves, but we'll only ever have our insecurities and hopeful daydreams. My insecurities call me an easy round. Weak, timid, and deficient in killer instinct. My daydreams, becoming ever more vivid, aspire to be like fireworks. Quiet, sneaky, and then, explosive. With style.

Eden interrupts my little fantasy with another pop in the face, then takes me down with practically no resistance because she timed it well and it's over before it started. I let her slam me to the mat, but then I come alive. She drives her shoulder into my chest while she walks her legs around my knees on her way to taking a dominant pin called side control. I push my hips away, use an underhook looped under her right arm to create distance and turn her away from me, and start to build back to my feet.

She frees her arm and drives into me again to wrestle me under her control, but I scramble, putting full, charged, chaotic energy into getting my feet under me, then behind me as she tries again to drive through. I reach a point of stability in my base and knee her in the ribs. She shrugs me off her upper body and throws a jab as we return to standing, but I shoot for her hip and take her down this time.

I'm pushing more energy her way than I ever have before. Eden's style is so technical, so precise and in control that it can feel more like a dance than a fight right up until she knocks you into next year, but I want this to feel like a fight. I want her to feel like she's in a fight. I expect her to back up or push me away with her lethal legs or even tell me to tone it down, but she doesn't. She matches my energy like it was always supposed to be this way, and I feel it click into place.

It *was* always supposed to be this way.

This is the difference between winning and surviving. You're not supposed to want to win cognitively, you're supposed to need to win viscerally. There's no split focus, no part held in reserve to wonder when it will end or how to get there in one piece. There is only this moment, and you must grant every second whatever it requires. There is no negotiating with it. It may have taken the Yard to force me to bring everything, but it belongs to me now.

Eden weathers my storm, my best like it's another day in the office, getting back to her feet, but I don't pause, don't sulk, don't doubt. I do it again. I shoot for her hip and drive. She sprawls, her heels shooting far behind her, her chest pushing my upper body toward the mat. Her arm loops around my neck to choke me in a guillotine, but my hand shoots automatically to defend.

She moves around to take my back, but I come up with that explosive energy again and spin into her before she can. I shoot for her hip yet again, but this time I get her, dragging her to the ground with a single leg takedown. I move to pass as she moves away for freedom. I remember my hands and hit her as I chase her to keep her on the ground. I throw a knee and feel it connect first with her hand, then her face. I wake up from my state and realize that was very much illegal.

"Shit, I'm sorry. Fuck. Are you okay?"

I threw it at rowdy sparring power which means half-hearted control, but a knee in the face is a knee in the face. I try to spot blood, but Eden doesn't even pause before she holds me where I am, grabbing my knee and forearm to keep me from abandoning the position to check on her.

"Wait. Stay."

I hold the position and look at how we're composed as she does the same.

"You can't do that anymore," she says. "But if you reversed it, weight on this side and throw the other leg, you'd have the same knee to the ribs."

I look down and picture what she's describing, then meet her eyes again.

"Knees to the body are legal, even on downed opponents," she says.

Of course I know this, but I can't blame her for explaining since I'm a big dumb silent lump. She wipes a little blood off her lip, not even acknowledging it. What have I been so afraid of all this time? Eden is as controlled and genuinely kind as they come, but she's a fucking savage. How did I miss that piece of her teachings?

"Does that expose my back too much?" I finally ask.

"Not if you stay north of my hips. Don't let me push you down. Throw the knee and posture up, you'll be okay. Then hammer fists to the face."

I go through it, and she's right of course.

"Got it. Are you okay?"

She wipes her lip and glances at the blood.

"Don't worry about it. Great round. Keep the intensity, lose the disqualifiers." She punches my arm and smiles. "Harlow's been coaching you?"

"The environment is pretty motivating, but yeah, I spent a lot of time training with Harlow."

"You're different," she says. "I like what it's doing to your fighting, but I miss seeing you smile. You sure you don't want to tell me what happened?"

"Shit just went sideways after that night. I pushed her too hard."

"Pushed her how?"

"To go legit with her promotion. To believe in herself." My chest feels heavier with every word.

"That doesn't sound so awful."

"It doesn't, but it was. I made her feel like she was beneath me. I hardly let her get in the door before I was ramming what I thought down her throat."

"I'm sure she knew you were worried and emotional."

I shake my head. "With everything she was dealing with, I didn't have the right to be the emotional one. And it doesn't change that I treated her like everyone always does. Like it's all so easy and her reasons aren't real. I acted like if she didn't agree with me right then and there something was wrong with her. It wasn't fair."

"Have you told her that?"

I shake my head. "Are you nuts?"

She laughs. "Oh, excuse me, that would be too simple."

"She doesn't want to see me. Even if she did, that won't be enough. She wants to know I'll be with her even if she doesn't stop the underground fights."

"And you won't?"

I tilt my head and stare her down. Like she doesn't have a bigger problem with that notion than anyone.

She shrugs. "What? You were fine with it before. I don't know. I'm being supportive."

"I know. Maybe I shouldn't care. She really does have her reasons, Eden. She's supporting like a million fucking people. Kids. Family. She's afraid to risk their livelihood, their safety. There's medical stuff involved too. It's not a small problem, and in her mind, she just can't justify the risk. I know she could do it, though. She's so focused and smart. It's not a greed thing. She gives most of it to her fighters and her family."

Eden's eyes are locked on mine, listening intensely yet deep in thought.

"I understand."

I smack her leg. "Gee, thanks. I understand too, but I still don't know if I can wonder every day if our world is going to come crashing down. God, if we could have just stayed in that place where we were happy and in love and didn't know what was coming next and that was okay. But I'm a big fucking idiot and ran my mouth and now we can't pretend it didn't happen. And if I can't fix it, isn't talking just torture?"

"Sometimes, yeah," Eden admits. "But, Laila…"

"What?"

"In love?"

I feel my cheeks flush, which is a phenomenon I thought I left in my past. "Yeah, well, it didn't stop me from ruining it."

"Laila, this is—"

"I should go. Thanks for the session. And the talk." I choke on the lump in my throat. "I just can't."

I pull her into a hug and get up before she can react. Before she can say things that will make me fall apart. Loving Harlow is still too real, and the hole she left behind isn't the neat, quiet type that erodes over time. It's the screaming gale of a jet with a wing ripped off.

Chapter Twenty-five

I've never liked walking to Vic's. You have to pass the record store, which always has a hoard of guys out front, and it usually takes a full block to stop hearing their comments. Vic makes the journey all the time without complaining, but I can hardly expect that of her now with her giant leg brace and crutches. I knock on her door and wait for her to figure out how to answer it. Just as I'm texting to ask her if she'd prefer I break in, the door swings open.

"Biiiiitch." She beams. "Come in."

"Aye aye, Captain. How you feeling?"

As soon as I'm inside I see that one of her roommates, Keith, is lying on the couch with one leg hanging off and an Xbox remote in his hand.

"Really, dude? You couldn't open the door for her?" I snap at him, but he doesn't seem to process it.

"See? Can't get treated like a lady even when you break your fucking leg anymore." Vic hobbles toward her bedroom.

"Come on, Keith."

He grunts, and I help Vic down onto her bed. She grimaces as she leans down to grab her brace by the strap, then slings her leg onto the bed. I take her crutches and lean them against the wall.

"How bad is it?"

She shakes her head almost imperceptibly. The smallness of the motion conveys the hugeness of the bad.

"Painful?"

"Painful, pathetic, slow, depressing, exhausting, expensive. But don't ask, I'm trying not to be a bitch about it."

"You're allowed a little bitching in this scenario."

"Okay, well, my life is over." She says it like it's meant to be funny, but the pain in her eyes is very real.

"Your life isn't over, Vic. You'll get better." I tilt my head. "Eventually."

She laughs at my insensitive addition. "Yeah, in a year."

"Hey, if you found out you had to serve a year in jail, you'd shrug it off."

"I'd take a year of jail over this in a heartbeat," she says.

"Wow, even with the food?"

"No contest."

"I'm sorry." I drop the playful tone.

The facade falls off her face. "Hey, you told me not to go back out there. I guess I should have listened."

"I should have called it before the third."

"I told you not to."

"You were out of it."

"I threatened you." She laughs. "It's not your fault, Laila. We both know damn well I would've wanted to go back in whether I was thinking straight or not. That's who I am. You even avenged me."

I roll my eyes. "Not enough."

"Hey," she says. "You're a really good friend. I'm sorry I haven't always been one."

"Are you on painkillers?"

"Of course I am, ass, but I'm trying to have a fuckin' moment."

"Sorry. Do it again."

"Nope. Too late." She shakes her head and laughs.

"Look, you've had my back in tough spots too. We're all good," I say.

"I was a jerk, and I was wrong when I said you shouldn't be a fighter. I'm glad you've already figured that out."

"You already smoothed that out too, Vic. Man, she knocked your brain around too, didn't she?"

"I said I was sorry, but I didn't say I was wrong. In my head you were still that kid who talked shit to Fat Roll Molly and then needed me to save you. I guess maybe that's who I wanted you to be. Saving your ass is really the only cool thing I ever did."

"Vic." I laugh at the memory. "It was Muffin Top Molly."

"Mean little bitch."

"Bashed my head into a pole."

"Yeah, but she picked on your brother, and you just did what you do. Didn't care that you didn't know how to fight or that she was twice your size. You had heart. That's what it's about. I had no right to say you weren't a fighter. You've always been a fighter."

"Wow, Vic." That was by far the most sincere thing she's ever said to me. "You do know this injury isn't terminal, right?"

"Jesus, Moretti, you're worse than I am. Look, I just didn't want you to have any leftover bullshit in your head when you go into your next fight. I hear it's for the UFC again."

"There's nothing official yet, but that's the hope. When I'm ready."

"Well, congratulations."

"Don't congratulate me yet."

She smiles. "Right. Well, don't forget I'm the one who taught you to stomp 'em in the stomach."

"I'm not going to be allowed to do that, but I'll remember you anyway."

"No stomach stomps? Jeez, can't do anything with these people." She rolls her eyes. I can't remember the last time she was so at ease. What an unexpected side effect.

"Saving my ass when I got myself in over my head is not the only cool thing you've ever done. It was just a perk. You're loyal and fun and you never cry about life even though you've been through hell. You're strong. And you'll get through this too."

"I guess I have to, don't I?" She squeezes my hand and nods. "Thank you."

"So," I say, letting the silence drag.

"So?"

"Have you seen her?"

"Of course," she says gently.

"And?"

"And what exactly are you looking for here?"

"Are things okay? Is she okay?"

"She's okay." Vic nods thoughtfully. "The bandages are off. Cut is still pretty gnarly, but no issues or anything, just healing. Tom's on the mend too. He's not okay, but he will be eventually."

"Any word from the cops?"

"One more time right after my surgery, but three weeks of nothing now has to be a good sign."

"And Harlow?"

Vic shrugs. "She didn't say. I think she's in the clear though."

There's a mixture of relief and disappointment in my chest. "So, it's just business as usual, then?"

"She didn't talk business with me. It's not like I can fight anytime soon. She was just checking on me."

"Did she say anything about me?" That question is so embarrassing, but I can't help myself.

"Just that you broke up."

"That's it?"

"Yeah, pretty much."

"Your friend tells you they just broke up, and you don't ask why?"

"She obviously didn't want to talk about it," Vic says.

I roll my eyes because Vic would have drilled me for an hour if I tried to get away with that.

"I'm sorry, your two friends are dating, and they break up, and you don't ask why? *You* don't ask why?"

"I assume you know why," she says.

"Of course I know why."

"So, what's the problem? I didn't ask because you're both my friends. I'm not trying to get into anything messy. I'm Switzerland, baby."

"It's not that messy, and fuck Switzerland. You were my friend first."

"Okay, so what happened?"

"I don't want to talk about it."

She rolls her eyes. "Great, you're an idiot. Did she sleep with someone?"

"No, God no."

"Did you?"

"Vic. No. I told you it's not that messy."

"Then why are you all in a twist?"

"I'm not." I sigh. "I just thought she'd say, I don't know, something. It's fine. I should go."

"Okay, freakshow. Call me when you're ready to tell me how you fumbled this one."

I flip her off and back out of the room. Her roommate is still comatose on the couch.

"Hey, asswipe. She needs help. Have you seen her trying to walk? It's like a fucking three-legged giraffe. It's sad. Get her some fucking water and answer the God damn door for her."

He holds up his hands. "Okay, okay."

I power walk back to my apartment, wishing one of those disgusting men would say something to me just so I can tell them off, but of course they don't. The first time in recorded history.

Harlow is going on with life like nothing happened, and life is letting her. Everyone is on the mend, no one has any hard feelings, the cops don't care, and she doesn't even feel the need to talk about any of it. Was it all that inconsequential? Was I that inconsequential? A complication she couldn't resist but is better off without? She's probably hosting fights this weekend. Watching the waters smooth and remembering how safe it all felt before.

I was the one to make it dangerous. I'm the one who got her to risk her agreement with Eden. I'm the one who almost fought Katarina on the roof. I'm the one who jumped in the cage at the warehouse. I was a menace to her precious security, and then I tried to make her let go of what she had left. I imagine she's well rid of me. I'm just a wild story she'll tell one day.

CHAPTER TWENTY-SIX

Even though Eden claimed she was impressed from the moment I came back, two months later she's still telling me to keep my head down and grind. Not to worry about a fight. She'll take care of it when the time is right. I don't know what she's waiting to see, but I've already resigned myself to stick this out no matter how long it takes.

Part of me is convinced this is a test designed to make sure I'm not still a quitter, that I won't throw a tantrum and walk away. It probably isn't, but I wish it were so I could show her I won't break even if she drags this out for a year. If it were a test, it would mean I could pass, and I don't have to stay that embarrassing person who shoved her best friend because she couldn't handle a loss.

I finish my fifth round with Chris. He's training for his third fight with the UFC and needs as many bodies as he can come by, even if some of us are women. Thankfully, he's a little guy and fights at just one hundred twenty-five pounds, but he's still much stronger than I am and athletic beyond belief. I managed to give him a hard enough time that he's breathing hard with his hands on his knees, and I'll take that. We bump gloves and I take a lap around the gym to walk my heart rate down.

I'm sweating and sucking wind too, but I feel good. Five rounds is no easy feat in general, but being able to sustain a formidable effort throughout them is the real trick, and I can do that now.

There are often unspoken pace breaks in the gym. Even in a real fight. Usually after a big exchange when you've both expended a lot of energy. A sort of reset. Thirty seconds of dancing around or a minute of letting a position on the ground go stagnant. I've stopped honoring those unspoken breaks. Now I use them to try to break my opponent, and it works.

"Looking good, Moretti. Got time for another round?"

It takes me a second to spot Parker about to step on the mats. Seeing him always makes my mind go to Dylan since he asked about the rising star and if I get to train with him. Thinking about Dylan invariably makes me think about Harlow. I'm finally getting used to the stab of pain that comes with that.

What I'm not used to, is hallucinating her in the Emerald Tiger waiting room. I shake my head and squint, waiting for my eyes to confess their mistake. But, no. It's her, leaving in a backwards hat.

"You don't have to look at me like I'm an alien. You can just say no," Parker says, but I'm not looking at him at all.

I rush over, trying to get a better look at the mystery person who looks an awful lot like the woman I love. Even from the back I could spot her a mile away. She opens the front door and disappears down the sidewalk. I jog off the mat, through the entryway, and out the door. She's already half a block away, but it's her. That tall frame, the strong arms, the loose jeans and muscle shirt.

What the hell is she doing at Emerald Tiger? Not seeing me, apparently. Unless she was. No, she wouldn't come all the way down here and lose her nerve. She wouldn't even choose to meet me here of all places. She knows where I live. She has my number. She's made use of neither. Parker raises his eyebrow at me when I go back inside.

"Not with the feet," he says, looking down. It's a well-known breach of martial arts etiquette to wear shoes on the mat. Less discussed but equally major is the rule not to go barefoot outside or in the bathrooms and then step on the mat again.

"Did you see that person leave just now? The woman?"

He smirks. "Yeah, I did."

"Ew, stop." I punch him in the arm as fast as I can with an urgent need to not see that carnal appreciation on his face.

He rubs his arm where I hit him a little too hard and laughs. "Yes, I saw her, jeez. Sorry, I thought you liked girls."

"I do like girls." My frustration skyrockets. I don't just like girls, I like *that* girl, but I don't want to get fist-bumped or something. "Just, no. That's not what we're doing. I'm asking what she was doing here."

"I don't know." He shrugs. "Never seen her before. She was in Eden's office. She looks like a fighter, maybe she's signing up."

"You saw her in Eden's office?"

"Yeah, she was in there when I came in."

"Was Eden in there too?" I glance over at her office door, but it's closed.

"Well, yeah. I don't think she was trying to steal the paperclips if that's what you're worried about."

"You're not funny," I snap, but it only makes him smile wider.

"What is the deal, Moretti?"

"Did you hear what they said?"

He shakes his head.

"Nothing? What about when she left? Did she say bye? Did they sound friendly? Was there tension?"

"Yeah, I think I'm going to go warm up now. You're scaring me."

"Parker!"

"I don't know, woman! I didn't hear anything. The door was closed when I came in, then the door opened, and she left. That's all I got, kid."

I start toward Eden's door to knock, but Parker speaks up again. "She's with someone else now. Sorry, I thought your obsession was singular. A guy went in there next, like five ten, young, dark hair, gym shorts, looked like he might be interested in the pens."

"You are not helping."

He smiles and bows onto the mats. "You owe me a round!" He jogs off and leaves me with my debilitating curiosity. I rush to my bag and dig out my phone as if there's going to be an explanation on it, but there isn't, just four messages from my brother.

Family dinner tonight. Angelo's. 7.

Bringing a girl. Need you. Buffer me.

Come on I asked nice.

WHERE ARE YOU?! NEED. BUFFER. CONFIRM!!

Not Harlow and not a good substitute, but I check the time anyway. It's six now, which means I can still make it. He's really losing it, which is hilarious even though the torture wasn't deliberate. I text him back.

What will you give me?

His response is instant. *You can have my firstborn. Just show up. Mom hates her already and they haven't even met yet.*

I start the walk home while I text. *I don't know if a firstborn is in your future if Mom hates her. What did she do?*

Nothing. I work with her and Mom is crashing out.

I smile at the image of Mom crashing out about Louis for once. I'd show up just to savor it.

Laila!! He texts again.

Yes, little brother. I will be there. Calm yourself.

THANK YOU.

I get home, take a shower, then make the walk to Angelo's. When I get there, Mom and Dad are standing outside together waiting for us. I smile at them and wave from across the parking lot and can't help but laugh at their bizarro relationship. When they were together their marriage seemed fake, and now that they're not their divorce seems fake.

Any time I see either of them, I see both of them. The rest of the time they live separate lives, but the way they stick together and play off each other when we do gather, I wonder what it's like to be too annoyed by someone to live with them but love them too much to let them go far.

As soon as I make it over to them, Louis and his date appear, which means they were hiding until they saw me. Louis is in a nice button-down shirt, which marks the pinnacle of his fashion. The girl on his arm is his usual type, petite, long dark hair, makeup, nails, all very girly.

"Hey." He hugs me tight. "Thanks for coming. This is Sarah." His thank you is so sincere even I can't come up with anything snotty to say.

"Of course, little brother. Nice to meet you, Sarah."

She looks nervous but sweet and very young. Mom won't like that. Louis is only twenty-three himself, but this girl looks like I should ID her. We manage the awkward greetings and find our way into a booth. A full minute of silence passes before Mom uses all her grace to break it.

"How old are you, Sarah?"

I choke on my laugh and look up in time to receive Louis's dagger eyes.

"I'm twenty," she says. "I'll be twenty-one next month."

"Twenty is good," I say. All four of them look at me weird. "What? It doesn't end in teen, you're a real adult, but you can't get in a bar yet. It's the pinnacle of responsibility."

"Yes, you two were marvels of responsibility at twenty," Dad says.

"Maybe not, but I'm sure Sarah is, right?" I look back to Louis.

"Oh, yeah. She has a great job. She's my best employee," he says.

I cringe, actually feeling sorry for him that he couldn't make it five minutes without bringing up the very thing that upsets Mom the most. That was very me of him.

"Well, that's wonderful," Dad says. Mom looks at him like he's stupid.

"Have you two reported your relationship to your manager? You should do that. It could protect you," Mom says.

"Oh, that could actually get us in trouble," Sarah says.

"Not as much as them finding out on their own. You haven't promoted her or given her a raise or anything have you?"

Louis shifts in his seat. I look at him with an expression I hope tells him to lie, but it's too late and obvious he has.

"I think I'm going to go to the restroom real fast," Sarah says. I nod at her that it's an excellent idea, and she walks away.

"Louis, did you give that girl a raise?" Mom hisses. "You can't do that. You can't abuse your power like that. That's exactly why they don't want these relationships in the workplace."

"Hey, at least he's using his powers for good," I say. "It would be worse if he fired her."

"She deserved the raise, Mom."

"Oh, you expect me to believe that girl, *that girl*, is gifted with hardware?"

"Louis's hardware, maybe." I catch a smile from Dad before Louis's betrayed face makes me feel bad.

"She's good with the customers," he says pointedly.

"What are you thinking, son?" Mom asks. "She's too young anyway. You're not going to end up with her, so what are you doing risking your job? You just got your promotion and the first thing you do is date your employee?"

"Mom, let's get through dinner at least," I say. "Get to know her maybe?"

"Yes, Maria, don't be rude to the poor girl," Dad says.

"I just don't understand the two of you. This one finally finds a nice girl and now you want to date a little troublemaker who's going to get you fired."

Her gesture at me saying I found a nice girl hits me like a physical impact. Isn't that just bittersweet. Mom actually approves of Harlow, and I'm not with her anymore.

"Hey, maybe a new topic, huh?" I say.

"Excuse me, are you Laila Moretti?" The server is standing over my right shoulder examining my face, but if I've ever seen him before, he made zero impression.

"Yes."

I feel my entire family sit up straighter. Sarah comes back and looks equally over-engaged.

"I saw you fight on *The Contender Series*."

I cringe. I hate being recognized from that fight. It blows me away anyone ever knows who I am, and they probably wouldn't outside of my neighborhood, but around here, everyone tuned in to see the local, and the local let them down big time.

"What about it?" Louis snaps, leaning forward protectively.

"Oh man, that's so cool," the server says. "I'm sure I'm not supposed to do this, but I have a poster for that fight in my car. One of the ones that was up on all the light poles around here. If I brought it in, do you think you'd be willing to sign it?"

I examine his face for signs he's fucking with me, but there aren't any.

"Uh, yeah. Sure. Really? Sure."

"Awesome. I love MMA. Did you see that girl you fought ended up debuting in the UFC at the next weight class?"

"Really?" No, I did not. "She's at one thirty-five now?"

He nods. "Yep, she said that weight cut was too brutal. She was obviously the bigger fighter in there with you."

"She was strong, but she did everything better that night. She deserved it."

"Well, I'm still proud someone from around here actually got on and got after it. I'll bring in that poster."

When I turn back to the table, I expect them to gripe about the fact that the distraction caused him to forget to take our order. Or if they're in the mood for it, to gripe about my fighting, but they actually look, something else. Their eyes are all sparkly.

"He recognized you from TV?" Mom asks.

"Yeah." At least this will distract them from Louis and Sarah. "Speaking of that, you know I've been training and working at Emerald Tiger again. I just wanted to let you know I think they'll be getting me another fight soon."

"Well, that's great," Mom says.

I'm too stunned to speak at first. "Come again?"

"It's what you want, right?"

"Yeah," I say carefully. "It is."

"Then it's great. Isn't it?"

"It is for me, yeah. I just didn't think you'd—"

"Honey, what's great for you is great for us. We just worry. How could we not? I used to think it was just a dangerous hobby of yours that would go away eventually, but obviously not. You want it to be your life one way or another, and you're clearly talented enough people know who you are. Just please, please be careful."

"Thanks, Mom." I can't even put more words together. I look over at Dad, then at Louis, and they both just smile and nod.

"And get me tickets," Louis says.

"I can do that."

"Now, Louis, what are we going to do about the mess you're in? Sarah, have you given it any thought? Aren't you worried?" Mom asks.

Louis's eyes meet mine across the table, but all I can do is shrug. I did my best work here running distraction and even bringing up fighting. I want to say they just love me more than him now, but I don't. He's more sensitive than he seems. I wonder if this is how he's always felt being the favorite. I've never had this kind of approval. I must be doing something right. Until they find out I lost Harlow, anyway.

Chapter Twenty-seven

I walk into Emerald Tiger at seven o'clock. I'm not a morning person by nature, but Eden offered to let me teach the early class to supplement the desk duties I lost to Ashley. Class isn't for half an hour, but it's been so long since I've taught, I'm actually nervous. When I round the corner to the MMA room, two guys are already stretching. I squint at the one on the right. I almost say his name but stop myself. I back off the mat and jog to Eden's office.

"Eden!" I pound on her door.

"Come in."

I burst inside and close the door behind me. "Is that Harlow's nephew on the mat?"

She looks up from the papers on her desk. "Probably, he signed up yesterday. Is that a problem?"

"Dylan. That's Dylan. Dylan Hayes. In my class?"

"His last name is Matthews, but yes, that's him."

"Really? He has his dad's name? That guy sucks." I remember now that his father didn't always suck, so I guess that makes sense, but Eden is looking at me like I'm spiraling.

"I was under the impression you liked him?" Eden asks.

"What?"

"Dylan. I moved around with him a little yesterday. He's good. Seems sweet, and he loves you."

"He's the sweetest, and really good. But he's Harlow's nephew."

"Do you not want him here?"

"No, he can be here. He should be here."

"Great. He's here."

"I saw Harlow here yesterday too." I say it like an accusation. "She was here to enroll Dylan, I take it? And you weren't even going to tell me? Neither of you? She can patch things up with you after all your shit but not me?"

"Laila, come sit down."

I slump into the chair across from her. "I know we broke up, okay? But still. She just comes to my school and enrolls Dylan and doesn't say a word?"

"I asked her to come," Eden says.

"What? Why?"

She opens her drawer and takes out a piece of paper, slides it across the desk. I pick it up and try to process it. It's a flyer. For Gladiator Combat League. Coming soon.

"Is this what I think it is?"

"I came across it and looked into it," Eden says. "It's real. It's hers."

I stare at the flyer closer. Of course it's hers. No one else launched a promotion that happens to be called Gladiator Combat League and happened to post it in our neighborhood. Yet I can't take in the information.

"There are flyers," I say, which couldn't be more obvious, but she nods. "And they're posted around town. Meaning this is legal."

She nods again.

"She did it."

"She did," Eden says. "It's in progress anyway. She hasn't had her first event yet."

"How do you know?"

"Because I talked to her."

My head is spinning. "Right. When you invited her here. Why did you invite her here?"

"I wanted to float an idea by her. And you."

I don't know why my heart stops. I don't have the first clue what this idea could be, but the simple fact that there is one dumps adrenaline through me.

"What idea?" The words barely come out.

"For you to headline her first event."

I feel my eyes go wide as all the thoughts tumble over each other.

"What?"

"Are you looking for me to repeat myself or my reasons, because I do have some good ones."

"Reasons, I guess." I'm not sure I'll hear a word over the screaming image in my head of me fighting in Harlow's event. Again. Only it won't be like before. She really did it. And I'd be her first headliner? Why would she trust me with that? I can't imagine she would. Unless Eden made her some kind of deal she couldn't refuse. Dylan. She'd do it for Dylan.

"Wait, no. Is this about Dylan? I can't do this to her."

"Huh? Dylan?" She shakes her head like the confusing thought is just an annoyance. "You can't help her have a successful launch?"

"No, of course I could do that. If she wanted me to, but she doesn't."

"How about you let me talk now?"

I sigh, drawing out the exhale. "Okay."

"I was keeping an eye on the upcoming *Ultimate Fighter* season to see if we could maybe get you a spot there, but they're going with featherweight men this season, so that's out this year. You've already done *The Contender Series*, and while you could potentially get back on, they typically like to let a good stretch of time pass first, and I can't have you just sitting around in the meantime. So, I was thinking the best road for you is to get you fighting for a smaller promotion, build your pro record, let them scout you there. I was thinking Invicta, maybe LFA."

"Oh," I say. "Okay, that makes sense."

"Then I find this flyer." She looks at me pointedly. "Obviously, they won't be as big as Invicta or LFA out of the gate, maybe ever, so this is up to you. However, I am pretty damn sure I can get a UFC scout in the audience to watch you, even at this. They want to see you again, and Harlow wouldn't lock you into a contract, meaning if and when they like you, you'll be free to sign."

I open my mouth, but I'm actually speechless.

"If you'd rather go with one of the other promotions I understand, and we can still do that. I just thought you might not hate the idea of helping Harlow get off the ground. I know it might be awkward, but—"

"I'll do it."

"Really?"

"Absolutely. If you really think I'd be helping. I mean, I'm nobody really."

"You are not nobody. Certainly not to her." Eden smirks.

"Hold on, I don't want her to do me a favor. Whose idea was this?"

"Laila, this is mutually beneficial but if anyone's doing anyone a favor, you're doing her one. She's just starting out, and she lost a lot of her fighters in the transition. She's actively scouting talent. You're not the only one I'm going to send her way."

"Really?" That's interesting.

"Yes, once I looked into everything and verified it's all above board, licenses, athletic commission, the full thing, I told Harlow our deal can go away. She can recruit here now. It will build up her talent pool and give some of our newer people a chance to have their first fights."

"And she said hey, wonderful, so can Dylan train here now then?"

Eden shrugs. "More or less."

"So, you're besties now?"

"I wouldn't say we're besties. Laila, this is a good thing."

"For Harlow, yeah, it's great."

"Okay, well if you don't think it's right for you, we can do something else."

"I said I'll do it," I snap.

"Okay, but you're mad. Talk to me. She did this for you. You get that, right?"

"Oh, she did not. She didn't even tell me."

Eden looks at me like I'm a puppy. Warm sympathetic eyes that say I love you but you're an idiot.

"I don't think she knew how," she says. "Or maybe she wanted it to be, I don't know, more, before she did."

"She's over it."

Eden rolls her eyes. "This was some of my finest work, Laila."

"I know, and I appreciate it. You and Harlow should be on good terms. You have the same mission for fighting and for this neighborhood. This is some magical Snow White shit for the two of you. I'm happy to fight for her, and I'm grateful you're getting me another shot."

"But you're going to pretend it means nothing about the two of you?"

"Who's pretending? Have I heard from Harlow? Even since you two had your little secret meeting? Did she bother to tell me herself or even wave at me when I was literally in the building?"

"Okay, but—"

"Not a peep."

She rolls her eyes again. "Fine, be stubborn."

"Real, not stubborn."

"You want to hear the last bit of news?"

"Jesus, there's more?"

"You'll like this part," she says.

"What is it?"

"Don't you want to know who you're fighting?"

That does pique my interest. "Who?"

"It's Katarina."

CHAPTER TWENTY-EIGHT

I've looked at Harlow's building with pain, longing, confusion, and anxiety for the last two months, but it's anger that finally drives me inside. Not your standard self-righteous anger, but the kind where frustration and confusion breed and overflow. I trail into the secured entry behind someone who gives me a look but decides I'm not worth the confrontation. I take the elevator up and knock before I can think better of it. Before I hear the giggle on the other side of the door. That might've been enough to make me second-guess myself, but she opens the door too fast, and then I'm staring at her gorgeous face.

Her smile falls away, replaced with something I decide to categorize as surprise to spare my own feelings. Her eyebrows raise over her lovely eyes, and her lips part just a little.

"Hi," she says.

"Hi, Laila!" A flash of Aspen passes behind Harlow, and I can't deny I take a breath of relief it wasn't a different sort of girl giggle I'd overheard.

"Hey," I say, feeling like I really shouldn't but incapable of ignoring the sweet greeting. She's much more lively than the last time I saw her, practically springing in the background like a gazelle, which I hope means she's been feeling better. "I'm sorry," I say to Harlow, which takes a lot of steam out of my plan to be stern with her.

"What's up?" It comes out so casual. She's so perfectly nice and normal it hurts.

"I heard congratulations are in order," I say, finding about a quarter of the heat I'd planned to deliver on the way over.

"I'll be right back," she says over her shoulder to Aspen, then steps into the hall and closes the door. She's just in a T-shirt and whitewashed jeans, but she looks good. It isn't fair. She isn't even trying. She's just at home with Aspen, yet she gets to look like that and steal half of my resolve to be mad at her up front.

"Thank you," she says.

I want to scoff at her for replying so simply when she must know I'm hurt. She wouldn't have come into the hall if she thought it was so simple. The silence builds, and she shows no sign she plans to say more.

"How could you not tell me?" I finally ask.

"We weren't speaking."

"We would have been if you'd called me. That's how phones work."

"Yes, but we haven't talked in two months," she says, softening just a little. "I didn't think you'd care."

"Harlow." Just the notion is devastating, but I don't feel the full impact because I find it incredibly hard to believe. "Of course I care. I'm so proud of you."

Something in her body language stiffens and pulls away as if that isn't the compliment I think it is. "I take it Eden talked to you? About the offer?"

"To headline? Yes, she did. I accepted."

She smiles. "Well, that's great. I'd shake your hand, but I don't think this needs to be any weirder."

"If you shake my fucking hand I will kick your ass."

She laughs. "How about just thanks? Again."

I want to kick her ass for that too. Thanks is for colleagues and acquaintances.

"Yeah, well, thanks for the chance to beat Katarina's ass finally. Although I can't believe you're letting her in your new promotion. Not that I have any right to an opinion. Sorry."

"No, you're right, it was a tough decision. To be honest I didn't think she'd want any part of it, but she has a pretty good pile of money saved up and said she could take a charity fight as long as it's to establish the belt." Harlow rolls her eyes at the term charity fight. "I would have said no, but too many of my fighters already walked, and I figure she does kind of owe me. I was still considering bumping her because I couldn't figure out who I could match her with without feeling like I was hosting a sacrifice until Eden turned up and threw your name out there."

"Ah, and then you decided a sacrifice wasn't the worst idea."

She smiles and shakes her head. "No, of course not. I'm just glad it's you. You know what you're dealing with. You can handle it. And I figured you probably still wanted a crack at her."

"Yeah, well, I'll try not to do anything fucked up to ruin it this time." I smile so she knows I'm playing around, but her expression stays serious.

"Look, I'm sorry I said you ruined the last one. It wasn't all on you. Katarina crossed the line, and I really was hosting an environment that didn't exactly say that kind of thing wouldn't fly. It was a shitty thing to put on you."

I shrug. "It wasn't *not* my fault. I should have thought about you and your business. I knew how important the night was to you, and I treated it like it didn't matter."

"Well, it was a wild night."

"So, you think Katarina will actually follow the rules?"

"I do." She nods. "We had a long talk, and she won't get very far if she tries not to. She'll be disqualified immediately. She'll still be an animal though. Especially with your history. So, you know. Be careful." She suddenly looks sheepish when she says it. It makes me want to kiss her, but then I remember we don't do that anymore. And then the pain takes my breath away.

"Harlow, why didn't you tell me?"

She looks at her feet, then over her shoulder like she's checking on Aspen even though the door is closed, then back at me.

"We broke up, Laila. I haven't heard from you either."

"You're hearing from me now."

"Now that I've become who you wanted me to be?"

I take a step backward. The pain is blending with annoyance that she sees it that way.

"You were already who I wanted. I loved you the way you were." I love her still, but I don't know if I can say that with her looking at me with such clear disbelief. Sure enough, she shakes her head and looks away.

"It's not a coincidence that you're here now, Laila. You loved what you thought I could be, and now I'm interesting again. I needed you to love me for me."

God, if she only knew how interesting she's always been. From the first time I saw her in that collapsing old house to the first time we kissed to the day she told me to leave her apartment. Yet I've never known my words were futile like I know it now.

"That's not true," I say anyway. "It wasn't that I didn't love you. I was afraid for you. Of losing you. The risks became too real that night, and things went sideways so fast. I never meant for us to split up though. I didn't want that."

"Then why didn't you call?"

"I thought I'd ruined it." I want to leave it at that. It's true, and it's been an obsessive symphony in my mind the last two months, but not the only one. "And I was still afraid."

Harlow holds eye contact for the longest, most breathless moment of my life. It feels like she has my whole world in her hands. I should have called. I should have come back, but she's right, I didn't. If being afraid is an excuse, I'm not sure it's a good one. She simply doesn't believe me, and I'm not sure I can blame her for not being impressed by the logic of "I let you go because I was afraid to lose you."

Her apartment door opens and Aspen peeks out. "You know you guys can come inside, right?"

I smile at her and wish that were true, but a glance at Harlow confirms it isn't.

"I'll stop taking your time. Congratulations, Harlow. I'm happy for you."

"You too. Make sure you beat Katarina for all of us. I'm going to have to pretend to be neutral, but you know I'm not."

I wish it was her complete recovery from me she was faking, but I nod and take what I can get. "Glad to hear it."

Chapter Twenty-nine

Even though my time working at Charlie's Chicken was laughably short, there's still something in the category of nostalgia I can't help but feel walking in. My uncle Tony opened it fifteen years ago, and it's become a staple of the neighborhood and the pride of our family. Yeah, it's a chicken joint, but it's beloved, and Tony has become truly successful because of it.

There wasn't an ounce of irony in my family's petitions for me to please just learn a thing or two from Tony. Aside from being the first in my family to figure out how to work for himself, he's also always been my favorite family member, and I've always wished I could muster some interest in his line of work. I've never been able to, and he's never held it against me.

"Hey, there she is," he shouts from the order window the moment I walk in. "Is it three already? I'll be right there, kiddo."

The dining room is pretty full, but not so much I can't find a table, so I pick one against the wall. I recognize some faces. The same ones I saw all the time when I worked here, some of the same ones from the Yard. One I'm pretty sure came in with Vic and Harlow the day Harlow rescued me from my misery, but I can't be sure. They can be a rowdy crowd, but they're loyal customers who ultimately do love Tony's place and mean no harm.

Tony comes out wiping his hands on his pants after washing them and pulls me into a hug. "Hey, my favorite niece."

"Your only niece."

"Yeah, and good thing or the others would be jealous."

His smile is bright white, his skin tan and smooth, his hair jet black. Mom is always going on about how thick and beautiful Tony's hair is. It used to drive my dad nuts. He still has a full head, which is more than a lot of guys his age can say, but there's no denying it's nowhere near as glorious as Tony's. Add to that Tony is a tall guy who always stayed in shape, and I like to hope I take after him genetically.

"So, what brings you in?" he asks. "Listen, kid, if you want your job back you know I'll always take care of you, but I got to tell you, I don't know if chicken is for you."

I can't help but smile at his sincere delivery. "You're right, it's probably best for both of us if I stay away from the fryers."

"You're doing okay, then? Your mom tells me you're fighting again."

I take out Harlow's flyer and put it on the table. "Yeah, for this organization."

"Never heard of them."

"No, they're brand new. And local. My friend is starting it, actually. She comes in here all the time. You probably know her."

"The one with the red stripes in her hair you used to always run around with?" He rolls his eyes with affection.

"No, not that one."

"Oh, good, because I don't know about that one and business."

I laugh. "No, this one is different. She's going to turn it into something great."

"Well, that's great. It won't hurt her having a superstar like you fighting for her, huh?" He punches my arm.

"Yeah, I hope I can pull the neighborhood in, at least."

"Of course you can. Who around here doesn't know and love you? Your mom already told me to get tickets when they come up. She doesn't know how to do all that, but we'll be there."

That derails my line of thought. "Wait, really? Mom wants to come?"

"Of course she does."

I'm sure he means that as the given he thinks it is, but Mom has never come to one of my fights or shown any interest in doing so. I've never pushed the issue and eventually quit even telling her when they were. She's not the first mother to not be able to watch her kid fight, so I even stopped taking it personally, but I can't pretend this doesn't lift me up.

"I didn't know that. I'll get you guys tickets."

"Good. And get an extra for your brother for this girl of his that your mom hates."

"Wow, she's going too? Brave."

"Only the strong survive." He winks. "But you're trying to ask me something. It's all over your face. What is it? What do you need?"

"I wanted to see if you'd maybe be interested in being a sponsor."

"For you?"

"No, for the league. Gladiator Combat."

He runs his hand over his chin. "A sponsor."

"She's run something like this before. It was really successful. This is going to be bigger."

I hear a snort over my shoulder and turn to find where it came from. One of the girls I've seen in the Yard is there, but she looks away, and I can't be positive it was meant for me.

"I don't know, kid. I do all right around here, but I don't know if I'm capable of bankrolling something like this."

"No, it's just starting out. It doesn't have to be a huge number. Whatever you feel like you could do. That's why it's an opportunity. You'd have to pay millions to be a sponsor of the UFC, but something like this right now, before it's a big deal, you could get in for way less. And just think, when it does become a big deal, they'll still be shouting out Charlie's Chicken."

"So, it's like advertising," he says.

"Exactly, take it from your advertising budget. You can write it off. It'll be great."

"I don't have an advertising budget. I haven't had to advertise in a long time, kid."

"So just think if you did."

He laughs, his good nature so endearing. He leans back in his chair, clearly thinking through how to make it work.

"I don't know if I see it, Laila. I mean, I have nothing to do with martial arts. Maybe if I sold gloves or something."

"Not true," I say. "They all hang out here all the time. You're one of their favorite spots."

"Who, the fighters? You're telling me professional athletes are in here eating fried chicken?"

"Yes, but not just the fighters, the whole scene. The audience. The coaches. You're right around the corner from where it started. You're a neighborhood staple, and this is a neighborhood promotion for now. They go to the events, and then they come here. They love you, Tony. Don't you want to be part of the community?"

"Don't do it, Tony. It's not going to make it." The girl behind me *was* scoffing at me, and now she's actually running her mouth.

I turn around. "Are you lost?"

I want to just stand up and deck her, but it turns out people don't love it when you do stuff like that in their place of business.

"Just saying," she says. "It's never going to make it. She should have kept it the same."

"Hey, don't make me kick you out," Tony says. "This is my niece. What's the matter with you?"

The girl holds up her hands and turns back to her friend, giggling as I close my eyes and swallow the anger.

Tony motions for me to cool off, and I nod at him that I'm under control. He stretches his leg out and thinks. "What would I get, exactly? Like a shout out on the mic a couple times?"

"You'll have to talk to Harlow about the specifics, but I know she'll work with you and make sure you're happy."

"You think she'd put the chicken on the shorts?"

I smile and try to contain my laughter. "Come again?"

"On the shorts. You guys always have all these logos all over you, right? Those are the sponsors? So would she put the Charlie's Chicken chicken on the shorts?"

Now I can't help the laughter, but I nod. "Yeah, I guess they do that sometimes."

"Well, hey, if she'd do that I might be interested."

I write down Harlow's number on the flyer and slide it over to him. "Ask her. I bet she says yes."

"All right, kid, I'll do it for you. And the chicken."

"And the chicken."

"Charlie is a cool chicken, okay? Don't mock Charlie."

"The chicken is Charlie?" I ask.

"Well, yeah, don't you think?"

"No, I thought the chicken was, well, the chicken in Charlie's Chicken. Not the Charlie. So, what? He's like a cannibal?"

"He's not eating himself, you nut."

"He's just cooking and selling his brethren?"

"Okay, you're making it weird. That's enough," he says.

"I didn't make it weird. You're making it weird."

"Oh, get out of here before you ruin my day. Jesus, Mary, and Joseph."

I get up and kiss him on the cheek. "Thank you, Tony."

"Yeah, yeah. Send me the details on your fight, kid. And kick some ass."

"I will."

I stand up in time to see the girl behind me stealing a glance again while her friends giggle and cover their mouths.

"You want to step outside or what?" I snap.

"Laila," Tony says, but I hold my hand up at him hoping he'll stay out of it.

"You used to fight in the Yard, right?" I ask.

"Yeah, that's right. So maybe be careful before you run your mouth," she says.

"If you were a real fighter, you'd be excited about what Harlow's doing. It's not bad enough you bailed on her, you have to run around town talking shit too?"

"I'm just calling it like I see it," she says. "We had a good thing going. We needed that money, and now she wants us to fight for practically nothing? Fuck her."

"Yeah well, you're an asshole. Harlow had your back. She had all our backs. When we had nothing, nowhere to fight, no options, no money, she came in and she paid you like a real professional. She didn't have to do that. Anyone else in her position would have put that money in their pocket and paid you like the desperate back alley nobody you are. You had a good thing because of Harlow."

"Yeah, and then she threw it all away to be just like the rest."

"No, she went out on a limb to give us something even better, something real, something safer we can build into a career, records we can actually talk about to other promotions, videos we can actually post online, and you abandon her and try to keep people from supporting her? All you idiots talk about supporting our own but the second someone tries to do something real you shit on them. She's going to make it without you, and you're going to feel like an idiot when she does because no one else would give you the time of day."

I nod at Tony, who is standing on guard to intervene, then head for the door. I'm prepared for the girls to come after me, but they don't. Only cowards try to stop other people from reaching, from trying. Harlow knew it would happen, and I knew she was probably right, but it still lights a fury inside me I can't contain to see her people abandon her knowing her dedication to giving those same exact people an opportunity. They don't deserve her, and it only strengthens my resolve to help her in any way I can.

My uncle's sponsorship was an idea that just came to me, that just felt right. After today, though, I feel compelled to outweigh the damage of the idiots who doubt her tenfold. She'd never ask for my help. She'd probably even tell me not to if she knew, but it doesn't mean I can't do what I do best. Run my mouth. To the fighters, to local businesses, to anyone who will listen and a few who'd rather not.

Chapter Thirty

There's something that feels weird about waking up in your own home on fight day. It feels like it should be more in some way. More glamorous. Everything else about a fight is so heightened, so intense, yet you just wake up in your ordinary bed with your ordinary sheets and your ordinary roommate who gives you their ordinary grunt when you say you'll see them later.

Getting in Eden's Acura helps. It's gorgeous and zips us across town like we're floating. She's quiet on the drive, letting me find a calm space in my mind. Sometimes that's what I need before a fight, while other times I'm prone to nervous chatter, and she always seems to know which is right.

The six weeks I've had for my fight camp have felt like an eternity, both because it's one of the most demanding things you can put yourself through and because I spent most of it wishing Harlow would call, which has a way of putting life in slow motion. I haven't heard from her, and I finally stopped expecting to, but I managed to send a few more sponsors her way, and this event now has double the original expected audience. If nothing else, I can't wait to see her in control of her dream tonight.

Eden parks in back of the venue and brings me through the staff entrance, information I assume went straight to her. As the main event, I go last, which means fights have been underway for an hour before I even show up. The seats are already full. I drop my bag in the fighter room and walk down the hall to peek out.

We're in an event center that normally operates as a popular nightclub, which means the lighting is amazing, and the feel is gritty and perfectly suited for fights. The octagon is in the center of the huge space and elevated, surrounded by chairs that look sold out. There's an open, industrial ceiling with exposed pipes run with colored track lights that reflect off the polished floor. There are three bars set up, one on each side of the room minus the side the fighters enter from on an elevated walkway. There are two cameramen catching the action cage-side, with a third overhead camera operated on a twenty-foot arm by a tech with a monitor.

Eden appears over my shoulder. "It looks great," she says.

"It's fucking amazing, isn't it?"

She smiles. "Yeah. She's going to be just fine."

We go back to the fighter room, and I start moving around, shadowboxing while Eden fishes through the bag for mitts. I didn't know what kind of setup would be available, if I'd have to share space with Katarina, but thankfully, there are two areas, one on each side of the walkout ramp. I wouldn't leave us in the same space if I was Harlow either.

As I move, my body loosens up quickly. It's cooperative these days, at its peak. I spent so much of my camp so sore and banged up I thought I was doing more harm than good, but now I'm ready. I'm a weapon, strong and fast and agile, if a little queasy. Eden tosses the mitts on the floor and walks over to wrap my hands. When I look up, I see Harlow behind her watching.

"Hey," I whisper. Eden looks over her shoulder, then back at me. She pauses before she puts the tape in my hands. I nod at her intense, questioning eye contact.

"I'll be right back. Forgot something in the car," she says.

Arguing right before a fight is about the worst thing you can do. Any distraction really. I wouldn't have been surprised if Eden had outright refused to let us speak, but evidently, she trusts me, and I trust Harlow. Even if things aren't right with us. She's leaning against the wall with that sly smile on her face when Eden passes her.

"Looking good, Moretti."

"I'm so proud of you," I say. She didn't seem to love it the last time I said that, but there are no other words. "It's awesome. What you've done. So fast. It's amazing out there."

She pushes off the wall and walks over. She takes the tape from me and holds her hand out for mine. I put my hand in hers, and she starts at my knuckles. The touch of her fingertips sends tingles through me.

"Word around town is I have you to thank for a lot of this," she says. "For your uncle's help, and the hardware shop, the fitness center. I even heard you reamed Olivia in Charlie's Chicken. She came back, you know?"

I shrug. "It was nothing."

"You know that's not true."

"Well, you know how hard it was for me to part with the Charlie's Chicken uniform. Now I get to wear it on my shorts again." I point to that ridiculous cartoon chicken on the right leg of the shorts Harlow sent over for me.

She smiles. "I put it on the canvas for him too."

"You're kidding. In the octagon?"

She smiles and nods. "I didn't tell him. I thought it would be cooler if he just saw it."

"He's going to love that. Thank you."

She finishes wrapping my wrist before she meets my eyes again. "Thank *you*."

"You didn't need it. I just wanted to."

She takes my other hand and starts to wrap it. "I did need it. Between everything you did and you fighting tonight, this happened because of you as much as me."

"I'll try to put on a good show."

She shakes her head. "Don't worry about that. You fight however you need to fight to protect yourself and to win. And if she does anything dirty, if she so much as accidentally grabs those goofy chicken shorts, I will jump in that fucking cage just like the great lawless Laila."

I pause. "Lawless Laila?"

"Yeah, not bad, huh?"

"I've never had a nickname."

"Do you want one?"

No one has ever seen me in a way that was fight name worthy, and the whole naming yourself thing never sat right with me. It feels like a gift.

"I do from you."

"I can have them announce you that way if you're serious, but you totally don't have to. It just slipped out."

"Do it."

She finishes my wrap, squeezing my hand before she lets it go. "Okay, I will. You better finish warming up."

I glance over my shoulder and see that Eden is back and putting on the mitts.

"I'll see you after?" I ask Harlow.

"Of course you will. I'll be the one putting the belt on you." She winks and disappears, and I turn back to face Eden while I put on my gloves.

"You good? We focused?"

"We're focused."

Eden puts me through a hard warmup. I picture Katarina in front of me. What I plan to do to her. What I know she wants to do to me. I see it all, from the easiest one-shot win to the bloodiest war. I'm ready, and I imagine her scared and human. That might be obvious, but I think I've imagined others to be gods. No more. I imagine her in a ball on the bathroom floor. Shaking like a leaf on the other side of the black curtain that separates us.

They signal me to the walkout tunnel. Eden stands at my shoulder.

"If I lose again, that'll be it for the UFC, won't it?"

"You did not go through what you've gone through to lose now," she says.

The nausea that comes with the pressure of being scouted is unmistakable and specific. It's hot and acidic. I've been beaten and bloodied and humiliated and taunted. None of it felt good. All of it was scary. But this, the feeling that put me on the floor the day of *The Contender Series*, isn't about any of that. It's about this moment, the one where everything I've ever wanted is at my fingertips, mine to grab or drop. My life condensed to one chaotic moment that hinges on instinct more than intellect, both in and out of my hands. The air feels too thick and sticky to go in and hitches in my throat.

"Laila? Stay with me," Eden says.

"I'm with you." I kick my fear in the teeth because there's nowhere else to be but here. I tell it to shut the fuck up. I've given everything to be here, and if I crawl inside myself now, I may as well never crawl back out.

"Good. What do we do with strong but messy?" she asks.

"Move and strike."

"Move and strike." She confirms the mantra that refers to a wide range of tactics. Fast footwork, creating angles, setting traps, feinting and counterstriking. Katarina might not be able to fight dirty, but she'll still try to make it ugly. My job is to be the matador to her bull.

"Lawless Laila Moretti!" The announcer's voice blasts through the speakers, and I power down the aisle. The room holds around five hundred, but they're a presence to be felt. The green overhead lights flash and dance, a shoutout to our gym as "Let's Go" by Trick Daddy plays.

Once the athletic commission staff member clears me to step inside the cage, I circle the octagon. I look out at the crowd, which is something I've never done. I've been too in my head, too focused on not throwing up or passing out, but I take in the moment and feel what Eden has said all along. Being here is a reward, not a mistake or a misfortune.

Katarina comes out to red lights and death metal. I can tell she had to actually cut weight to be in the same division with me, something she wouldn't have had to bother with in the Yard. When she joins me in the cage she makes her favorite throat slitting motion. I forego the urge to flip her off and just smirk at her. The ref calls us to the center.

"I'm surprised you showed up, Moretti," she says.

"Hey, no cross talk. You've both received and agreed to the rules. You will obey the rules at all times. Violations will result in a warning, a point being taken away, or disqualification at my discretion. You will protect yourself at all times. You will obey my commands at all times. The fight is scheduled for a possible three five-minute rounds. Are we ready?"

We both nod.

"If you want to touch gloves, do it now."

We back away without a hint of consideration. The ref looks to each of us for a nod one more time, then yells, "Fight!"

Katarina comes out like a cannon to take the middle of the octagon. I meet her there and open the fight with a right hand as hard as I can throw it. I want her to respect me, fast. Before she starts trying to muscle me around. To my surprise, it actually hits her right on the cheek. She tries to roll with it but stumbles back. The crowd explodes at the early action as I chase her down.

I hit her with a left shovel hook, a cross between a hook and an uppercut to track down her turning face. Her chin pops up and I follow with an overhand right. My adrenaline spikes as it lands, and she stumbles over her heels to the canvas. The idea of ending it this fast fills me with reckless energy, but I wrestle it under control and watch her feet to make sure I don't take a kick to the face. She's hurt, but it's early, which means she's full of energy and strength. Counting her out too soon could be fatal.

I grab her ankle to control her foot, pull it to my left with the intention of passing to my right, but she picks her hips up and launches the other foot at me as hard as she can, and I have to let go. Her eyes are alert as she tries to kick me in the knee, a move that is technically legal but regarded as shitty and uncool. No surprise there. I manage to pull away before she connects and kick her thigh hard in return.

I take a chance and dive for the pass, leading with a right hand at her face. Her arms go up to protect her head, her knees come to her chest to try to stop me from passing her legs. I throw elbows at her head to distract her while I work on passing. She tries to wrap her legs around me in a position called guard. I slam her knee to the canvas and try to slide over it into side control.

She frames her arms against me and backs her hips away, trying to create space with a desperate urgency. I back off just a little to make her think she can get up. She takes the bait and tries, and I throw a knee at her face as soon as her hands come off the canvas.

She pulls back and takes it mostly to the chest. I shove her into the fence like I did the night she ripped Vic's knee to pieces and throw an elbow at her head the same way too. I remember Eden's advice to work the body, but I want to knock her out, and it feels an awful lot like I'm about to.

I go for the body as hard as I can. A left hook, which is the punch that produces the infamous and debilitating liver shot if you land it right. She doesn't go down, but I keep swinging. I try to put her away all the way to the bell, spending all my energy without reservation. She won't go down, and when the bell sounds, she straightens up and acts like nothing happened.

Not wearing your pain, damage, or discouragement is a bona fide tactic designed to make your opponent think you're invincible. It can work in the right moment against the right person. It might have worked on me just a year ago, but I know I landed hard, and I know it was not Katarina's game plan to get rocked in the first round without returning a single significant punch.

I go to my corner where Eden is waiting for me. She kneels in front of me.

"Gorgeous," she says. "She's going to try to regroup big here. Move and counter. Keep the momentum. Let's stay off the ground. You've got her on the feet no problem. Keep it sharp and clean."

I nod and stand up to answer the bell for the second round. When it sounds, Katarina barrels for the center again, her hands high to protect her face. I come in and kick for the body to slide under her high guard. She steps to the left and throws a hard right. It hits my gloves before my face but has enough power to knock my head back. She follows the strike through to a takedown attempt, her right arm draping over my left shoulder and clasping the other hand behind my back. She drops her hips and yanks, trying to drag me down.

I stumble but bear her weight, correcting my posture as she tries harder to drag me. I fling my elbow toward her face, and it connects. She eats the impact, set on pulling me down, but I have my feet now and throw the elbow a second time much harder. She splits open over her right eyebrow. I feel a rush of excitement as I move to step out, but she doesn't fall to the canvas idly, she falls on my ankle and clings to it as I try to step away. She yanks me backward and climbs up to a better grip higher on my leg, then flings her weight down again. Her technique is shit, but her strength is not, and no matter how I might resent the graceless effort, it finally prevails. I fall.

She continues climbing my body, and no matter how I try to back away, she is slowly, wildly taking mount. I throw punches from the bottom, a tactic that doesn't work very well but has always felt like a fuck you to me. I push at her knees that are locked on the outside of my hips trying to create enough space to wiggle out, but her legs are strong, and she's locked on.

When she has the position secured to her satisfaction, she postures up, and I brace for a very bad situation. Her hands land heavy and fast. I cover up and move my head to evade it the best I can. There's no avoiding getting hit in moments like this. There's just avoiding devastation. My job is to make her miss, to not be where she thinks I will in a way that's slick enough to disrupt her balance and give me a chance to escape.

But the shots are landing harder and harder. She hits the side of my head. Everything goes fuzzy and static. When I adjust, she hits me in the face. When I cover my face, she goes to the sides again, and on and on. I duck and cover and buck my hips to throw her off, but she's too heavy, too strong, and a dog with a bone.

An elbow slams down. I feel my brow split. I feel the skin of my cheek becoming thin and squishy with scrapes and fluid. I'm losing this round as dramatically as I won the first, but all I care about is not letting the ref stop it. I can't lose. Not just for Vic and Harlow and Eden and my poor mother who's probably covering her eyes right now. Not because I won't get a contract and not because the neighborhood will talk shit when I walk by. I can't lose because I'm the better fighter, and this is mine.

I breathe. Absorb the impact. Feel the blood rolling down my face into my ear. And then I think. I time it. I watch the fist come. I don't move until all her weight is in it, and then I duck to the right. Her fist brushes past me and hits the canvas. I launch up and wrap my arms around her, locking her against me with my head on her ribs so she can't punch again. I bridge my hips as hard as I can throw my weight over my left shoulder, pushing through.

It feels like I hit a wall where I can't overpower her, but I gather my strength and push through it anyway. A second explodes into an hour where we're locked with equal leverage in a battle of will. She's leaning forward just enough. I feel her draining. I feel her breaking, and I push again with the last of my strength. She goes over. I'm on top.

Blood falls from my face onto her stomach and Eden shouts that I only have ten seconds, but I hit her as hard as I can until the buzzer sounds and the ref yells at us to separate. I stand and go to my corner. Like nothing happened. I lost the round terribly, but getting out even for those ten seconds feels like everything, and I walk to the corner calm.

I face Eden as the cutman works on me. Her eyes are calm, serene even like they always are. I can see she knows I'm not the same fighter that crumbled a year ago. No matter what happens in the next five minutes, I'll be at Emerald Tiger tomorrow, and I think her knowing that means more to me than her knowing I'll win.

"How's the gas tank?" she asks.

"I've got more." It didn't feel that way a minute ago, but I'm already recovering.

"Okay, I want you keep the pace high. Keep her busy. She's going to try that football tackle shit again by the end. It's the only place she has a chance. Don't be flatfooted ever. Move, move, move, and when she tries just get the hell out of there, I don't care how ugly it is. Stay on your feet and the big shot will come to you. If you end up on the ground, attack. Stay in front of it."

I nod and stand up as the break times out.

Eden grabs my shoulders before she leaves the cage. "Trust yourself. You are better than she is. Make her feel it."

The bell sounds for the third time, and I launch to the center. Katarina comes out slower, not like she's tired or hurt, but like she's trying to show the audience she isn't worried, like she'll get to me when she feels like it. I step forward and kick her as hard as I can. I drill it into her side so hard my shin screams when it clashes against the piece of her forearm that sneaks into my way. I pop her in the mouth with a jab while she's still trying to absorb the kick.

I circle to the left and pop her with the jab again, and a cross to the body, then bounce away. She marches toward me with that same attitude. I imagine she thinks this unfeeling, unmoved, unhurried, aura is intimidating, but I just pop her in the face and move again.

And then, she explodes. She shoots to her front knee and flings her arms out for my leg. I meet her shoulders with my hands and push her toward the canvas so hard and fast she faceplants. I hit her in the face five more times as she tries to build back to her hands and knees, and then I jump on her back.

I'm supposed to stay on my feet. If I somehow lose this position, I'll be on the ground with her where there's no telling what could happen. She could wind down the clock and squeak out a decision win, but I'm already on her back. The impulse was so strong I'm strapped onto her before I can even think about it, but it feels right. I sink my hooks in and latch on hard to secure the position in a way that renders her strength meaningless.

I don't care that we're on the ground, I've got her. I've got her here as much as I did on the feet. I'm better, and I'm not afraid. I punch her in the side of the head to distract her, and her hands shoot up just like I hoped they would. Enough I can loop my left arm under her chin with vicious speed. I clamp down my left hand on my right bicep, lock my right hand behind her head, and squeeze, pushing my forehead against the back of her head as I constrict the choke.

It's as clean a choke as I've ever gotten. It's a matter of how long she wants to struggle and if she'd rather tap or go unconscious, but she's not getting out. I beam as I take in the moment. Her thrashing isn't threat enough to even distract me. I constrict tighter and tighter slowly to give her a chance to tap, a habit though she'd never do the same. I hear a strangled sound in her throat.

Her hand hovers over my arm. I hold.

She taps.

The ref waves his hands and pulls my grip off her to end the fight.

I let her go and leap to my feet, throwing my fist in the air as Eden jumps in the cage and hugs me while we yell. I tune into the sound of the crowd screaming for me, and it couldn't mean more if there were twenty thousand of them. I don't even know if the UFC scout showed, but this is my neighborhood, my family, my home.

I look back to Katarina, who's still coming to terms on the canvas. Her coach pats her chest and pulls her to her feet. When she has the confidence to stand, she comes over and reluctantly nods. She doesn't manage anything as noble as "good fight" or "sorry I destroyed your friend's knee," but I nod back.

The announcer steps into the octagon with a microphone. "Ladies and gentlemen, presenting Gladiator Combat League's very first flyweight champion, Lawless Laila Moretti!"

Harlow steps into the octagon with a very impressive championship belt over her shoulder, but I can hardly look away from her sparkling eyes long enough to see it. She circles behind me and straps the belt around my waist. Her soft hair brushes against the side of my face, and her warm smell makes me close my eyes.

"Congratulations," she says by my ear in a voice that travels straight through my entire being. I want to turn around and kiss her until she melts in my arms, but I can't. I don't.

I just whisper, "Thank you."

"I'll meet you in back," she says even quieter, and then she walks back out of the cage.

I want to stumble not so discreetly after her right now, but the announcer comes over with the mic, and I realize I owe him a quick interview. My impatience with that notion barely manages to take shape because next I see my entire family standing in the front row, beaming and whooping like idiots. I shake my head, but I can't stop smiling. I lean into the mic before he even asks me a question because first thing's first.

"I'm okay, Mom."

She blows me a kiss. I flex and point at my belt for my brother, Tony, and Dad, who all flex back and whoop some more. My whole pack came through.

CHAPTER THIRTY-ONE

It takes all my self-control not to run to the back after I leave the octagon. A lot of self-control anyway. My aching body does slow me down some too. The adrenaline masks most things in the moment, but it doesn't take long for them to start surfacing. I don't have the faintest idea when or how I hurt my ankle, but a limp is creeping into my step.

When I pass through the curtain into the back, Harlow is sitting on the table along the back wall. She smiles when I come through.

"All hail the champ."

I remember the belt across my waist, a huge, weighty object after the usual fashion of such icons. I take it off and look at it for the first time. The belt itself is black while the face is gold with a raised depiction of the Gladiator Combat League logo and the words Flyweight Champion. It's beautifully done. I imagine the belt will evolve and get more and more impressive over the years as is typical, but having the original will only get more and more special.

"You like it?" she asks.

I drape it over my shoulder and make a show of feeling the weight. "Mmm, yep. Feels good. How do I look?"

"Gorgeous."

I smile, surprised. "Gorgeous?"

"Sorry. You were probably looking for badass, huh? You look badass too. Just, you know, also gorgeous."

She gives me that mischievous smile I've missed so much. The one that makes my heart hammer in my chest, which is really not a fair thing to do to me given the athletic feat I just completed.

"You're looking pretty gorgeous yourself," I say.

I half expect her smile to disappear and to find out that flirtatious comment was actually just a nice thing to say to someone in a big moment, but her eyes are still locked on mine.

"You think so?"

She leans forward, resting her elbows on her knees. My eyes drop to her lips, and I can't be bothered to hide it. It feels surreal. As much as I know what I see in her eyes, I'm afraid to be wrong.

I step closer and set the belt down on the table beside her.

"Tired of it already?"

My throat feels like it's closing. My body tries to intervene in the suicide mission that seems to want to force its way out of me. The thing is, I don't mind jumping off the edge for her.

"You're the prize I want, Harlow."

Her lips part, and I watch the impact of my words penetrate her before I close the last of the distance between us. Her lips meet mine soft and slow, but a shock of warmth and energy ignites. She breathes in and kisses me deeper, her hand finding the small of my back and pulling me closer. I step between her legs and kiss her, sinking into it slowly at first, then fast and hard. A dizzy, dreamy, fog floods my head. Her smell and touch and taste take over.

I slide my tongue into her mouth and feel her fingers tighten in my hair. Her cool fingers trail down to touch the back of my neck, then her palms rest on my chest as she kisses me with a fire that saturates every inch of me. I've never been kissed like this. I've never kissed anyone like this.

Our time apart feels like nothing and everything, a starved convergence while nothing was lost. I overflow into her, my love and longing too much to contain, and she catches me, holds me. When our lips part we're breathless and tangled, our foreheads touching and our hands clinging.

"Is this a post-fight excitement thing?" she asks, a smirk on her face.

"This is an I love you thing."

"Come home with me?" she whispers.

Footsteps sound behind me, and when I turn, Eden is walking in.

"Well, hello there." She smiles smugly.

"Hey." I step out from between Harlow's legs and face Eden while Harlow swipes her lower lip with her thumb and tries to hide her smile.

"You kids." Eden shakes her head and goes to her gym bag, tossing things inside and zipping it up. "Don't mind me."

"Don't be silly," I say.

She zips the bag and comes over to hug me, the knowing smile never leaving her face.

"You did amazing. I'm so proud of you." She turns to Harlow. "And you. Unbelievable first event."

"I owe that to you two."

"Not to mention yourself," Eden says. "You're putting together something really special."

"Thank you, Eden."

"You taking this one home, I'm guessing?" Eden pretends to punch me, but I can feel her experience with being this banged up in the way she barely touches me.

Harlow smiles warmly as she looks at me for an answer.

"Yes," I say. I look back to Eden. "Is that okay?"

"Of course it's okay." She laughs. "I think Harlow is qualified to take care of you. Make her take an ice bath," she says, then looks back to me. "I know it's not the vibe, but you'll thank yourself tomorrow."

She leans in and kisses me on the cheek, then hugs Harlow before she goes. She starts to leave, then calls over her shoulder. "Rest up, Champ. Party next Saturday!"

Happiness starts to take the place of relief as it all sinks in. Harlow squints like she's trying to read my mind, then picks up my bag.

"My place okay?"

"Yes."

"Let the doctor check you out. Then I'll take care of you."

I go through the routine, my mind racing with the possibilities back at Harlow's. The doctor examines me, deeming my ankle likely sprained but recommending an x-ray as a precaution, something I'll deal with tomorrow. None of my cuts or scrapes are major, and I can track a light with my eyes with the best of them, so she clears me to go home.

After a frenzied but short reunion with my family—they encourage me to rest up—Harlow drives us back. Her hand rests on my thigh in the car, and it's like there are so many things to say we can't get any of them out. When we get to her apartment, she carries my bag again and lets me drape my arm over her shoulder to support part of my weight as I hobble inside. The view from her apartment greets me—a magical, warm reminder of how Harlow has always made me feel.

She gets me to the couch and sits beside me while I stretch my legs over her lap. She inspects me, rubbing my sore thighs while carefully going around the bruises and scrapes.

"Tell me when you're ready for that ice bath, and I'll get it ready."

I imagine the freezing water and the way it locks your chest up. "Eden was right, it's really not the vibe."

"No, but it will help you, and I promised to take care of you."

"And why would you do that?" I whisper.

"It turns out I love you too," she says. "So much I can't see straight sometimes."

"You know I loved you before any of this, right? With it, without it. I need you to know that. I wanted it for you because you deserve it, but I already loved you."

"I've never had anyone want more for me. My family was afraid for me to gamble what I had. They thought it was a miracle I got lucky once and thought more was impossible. They wanted me to protect it. That was their way of loving me. It took me some time to understand your way was just different. A braver way."

"I don't know how brave I was. I was so impatient with you because I was afraid. I was thinking of you stabbed and in jail and all the worst things and somehow instead of saying that, I insulted you. I don't want you to ever think I don't respect you," I say. "What you do for your family, how you make your decisions."

"I know, Laila. It's okay. I was scared too. That I couldn't measure up to what you wanted. That you didn't understand me. But then you were still trying to help my dream come true when we weren't even together, and I realized you're actually the first person to understand how much this means to me, let alone care like you do. I'm sorry it took me so long to get around myself. But I'm here now."

I sit up to lean closer to her. "Here, like, with me?"

"Yes, with you."

"No, like, with me as in—"

She shakes her head and presses her lips to mine before I can finish. The rush takes me again, and I kiss her back knowing this kiss, her kiss, is the only one I'll ever need. When she parts, she leaves her hand on my neck and looks in my eyes.

"As in only with you. As in I'm in love with you." She kisses my forehead. "As in I want to be your girlfriend and run your ice bath and make love to you and hang out with your crazy family and pick you up from jail when you jump in cages."

"Oh, thank God because I didn't have it in me to break it to my mother that we're not together."

She laughs. "Well, now you don't have to. As long as you want me back."

"Of course, I want you back, you menace." I kiss her again, finding her body with my hands and searching it, remembering her. Claiming her. I move to straddle her and am met with a flashing pain in my ankle, but I don't care. She grabs me back, holding me against her as she kisses me, then picks me up, standing with me wrapped around her, and takes me to the bed.

"You are supposed to be resting," she says. "And taking that ice bath."

"That's about the only way you're going to cool me off."

"Don't worry, I'll warm you back up."

"You're relentless."

"I'm true to my word."

She kisses me again. Harlow has always made me run hot. She could make me melt that ice bath in a minute she drives me so crazy. The fact that she'll be around doing that to me all the time, that I get to hold her and love her and share life with her is a gift, and it's better than anything that can be achieved.

"Fine, we can be responsible. As long as you promise to be irresponsible after."

"Oh, I promise."

Chapter Thirty-two

S imone, you're coming to my fucking party," I shout at her room as I cross the apartment to answer the door.

Harlow smiles before she steps inside and kisses me. "Hey. You ready? I left Vic in the car."

"Simooooooone."

She rounds the corner rolling her eyes. "I can just walk if you're so impatient."

"Oh no, I'm not giving you the chance to wiggle out."

She grabs her key and pulls on her jacket. "There. Happy?"

She looks beautiful with her hair all wild and her outfit all intentional. She has a funky fun style, which is totally lost on her computer screen.

"Yes, thank you for coming. I'll try to keep Vic from humping your leg," I say.

Harlow snorts before I give her a look and she nods. "Totally, we will."

We pile into the Mercedes. We'd normally walk, but Vic is still not great at the task even though she's out of the leg brace now.

"Hey, Champ!" she yells when I get in the car. "And *hello*," she says to Simone when she joins her in the back.

"Be good," I say. Harlow shakes her head and zips us down the short drive, then helps yank Vic out of the back.

When we have parties at Emerald Tiger, we use the MMA room, which is around the corner when you go inside, so I don't expect to see anything special when I open the door. But when I do there's a huge crowd to greet me whooping and shouting. I can't help but look over at Harlow in shock.

My family is here, which feels a lot like her work. Her family is too, not just Dylan but Aspen and Harlow's sister and all the little ones. Brooklyn, Parker, Mateo, and everyone else from the gym, dozens of fighters and students and even some faces from the Yard. Harlow smiles and nudges me inside with a hand on my back.

My mom takes my face in both hands and kisses me on each cheek before handing me off to Dad, who pulls me into a big hug.

"You did good, kid."

The fighters jostle me and hold my Gladiator Combat belt up. I dropped it off yesterday for Eden to add to the display of the many accomplishments members of this gym have produced, but for now they're still hoisting it in the air and howling like wolves.

Eden hears the commotion and comes out from her office smiling. She hugs me, then hops on top of the front desk.

"Excuse me, attention, please. Now that the guest of honor is here, I have an announcement."

The chatter quiets to a simmer, and we all squeeze together.

"As Miss Laila Moretti's manager, it's my job to find, negotiate, and present the very best opportunities," Eden says. "After her complete badass behavior last week becoming Gladiator Combat League's first flyweight champion, she's made my job really easy. Laila, welcome to the UFC."

My brother's arms squeeze around my waist, and he lifts me up as the cheers sound. It's the sweetest thing I've ever experienced. Eden jumps down from the desk and comes over.

"It came in last night, but I thought you'd like to hear it like this."

I throw my arms around her neck and squeeze. "Thank you, Eden."

"You earned it, Laila. I always knew you could do it. It's just the beginning."

The procession of people congratulating me, hugging me and slapping my back is overwhelming. It feels so good to have my family back. When I walked away from all this, that was the stupidest thing I tried to leave behind. These people are my foundation, my support, and my friends. They're what makes everything worth it. They're what gives it meaning. Holding a belt or a UFC contract doesn't even feel good until you can share it with the ones who love you and watched the hell you went through to get it.

I finally get a long enough break to look up. I search for Harlow and find her in some kind of passionate exchange with Brooklyn. She looks so right here, talking with Brooklyn and Eden and all the other fighters. She should have always been here, and it feels like a cosmic injustice has been righted. She comes over when she catches me watching her.

"I'm sorry. I got buried," I say.

"Don't be. They're doing exactly what they should."

"It doesn't feel real."

"It will." She smiles.

"Do you mind?" I ask. "If I take the UFC contract?"

I've wanted the UFC for as long as I can remember, and she's known that since I met her, but there's something bittersweet about having to leave Gladiator Combat to do it, especially since it means vacating her championship after just one fight, but her smile is so warm and genuine it soothes me on the deepest level.

"Laila, how could I mind? I'm so happy for you. Of course you're going to go to the UFC."

"Are you sure?"

"As long as you still come home to me." She leans over and kisses me, her lips soft and sweet and familiar.

"I'd give it all up to come home to you."

"But you don't have to." She smiles. "And don't worry, once word gets out getting the belt from Gladiator got you a contract with the UFC, I don't think I'll be short on fighters for long. You are elite, and you deserve to fight on the biggest stage in the world. Don't think for a second I'm anything but happy for you."

I throw my arms around her, resting my head against her chest and breathing her in. She squeezes me, and I've never felt so whole.

Before the party ends, Eden pulls us all together for a picture. They drape my belt over my shoulder and put me front and center with the whole gang behind me. It might be the one that goes on the gym wall, but my favorite is the one after. Harlow puts an arm around my neck to choke me, Brooklyn pretends to kick Vic's busted knee, Eden lets Dylan climb on her back, and my mom pretends to sucker punch my dad. That picture is my life in all its beautiful chaos.

About the Author

Nicole Disney is an award-winning author writing across multiple genres of lesbian fiction, all linked by a fascination with the hidden worlds beneath everyday life. Her stories explore gang life, domestic violence, addiction, poverty, and professional fighting, always through the lens of strong, complex women. With a background in martial arts as both a student and former instructor, she writes gritty, character-driven stories about love, identity, and loyalty. When she's not writing, she's usually traveling, connecting with new people, or finding meaning in quiet moments.

Books Available from Bold Strokes Books

Anywhere with You by Margo Glynn. On a road trip through the Great American Southwest, two friends discover nature, hope, and each other. (978-1-63679-907-0)

Burning Bridges by Lesley Davis. Can Clancy and Jude crack the case of nine missing women—and the secrets of their own hearts? (978-1-63679-872-1)

Dreams Entangled by Sophia Kell Hagin. Amid self-doubt, secrets, a pandemic, fear of attack and attempted murder, Pirin and Gracie's attraction turns to love and their lives will never be the same. (978-1-63679-892-9)

Echoes of Love by Catherine Lane. As Hazel's and Jo's paths intertwine, they're swept up in a whirlwind of long-buried secrets, sizzling chemistry, and memories that won't be denied. (978-1-63679-835-6)

Moonlight Obsession by Sheri Lewis Wohl. All it takes to stop a clever killer is moonlight, love, and a silver bullet. (978-1-63679-831-8)

My Boyfriend's Wife by Joy Argento. Amid betrayal and heartbreak, can two women discover a love that could heal their pasts and rewrite their futures? (978-1-63679-866-0)

Tapout by Nicole Disney. A struggling MMA fighter finds her edge in an underground ring, but as she falls for the magnetic and ambitious promoter behind the matches, their dangerous world threatens to destroy everything they've fought to rebuild. (978-1-63679-924-7)

The Fame Game by Ronica Black. Wild child Hollywood actress Luna Kirkman begins dating Hollywood's leading man, only to fall for his straitlaced sister instead. (978-1-63679-858-5)

An Extraordinary Passion by Kit Meredith. An autistic podcaster must decide whether to take a chance on her polyamorous guest and indulge their shared passion, despite her history. (978-1-63679-679-6)

That's Amore! by Georgia Beers. The romantic city of Rome should inspire Lily's passion for writing, if she can look away from Marina Troiani, her witty, smart, and unassumingly beautiful Italian tour guide. (978-1-63679-841-7)

The Unexpected Heiress by Cassidy Crane. When a cynical opportunist meets a shy but spirited heiress, the last thing she plans is for her heart to get involved. (978-1-63679-833-2)

Through Sky and Stars by Tessa Croft. Can Val and Nicole's love cross space and time to change the fate of humanity? (978-1-63679-862-2)

Uncomplicate It by Kel McCord. When an office attraction threatens her career, Hollis Reed's carefully laid plans demand revision. (978-1-63679-864-6)

Vanguard by Gun Brooke. Beth Wild, Subterranean freedom fighter, is in the crosshairs when she fights for her people and risks her heart for loving the exacting Celestial dissident leader, LaSierra Delmonte. (978-1-63679-818-9)

Wild Night Rising by Barbara Ann Wright. Riding Harleys instead of horses, the Wild Hunt of myth is once again unleashed upon the world. Their ousted leader and a fey cop must join forces to rein in the ride of terror. (978-1-63679-749-6)

Heart's Appraisal by Jo Hemmingwood. Andy and Hazel can't deny their attraction, but they'll never agree on the place they call home. (978-1-63679-856-1)

Behold My Heart by Ronica Black. Alora Anders is a highly successful artist who's losing her vision. Devastated, she hires Bodie Banks, a young struggling sculptor as a live-in assistant. Can Alora open her mind and her heart to accept Bodie into her life? (978-1-63679-810-3)

Fearless Hearts by Radclyffe. One wounded woman, one determined to protect her—and a summertime of risk, danger, and desire. (978-1-63679-837-0)

Forever Family by L.M. Rose. Two friends come together after tragedy to raise a baby, finding love along the way. (978-1-63679-868-4)

Stranger in the Sand by Renee Roman. Grace Langley is haunted by guilt. Fagan Shaw wishes she could remember her past. Will finding each other bring the closure they're looking for in order to have a brighter future? (978-1-63679-802-8)

The Nursing Home Hoax by Shelley Thrasher and Ann Faulkner. In this fresh take for grown-ups on the classic Nancy Drew series, crime-solving duo Taylor and Marilee investigate suspicious activity at a small East Texas nursing home. (978-1-63679-806-6)

The Rise and Fall of Conner Cody by Chelsey Lynford. A successful yet lonely Hollywood starlet must decide if she can let go of old wounds and accept a chance at family, friendship, and the love of a lifetime. (978-1-63679-739-7)

A Conflict of Interest by Morgan Adams. Tensions rise when a one-night stand becomes a major conflict of interest between an up-and-coming senior associate and a dedicated cardiac surgeon. (978-1-63679-870-7)

A Magnificent Disturbance by Lee Lynch. These everyday dykes and their friends will stop at nothing to see the women's clinic thrive and, in the process, their ideals, their wounds, and a steadfast allegiance to one another make them heroes. (978-1-63679-031-2)

A Marvelous Murder by David S. Pederson. When a hated director is found dead in his locked study, movie star Victor Marvel, his boyfriend Griff, and friend Eve seek to uncover what really happened to Orland Orcott. (978-1-63679-798-4)

Big Corpse on Campus by Karis Walsh. When University Police Officer Cappy Flannery investigates what looks like a clear-cut suicide, she discovers that the case—and her feelings for librarian Jazz—are more complicated than she expected. (978-1-63679-852-3)

Charity Case by Jean Copeland. Bad girl Lindsay Chase came home to Connecticut for a fresh start, but an old, risky habit provides the chance to save the day for her new love, Ellie. (978-1-63679-593-5)

Moments to Treasure by Ali Vali. Levi Montbard and Yasmine Hassani have found a vast Templar treasure, but there is much more to the story—and what is left to be found. (978-1-63679-473-0)

The Stolen Girl by Cari Hunter. Detective Inspector Jo Shaw is determined to prove she's fit for work after an injury that almost killed her, but a new case brings her up against people who will do anything to preserve their own interests, putting Jo—and those closest to her—directly in the line of fire. (978-1-63679-822-6)